Family Trust

Ian Walker

First published in Great Britain 2023 by Ian Walker
Facebook: Ian Walker – Author • @thebrewerystoryteller

First edition April 2023

Editing/publishing: Speak Euníque
Facebook: Speak Euníque
Contact: eunicewalker@mac.com

Original cover art: Ock Draws
Twitter @OckDraws – Instagram @ock_draws
Facebook: Ock Draws

ISBN 9798391650447

Also by Ian Walker

If only they could talk
Doppelgänger
Bitter End
Hair of the Dog

Disclaimer

This is a work of fiction and, except in the case of historical fact, any resemblance to **actual persons, living or dead,** is purely coincidental.

Prologue

You may have known a man all your life, but do you really know him? Even if outwardly, he appears to be a 'really good bloke', a true friend, a great family man, a man who will support you when things are tough, is that what he's really like? Perhaps he only appears that way because that's what people expect of him. The real person might be completely different. He may hate his life and all the things that constrain him, things like his job, his wife and his kids, all of which are slowly suffocating the life out of him.

Perhaps he secretly wishes he was free of them all? You'd never know if that's the case, of course, because men don't talk about things like that. Instead, they prefer to talk about things like beer and football, or anything else that doesn't let their friends know the truth about the way they're feeling.

So what would happen if he was given the chance to be freed from all his responsibilities? Would he take it and just walk away from everything? Or would he remain loyal to his commitments? It's an interesting dilemma, which for most people is purely theoretical. But that's what happened to Andy Bradbury. He was one of the few people who was given a way out of his boring life. That was back in 1979 and, to this day, his family are still feeling the consequences of his decision.

Chapter 1

Saturday, May 19th, 1979
Chesterfield v Gillingham

In a Gillingham home
They look in the dustbin for something to eat
They find a dead rat and they think it's a treat
In a Gillingham home

The fans on the kop were in fine voice despite the dismal scoreline. In fact, the match was not going well at all for the home supporters, and the situation was about to get a whole lot worse. That was because the Gillingham number nine had broken free on goal. A few seconds later, he deftly tucked the ball away into the corner of the net, giving Phil Tingay in the Chesterfield goal no chance. The Gillingham players celebrated whilst their small contingent of fans cheered their team. It was the team's second goal of the game. Meanwhile, Chesterfield had barely had a shot on target the whole match.

"You're going to get your fucking heads kicked in," came the reply from the kop.

It was their standard response whenever the away supporters cheered after their team had scored. Not that they ever carried out their promise to kick anybody's head in, and they definitely wouldn't be doing so today. This was the last home game of the season and both teams had absolutely nothing to play for. Also, Gillingham had only brought 35 supporters with them and most of those were related to the players. They were hardly the type of people who'd be spoiling for a fight once the match had finished.

"Shall we leave this pile of crap and just go?" Dave asked his two friends standing next to him. "There's a pint waiting in the bar with my name on it."

Dave and his friends rarely left the ground early. But with 89 minutes played and their team 2-0 down in a meaningless match at the end of the season, it seemed like a good suggestion.

A few minutes later while Tony, Andy and Dave were going through the exit, they heard the referee blowing the final whistle. It was met by another faint cheer from the mums and dads of the Gillingham players.

They sauntered into Saltergate Social Club and ordered three pints of bitter. Under normal circumstances, it would be at least a ten-minute wait before getting served. But the crowd had been so poor that day, there wasn't even a queue at the bar. There were also plenty of vacant tables. Bitter in hand, they sat down at one of the tables.

"We've been rubbish all season, but today was one of the worst performances by Town I've seen in a long time," said Andy.

The correct name for their club was just plain old Chesterfield Football Club, not Chesterfield Town. But that had never stopped the diehard supporters from referring to them as Town. They believed it distinguished the true fans from everybody else. After all, everyone knew Chesterfield's nickname was the Spireites. But only a local would ever refer to them as Town.

"Bloody Rod Fern looked like he was already on the beach in Benidorm," Andy continued. "I wouldn't be at all surprised if Arthur Cox decides to get rid of him before next season."

Arthur Cox was the Chesterfield manager. He had a reputation as a strict disciplinarian and someone who wouldn't hesitate to give a player the boot if their performance was not up to his standards.

The other two both nodded despite the fact they all knew Rod Fern was the best player in the Chesterfield team. He used to play for Leicester City in the first division and had even taken part in an FA Cup final at Wembley. That made him stand out head and shoulders above the rest of the Chesterfield squad, which was mainly made up of journeymen pros.

The majority of the team were average at best and were destined to follow the same career path as most third division players in the 1970s. In other words, once they stopped pulling the opposition's shirts, they would be pulling pints as pub landlords. They would be drinking too much and piling on the pounds. In the case of Chesterfield's squad, it looked as if some of them had started already.

"I was thinking of bringing our Vince to the games next season," Dave announced. "Only, I'm having second thoughts now, due to all the swearing."

Vince was Dave's eight-year-old son who had just started playing in goal for Birdholme juniors on Sunday mornings.

"Bloody typical," cut in Andy. "You're more concerned about the bad language than you are about the threat to kick somebody's head in."

"That's because it very rarely happens," Dave replied. "You know full well there's hardly any violence at Chesterfield matches."

He was right, of course. In fact, the only trouble they'd seen in recent years was during a match against Sheffield Wednesday. A group of Wednesday fans had run onto the pitch in an attempt to attack the Chesterfield kop. In an act of bravado, the home supporters had been chanting, "Come over here if you think you're hard enough."

Unfortunately for them, a large proportion of the Sheffield Wednesday fans were hard enough and had consequently chosen to take up this particular challenge. As a result, the kop soon resembled a scene reminiscent of Moses parting the Red Sea, with the Chesterfield supporters running off in all directions. It was the ultimate humiliation for the home fans, surrendering their beloved kop to the dreaded *dee dars. Dee dar* was the derogatory name given by people from Chesterfield to their neighbours from South Yorkshire.

"Your Vince can have my place," added Andy. "I'm sick and tired of watching this load of rubbish. Next year, I'm going to buy a season ticket at one of the big clubs."

"Come off it, Andy," said Tony. "Are you really going to travel to Manchester or Liverpool every Saturday?"

"I was actually thinking of going to watch Nottingham Forest," he replied. "I'm a big fan of Brian Clough and have been ever since he was at Derby County. Now that he's signed Trevor Francis, I don't think any other team will be able to live with Forest next season. You see if I'm not right."

They obviously didn't take him seriously. For despite everything they might say, neither of them would ever dream of switching allegiances where football was concerned. You supported the team your dad supported, the local team you first went to watch when you were too small to see past the people standing in front of you.

Supporting a football team has nothing to do with success. It has everything to do with who you are, where you come from and being a part of the local community. That's unless you happened to be a Manchester United supporter, of course.

"Now let's just be serious for a minute, guys," said Dave. "Are we all going to the Mansfield match on Monday?"

They didn't usually go to away games, but there were a few exceptions. They nearly always went to away matches at both the Sheffield clubs and sometimes even went to see the Spireites play at Rotherham United and Notts County. However, the one away fixture they never missed was at Mansfield Town. Mansfield was only twelve miles down the road and the rivalry between the two teams was intense. The fact that Dave was even asking the question just went to show what a poor season the Spireites were having that year. Despite this, it only took them about half a second before agreeing that they would all go.

"We may as well prolong the agony for one more match," sighed Tony. "After all, you've got to be a bloody masochist to support a team like Chesterfield."

"You know, there's absolutely nothing I like about Mansfield," said Andy. "For a start, there's the fact it's in Nottinghamshire rather than Derbyshire."

"Pardon?" replied Tony somewhat surprised by Andy's outburst. "I thought you said a few minutes ago you were going to switch your allegiance to Nottingham Forest. Just in case you didn't realise it, Nottingham is also in Nottinghamshire. The clue is in the name."

"Okay, so there's one good thing in Nottinghamshire," said Andy. "But nothing useful has ever come out of Mansfield. It's a cultural desert."

Andy was oblivious to the irony of him drinking a pint of his favourite Mansfield Bitter at the time. This hadn't gone unnoticed by Tony, though.

"Another pint of Mansfield, Andy?" he asked him.

"I don't mind if I do," he replied, totally unaware that Tony was taking the mickey out of him.

Tony jumped up and made his way to the bar where he ordered three more pints.

"Look," said Andy whilst glancing at the TV. "Bury have beaten Peterborough United, and that means Peterborough have been relegated."

Chesterfield may have been destined to finish the season near the bottom of the league table, but at least they hadn't been involved in a last-minute battle to avoid relegation. They'd been safe from the drop with two games to go.

"You know, I've always wondered why Peterborough are called the Posh," said Dave. "If that was Chelsea's nickname, I could understand it. But why Peterborough?"

"That's easy," joked Andy. "Posh stands for Peterborough is an old shit hole."

This almost caused Tony to spill the three pints he was carrying as he arrived back from the bar.

"Anyway," Andy continued. "Chelsea's nickname is the Pensioners, which isn't surprising since they play like a team of old men."

"At least it's obvious why we are known as the Spireites," said Dave. "But some of the other teams' nicknames are just plain weird. For example, I've always wondered why Everton are known as the Toffees."

"Because they're named after the local sweet factory that also makes Everton mints," Andy replied.

"In which case, they should be called the Mintoes," added Tony.

"I think the team with the most perfect nickname is Northampton Town," Dave cut in.

"Why's that?" asked Tony.

"Because they're called the Cobblers and that about sums them up, a load of old cobblers."

A long debate followed about which team had the best nickname. Dave put a strong case forward for Forfar Athletic, whose supporters were known as the Loons. But eventually, they agreed on Hartlepool United's nickname, the Monkey Hangers.

"If you're all finished," said Andy, indicating that the discussion was over, "I suggest we move on to the Boythorpe Inn. So down your pints lads."

"You seem very keen to get to the Boythorpe Inn, Andy," added Tony after taking a final mouthful of his beer. "I wonder if it's got something to do with the lovely Joanne and her massive jugs."

He was referring to the pub's barmaid, whose large chest and low-cut tops made her look as if she had a couple of bald men stuffed down the front of her blouse.

"Bugger off, Tony," said Andy. "You know full well that we always go there on the way home."

The routine on a match day was always the same. Dave and Andy were next-door neighbours and they both lived on St Augustines Rise about a mile and a half from the ground. Tony lived with his wife and two cats on St Augustines Drive about 400 yards nearer to both the town centre and to Chesterfield's Saltergate ground. The two neighbours would set off for the match at about a quarter past two and collect Tony on the way there. One of them would buy a programme from a vendor outside the ground before they made their way to their usual spot on the terraces.

After the match, it was always two pints of Mansfield Bitter in the Saltergate Social Club followed by a pint of Stones in the Boythorpe Inn on Boythorpe Road. The second stop was primarily for practical reasons. It would be really uncomfortable to walk one and a half miles after having drunk three pints of beer in the club. The Boythorpe Inn therefore provided a convenient comfort break at the halfway point. However, Tony liked to wind Andy up by implying it was a different sort of comfort he was after. It was the type that came in the form of Joanne, the busty barmaid.

They entered the Boythorpe Inn and Andy, whose round it was, went up to the bar.

"What can I get you, duck?" asked Joanne.

She was actually from Swindon and had only lived in Chesterfield for five years. But she was already sounding like a local.

"Three pints of bitter and one fo' y'self," replied Andy.

Tony knowingly winked at Dave.

"Ask her what team she supports, Andy," shouted Tony. "What's the betting it's Bristol City?"

This was a common joke between Tony and Dave who often referred to Joanne as Miss Bristol on account of her Double D cup size. Bristol City was, after all, rhyming slang for titty.

Andy returned from the bar with three pints looking flustered.

"Stop it, will you, lads?" he pleaded. "Joanne's a really nice girl and she gets upset when people poke fun at her. She can't help it if she's got really large fun bags."

"Yu wanna watch it with that one, Andy," added Dave with a smug look on his face. "She'll eat you alive. There's only one woman who frightens me more than she does and that's Maggie bloody Thatcher."

Sixteen days earlier, Margaret Thatcher had become Britain's first female Prime Minister. She was already proving to be a controversial figure.

Mrs Thatcher had acquired the nickname of Maggie Thatcher, the Milk Snatcher when, as Education Secretary, she had abolished free milk for schoolchildren aged between seven and eleven. She was not at all popular in left-leaning towns like Chesterfield.

"Hey, there's nothing wrong with Maggie," said Andy. "I voted for her the other week."

Tony and Dave's jaws dropped. They couldn't hide their surprise and just sat there without saying anything. Eventually, it was Tony who broke the silence.

"Yu did what?" he asked.

"I voted for Maggie," replied Andy.

"Bloody Tory bastard," commented a man wearing a flat cap who was supping a pint at the next table.

"Why would you want to do that?" asked Tony in a hushed voice. "You've been a Labour supporter all your life, just like me and Dave. What's wrong with Eric Varley?"

"Absolutely nothing," whispered Andy. "I've got nothing against Eric, he's a good local MP. It's Jim Callaghan and the Labour party in general that I'm sick of. Look at the winter of discontent we've just been through. Labour and the unions are flushing this country down the toilet. At least, Maggie is prepared to stand up to the commie union leaders. She's the only person in this country who is prepared to do something about them."

"Christ Almighty, Andy," said Dave. "You're from a working-class background. You live in a council house for fuck's sake. People from the St Augustines estate don't vote Tory."

"You know full well that Maggie has promised to reward skilled craftsmen like us," Andy replied. "And she's promised to give us the right to buy our council houses."

"You sound like a bloody party-political broadcast," said Tony, "and I for one have had enough of them lately. So let's change the subject, please."

Secretly, both Tony and Dave knew that what Andy was saying had some truth in it. Of the three of them, only Dave was a member of a trades union and even he was a foreman. He'd been promoted to that role after three years of working at the Tube Works on Derby Road. Andy was a mechanic and he worked at Walton Motors. Tony was the entrepreneur of the trio, as he was a self-employed French polisher. In fact, all three of them were in Maggie's sights as potential Tory voters. Not that Dave or Tony had ever considered voting Conservative. Well, not so far at any rate.

In an attempt to steer the conversation away from politics, Tony asked, "So where are you thinking of going for your holidays this year, Andy?"

Andy gave him a quizzical look before replying.

"Bloody hell, I thought for a minute there I was at the barber's having me hair cut."

He smiled and added, "Actually, I was thinking of going abroad to Spain."

"Fucking hell, it's no surprise you voted Tory," Tony replied. "The rest of us have to put up with a wet week in Skegness."

After a few minutes stuck in the murky world of politics, Tony had successfully steered the conversation back into more tranquil waters.

It was now nearly half past six. They finished the rest of their pints and headed home. Saturday night was always the lads' night out, irrespective of whether or not there had been a home match in the afternoon. This evening, it would be Tony's turn to call on the other two before they made their way to the Walton Hotel for a few pints of Home Bitter.

That would be in about an hour and a half, which gave them plenty of time to eat their evening meal and watch a bit of telly before going out again.

Andy's wife Sharon was already in the kitchen cooking supper when he arrived home. Sharon had a Saturday job in Boots and had only gotten home herself half an hour earlier. Tony's wife Lynne always looked after her boys on a Saturday. It was the one day of the week that Sharon really looked forward to. Two little ones, both of them under the age of five, kept her busy on every other day and, on top of that, she also had all the housework to do. At least by working on a Saturday, it gave her a short break from her humdrum life. Not only that, but her job did bring in a little extra money.

"What's for tea?" Andy asked her as he came through the door.

"Sausage and mash," Sharon replied, "and I've bought you a copy of *The Green Un*. It's on the table."

The Green Un was the name of a local paper that came out every Saturday evening. It was predominantly a sports paper with reports from all the matches involving teams from the Sheffield region, including the Chesterfield game. It miraculously always managed to be out soon after all the matches finished.

Andy came into the kitchen and grabbed his wife's arse.

"I'll have none of that," said Sharon slapping his hand.

Andy could take a hint. He sat down at the table and began reading his paper instead. Soon Sharon started complaining about one of her favourite subjects.

"Lynne's spoiling the boys again," she said. "I've told you time and time again that she's doing it deliberately in order to make them want to spend more time with her. You won't believe what she's done this time. She's only gone and bought a Sodastream so that they can have unlimited fizzy drinks. Now they want to know why they can't have one at home. It's not on, Andy."

Andy had heard similar stories many times before, along with Sharon's threat to find someone else to look after the boys on a Saturday. It was an empty threat and both of them knew it. Lynne didn't charge them anything and Sharon and Andy couldn't afford a child minder. As a result, Andy had learned to ignore Sharon's moans and pretty soon she changed the subject to something far closer to Andy's heart.

"So how was today's match?" she asked.

"Crap, we lost 2-0," replied Andy, now totally engrossed in his paper.

"Well, my day was pretty shitty as well," Sharon went on. "We had a power cut at lunchtime and none of the tills would work. Some of the customers were getting really angry with us. I mean, it's not as if there was anything we could do about it. It had to happen when we were really busy. Sod's law, I suppose. It took over an hour before the power came back on again."

Sharon noticed that Andy had lost interest in what she had to say.

"Andy! Are you listening to me?" she said in an angry voice.

But Andy was staring at his paper and his hands were trembling. When he finally did speak, it was as if he was in a trance.

"Bloody hell," he said.

"BLOODY HELL," he repeated.

Andy wasn't going to the Walton Hotel that evening. He wasn't going to the Mansfield match on Monday either. In fact, he was never going to see Chesterfield play again. In a few seconds, his life had changed forever.

Chapter 2

Monday, July 15th, 2019

"Stop fighting you two," shouted Louise in the direction of her sons' bedroom.

The two boys were making one hell of a racket. Although they got on most of the time, sharing a bedroom wasn't ideal. Arguments were bound to break out occasionally. This time it was over which game they were going to play on the Xbox. Noel wanted to play FIFA 19 whereas his younger brother, Josh preferred Lego Jurassic World. It wasn't a major dispute, and after a few screams, yells and groans, it was all over.

Sibling disputes usually end with the elder brother getting his way and this disagreement was no exception. Consequently, Manchester United were soon kicking off in their match against Forest Green Rovers. It would be a one-sided affair if it was taking place in the real world. But not in the virtual world of the Xbox.

Meanwhile, Louise was cooking supper downstairs in readiness for when Mark, her husband, got home from work. They had met when they were both young teachers at St Boniface's Girls' School in Reigate, or St Drop 'Ems as it was known by the local boys. Mark taught Chemistry and Louise was a Maths teacher. It wasn't exactly love at first sight. But after they'd drunk too much Australian shiraz at the staff Christmas party, they found themselves snogging in the sixth form cloakroom. The rest was history. Six months later, they were engaged and had bought the two-bedroomed terraced house in Priory Road where they still lived. They were married the following year and, eighteen months later, Noel was born on Christmas day, with Josh making an appearance two years later.

Louise had given up work when she was pregnant with Noel and had returned part-time after Josh had started school. Even so, it didn't take a Maths teacher to work out that, with one and a half wages now supporting the four of them, they were never going to be as well off as they had been before.

Not that she ever regretted having the boys. Despite all the arguments and tantrums, she loved them both dearly. Secretly, she would have liked to have tried for a daughter, a third child to add balance to the family, and change the fact that she was always outnumbered three to one. But then reality would cut in. They lived in a two-bedroomed terraced house, which was already too small for the four of them. It would be impossible to squeeze a third child into their small living space. Not only that, but she'd turned forty the previous year and the family needed her income, even though she usually referred to it as a pittance.

"Don't be silly," she said to herself. "You're middle-aged. Be content with your two little men."

Mind you, they weren't so little anymore. Noel was twelve and was experiencing a growth spurt. Josh was ten and still quite small for his age, but he would soon be catching up with his brother and probably overtake him. Who would decide which Xbox game they'd be playing when that happened?

Mark and Louise had often discussed moving to a three-bedroomed house. But Reigate was so expensive that they couldn't afford to move. Even their small, terraced house was now worth over a quarter of a million pounds. Consequently, they were limited to looking longingly at larger properties on Rightmove, without the slightest hope of being able to make an offer on any of them.

At one stage, they had considered moving to Horley, close to Gatwick Airport, as property prices were slightly cheaper there. But they liked Reigate. Mark could walk to work from their current house. All their friends lived close by, and the boys were settled in their school. As a result, Noel and Josh were going to have to continue sharing a room for the foreseeable future.

Today was Tuesday, which meant Mark would be late home from work, as he took after-school tennis classes during the summer term. It was the last session of the year as the local schools would all be breaking up for the summer holidays on Friday. Teaching had its frustrations. But it also had the big perk of long holidays. It would be another six weeks before they both had to return to work.

Louise continued to prepare the chicken casserole for their supper. Mark often said that it was winter food, not really suitable for July. But both boys liked it and, besides, the weather that day was dull, overcast and cold. In many ways, it was a typical English summer's day.

She heard the front door shut and shortly afterwards Mark entered the kitchen and gave her a kiss.

"What are we having for supper tonight?" he asked her.

"It's chicken casserole and I've bought us a vanilla cheesecake as a special treat," she replied.

"Mmmm," said Mark tactfully. "Can I do anything to help?"

"Not really, unless you want to get me a glass of wine," Louise replied.

Mark got a couple of glasses from the cupboard and opened a bottle of Chilean merlot.

"Your post is on the sideboard in the living room and, oh, your brother phoned. He asked if you could phone him back."

"Bloody hell, that's a rarity," Mark replied. "Did he say what he wanted?"

It was more than a rarity. Pete never phoned Mark. In fact, the two brothers hardly spoke at all. The last time was back in April when they had attended their mother's funeral. It wasn't that they didn't get on. It was just that they had very little in common, and the fact that Pete lived over two hours away in Stroud didn't help.

"He must have forgotten that you take tennis classes after school on Tuesdays," said Louise. "He just asked if you would phone him back."

"Well, I'm sure it can wait until after supper," said Mark as he started to open his mail.

The post was the usual collection of bills, junk mail and one envelope that Mark didn't recognise. He decided to open that one first, and after reading for a few minutes, he looked up.

"Bloody hell, I don't believe it," he shouted out.

"What is it, love?" Louise shouted back from the kitchen.

Mark walked over to show her. "This letter says I'm a beneficiary of a £5 million family trust fund."

"That's nothing," Louise replied, "I had an email this morning telling me I had won $28 million in the Nigerian State Lottery. All I had to do was to send $1,000 to a Mr IMA Fraudster in Abbueja to cover administration costs and the money would be forwarded directly into my bank account. I was absolutely amazed, especially since I hadn't bought a ticket and he'd spelt Abuja wrong."

Mark pulled a face at her, as he knew she was having him on.

"This one looks genuine enough, though," he continued. "It's from a solicitor in Derbyshire and it refers to my late father. Here, take a look and see what you think."

Mark passed the letter to Louise. It said:

Knight and Son
Solicitors and Commissioners for Oaths
12 Riber View, Matlock, Derbyshire DE4 7JH
Tel 01629 583127

July 24th, 2019

Mr Mark Bradbury
7 Priory Rd
Reigate
Surrey
RH2 3BQ

Ref: Bradbury Family Trust

Dear Mr Bradbury,

We act as trustees for a family trust fund, which was established by A S Bradbury in 1984.

In line with my responsibilities as trustee, I am instructed to inform you that you are a potential beneficiary of this fund, the assets of which now exceed £5 million.

I must warn you that the terms under which this trust fund was established are by no means straightforward. One of the conditions is that you attend a six-day residential course, during which time you will be asked to participate in various challenges. The amount you receive from the fund is dependent on how well you perform.

The aforementioned challenges, which are mental rather than physical in nature, will take place between Friday August 30th and Thursday September 5th, 2019 at the following venue:

Striding Hall
Harper Hill Lane
Wingerworth
Chesterfield
S42 2ZX

I would be grateful if you could confirm your attendance by emailing me at knightandsonsolicitors@mac.com.

Two rooms have been reserved for you at Striding Hall, one for yourself and your wife, and one for your sons. I kindly request that you aim to arrive at around 5pm on August 30th, as dinner has been booked for 6.30pm.

Please note that all expenses during your stay at Striding Hall will be covered by the trust fund.

Should you have any queries, please do not hesitate to contact me, although I must inform you that, under the terms of the trust fund, I am limited as to how much I can reveal.

I look forward to meeting you on August 30th.

Yours sincerely,

James Knight LLB

PS. Please find enclosed a brochure with details about Striding Hall and its facilities.

"It's probably just a scam in order to sell you timeshare," said Louise, "a bit like the one they conned us into attending when we were in Florida. That's five hours of my life that I won't get back again."

Mark read the letter a second time.

"I don't think so," he replied. "This takes place over six days rather than five hours, and the letter states that our expenses are all covered. When I think about it, it probably explains why Pete phoned. What's the betting that he's received the same letter?"

"Well, I hope it's not a scam as the hotel looks really nice," said Louise looking at the brochure. "It says here it has a spa."

Louise passed the letter and the brochure back to Mark.

"The only thing I know about your father is that he was killed when you were little," she commented. "Was he really wealthy enough to set up a £5 million trust fund for you and Pete?"

Mark exhaled slowly.

"I never knew my birth father," he explained. "That's because he abandoned me along with my mother and brother when I was only two years old. I guess I should have told you about him before. But it didn't seem necessary because he never really featured in my life. My father was born and brought up on a council estate in Chesterfield and he worked in a local garage. However, he did become wealthy. Not because of anything he did, but because he won a massive sum of money on the football pools in 1979."

Chapter 3

Monday, July 15th, 2019

"I've always known that your mum and dad had split up when you were little and your mum remarried a few years later," said Louise. "But in all the years I've known you, you've never spoken about your birth father."

"It was so long ago and I was very young at the time," Mark replied. "I don't remember him at all. In fact, neither does Pete who was only four himself when our father left us. As far as I am concerned, Clive is my real dad. After all, it was he who brought us up after Mum married him. He has always been a loving father to both of us. He may not be my biological dad, but in every other way, he was everything a dad should be. I couldn't have wished for a better father."

It was a difficult subject for Mark to talk about, but he continued, nevertheless.

"The only thing my birth father ever gave me was my surname. I know very little about him or my early life in Chesterfield. The small amount I do know, I've learnt from my mother."

"I knew you were born in Chesterfield," added Louise. "For a start, it's written in your passport."

"Exactly," said Mark. "But what you don't know is that my parents met whilst they were on holiday in Cornwall in the summer of 1974. They had a whirlwind romance and got married two months later. At first, they moved in with my father's parents, which can't have been ideal. But when Mum discovered she was pregnant with Pete, the council rehoused them, not far away from where my grandparents lived. I was born two years later and, in 1979, my father had his pools win. It was literally a dream come true. A family from a council estate were suddenly rich beyond their wildest dreams. But pretty soon, the dream turned into a nightmare for Mum. My father had been having an affair with a barmaid from a local pub and a week later, the two of them ran off to Spain together. That was after he had transferred all the money into a Spanish bank account."

"You mean he left you, Pete and your Mum with absolutely nothing?" added Louise.

"That's correct. You see, Spain wasn't part of the EU back then and didn't have an extradition treaty with the UK. That was why the Costa del Sol was nicknamed the Costa del Crime. Loads of British criminals escaped the country and went to live there. They were beyond the reach of British justice, as was my father. Half the money he'd taken belonged to my mother and because he'd absconded to Spain, she had absolutely no chance of getting her hands on it. By the time Spain joined the EU in 1986, my father had died and the money had all gone."

"So how come you ended up living in the Cotswolds?" asked Louise.

"Mum came from Nailsworth and, after my father abandoned her, she moved back to Gloucestershire to live with her parents. She said she had no reason to remain in Chesterfield and she couldn't cope with all the gossip. So she just upped and left. Once back in Nailsworth, she got a job as housekeeper for Clive, the local doctor. Six years later, she married him and was very happy, despite the fact that he was fifteen years older than her. You know as well as I do that she was never the same after he passed away in 2011."

"Mind you, I'm not surprised that she was never the same," added Louise. "It was probably caused by Clive's children from his first marriage trying to sell the house without any regards for his wishes or for those of your mum. I remember those days very well indeed."

"They were never going to achieve that," Nigel replied. "Clive had stipulated in his will that Mum could stay in that house for as long as she wanted. His children would only inherit it after she'd either died or had moved out voluntarily."

"So what happened to your father and all his relatives?" asked Louise. "Did your grandparents never try to contact you?"

"My father died in a head-on crash in 1984. Both he and his girlfriend were killed outright. He'd spent a lot of the money by then and I understand that the relatives of other people involved in the accident sued his estate. He wasn't insured, you see, as he had lost his driving licence after being caught speeding. The court found in their favour and consequently they got the rest of his money. One of the people in the other car had also died and another had life-changing injuries. So the compensation would have been massive. That was why there was no money left."

"Mark, I've known you for fifteen years, and you've never told me about any of this."

"To tell you the truth, I'd forgotten about it until the letter brought it all back again."

Louise put her arm around his shoulder.

"As for my father's family," he added. "I understand that my grandparents wanted nothing to do with Pete and me once their precious son had deserted us. Mum told me they both died shortly afterwards and since my father was an only child, it meant there was never going to be a happy reconciliation with the rest of my family. You know, sometimes I wonder how I would have turned out if my father hadn't won the pools. Would I have been a different person if I'd been brought up on a council estate in Chesterfield, rather than in a middle-class home in the Cotswolds? Would I still have been a teacher? Or would I have done something completely different instead? My father was a car mechanic. Perhaps I might have become one as well."

"There's no point in beating yourself up about it," said Louise whilst giving him a hug. "You will never know the answer to that one. There are plenty of teachers who were brought up on council estates. The chances are that you would have gone into education no matter where you came from. It's the way you are. It's your vocation in life."

"I guess you're right," said Mark. "Anyway, I've changed my mind about phoning Pete after supper. Do I have enough time to phone him before you serve it?"

"Yes, the casserole won't be ready for another half an hour," replied Louise. "You'll have plenty of time if you phone him right now."

Mark kissed her and went and got the phone. He dialled his brother's number.

Pete and Mark were as different as chalk and cheese. Mark was quiet and reserved in public, whereas Pete was brash and outspoken. Mark was keen on football and still supported Forest Green Rovers, his local team from the Cotswolds. Pete, however, was a rugby fan, an egg chaser as Mark called him. He supported Bath Rugby Club.

Most rugby fans from Nailsworth supported Gloucester. But at the time Pete had become interested in rugby, Bath had been the most successful team in England. Hence the reason why he had decided to support them instead.

"It's the rugby equivalent of supporting Manchester United," Mark said at the time.

Pete was keen to point out that Nailsworth was only 26 miles away from Bath.

"It's not exactly on the other side of the country, you know," he'd replied with disdain. "Or the other side of the world in the case of most Manchester United fans."

Mark had moved to Reigate after studying Chemistry at Warwick University followed by a one-year teacher-training course in Reading. In contrast, Pete had never ventured far from home. After leaving school, he'd gone to Stroud College where he'd qualified with a BTEC in business studies. He'd got a job as a management trainee for the West Country Cider Company, eventually becoming one of their salesmen. Three years later, he was promoted to area sales manager. However, his career stalled after that. West Country Cider was only a small company, and any further progression was limited to what's known as 'dead man's shoes'. His career wasn't going anywhere unless his boss decided to retire, which was unlikely as he was only 49.

Pete had considered applying for jobs with other larger firms. But that would involve relocating, which was something he had no desire to do. He lived in a decent size semi-detached house in Stroud, only three miles away from the Nailsworth property where he'd been brought up. He was a local Conservative councillor, a pillar of the community, a big fish in a small pond. He was never going to move for the sake of his career. He wanted to stay in Stroud, working for West Country Cider for as long as it took to get one more promotion that would give him a seat on the board.

Pete had been married to Wendy for nineteen years. They had two children. Jack was seventeen and studying for his A levels at Marling school. Hannah was fifteen and was a pupil at Stroud High School. Both of them were doing really well, which pleased Pete and Wendy. According to Jack's teachers, he should easily get the grades he needed to get into one of the better universities.

Hannah was due to sit her GCSEs the following year and was a bright girl. Her parents had no doubts about her ability to progress to the sixth form, just like her brother.

Pete's wife Wendy was five years younger than he was. She had originally been one of the receptionists in the practice where Pete and Mark's stepfather worked as a GP. She'd started working there aged eighteen and had immediately caught Pete's eye. They had begun dating and a year and a half later they were married. Two years after that, Jack was born and Wendy never went back to work again. She became a full-time mother and a 'domestic goddess', as she liked to refer to herself. Just like Nigella Lawson.

In fact, Wendy was quite like her favourite celebrity chef, providing you took away Nigella's sex appeal, cooking ability and her big lips. For Wendy's lips were very thin and, when you combined that with her small circumcision mouth, it made her look cold and uncaring.

More recently, Wendy had started making a range of cheeses and selling them at the Stroud Farmers' Market. She was particularly proud of her Double Gloucester, which had won a silver medal at the 2019 British Cheese Awards.

It was Wendy who answered the phone.

"Hi, Wendy," said Mark, "I believe Pete phoned me earlier."

"That's right," she replied. "He's been trying to get hold of you all day, only your mobile was switched off."

"Well, it's always switched off when I'm at school. Not only that, but I take tennis lessons after classes have finished on Tuesdays. It was half past five before I switched it back on again."

"Well, not to worry," she added. "He can speak to you now. I'll just go and get him."

There was a brief moment of silence before Mark heard the sound of the handset being picked up from the side table where Mark knew Pete and Wendy kept their phone.

"Hi, Mark," came the voice on the other end of the line. "I'd forgotten you took tennis classes on a Tuesday. Actually, I thought you had already broken up."

"Not until Friday, unfortunately," Mark replied. "I can't wait."

"Well, you know what they say about the teaching profession," added Pete. "You spend half your time on holiday, half drinking tea in the staff room and only 10% of your time teaching."

"That adds up to 110%," said Mark.

"Precisely, and to think it was a Maths teacher who originally told me that story. Not Louise, I hasten to add. I'm sure she can add up."

Mark shouldn't let his brother's jibes about his profession get to him. But Pete always managed to wind him up.

"Teaching isn't a doddle, you know. You're forgetting about all the marking we have to do at home."

"Oh, come on," replied Pete. "You know as well as I do you don't ever read the kids' homework. All you do is write at the bottom 'Must do better, try again'. Then after they hand it back again, you say, 'Still not good enough, try once more'. Finally, when they hand it back a third time, you scrawl 'Much better' and give them a star. Everybody's happy, the kid thinks he's a genius and never realises that you hadn't even read the load of old drivel he'd written."

It wasn't the first time Pete had said this to Mark. Most of their conversations started off in such a vein, which was one of the reasons why they didn't speak that often. Mark was tempted to remind Pete that he taught Chemistry, and whilst such practices might be possible in the Arts subjects, where pupils had to write essays, it was not feasible in the Sciences. But before he had time to speak, Pete had changed the subject.

"Anyway," he said, "that wasn't what I wanted to speak to you about. Did you get a letter from a solicitor in Derbyshire today?"

"Yes," replied Mark, "I've just finished reading it. What did you make of it?"

"I was working at home this morning and I opened it as soon as the post was delivered. At first, I thought it must be some kind of hoax. So I looked up the solicitors on Google and discovered they are a bona fide firm of country solicitors in Matlock. Consequently, I phoned them up and spoke to Mr Knight."

"And what did he say?" Mark asked eagerly.

"He wasn't able to expand much on what he'd written in his letter. However, he did tell me that the trust fund was set up in 1984 and the beneficiaries are the children of Andrew Bradbury. In other words, you and me."

"Okay. So why the challenges?" Mark continued. "Why doesn't the trust fund just divide the money up between the two of us?"

"He said the challenges had been specifically designed to teach us about our family history and about the county where we were born."

"Why?" asked Mark.

"He wouldn't say. He just said that his role was purely to ensure the terms of the trust fund were carried out, not to question those terms."

"But surely that could be achieved by simply telling us about our family history, not by setting us challenges. Mind you, I've got a far bigger question. Why was the trust fund set up in 1984, the same year our father died, and how come it is valued at £5 million? That must be far more than he had won on the pools. Not that I know how much that was. Do you?"

"I haven't got the faintest idea," replied Pete. "However, Mr Knight was able to shed some light on your second point. He told me that the trust fund was set up with a far smaller amount of money. But with prudent investment over the past 35 years, the sum has grown to the £5 million it is worth today. As for the reasons why our father set it up in the year he died, I can only speculate that he had some kind of premonition something might happen to him. So he decided to take some of his money out of Spain in order to provide for our future."

"Sorry, you are asking me to believe that the man who walked out of our lives in 1979, taking all his money with him, should decide five years later to invest in our future just in case he was about to die? I don't believe it. Anyway, here's another question. Why did we have to wait 35 years before finding out about it?"

"I think I know the answer to that one," said Pete. "It must be to do with Mum's death. Since she was entitled to half his money, he must have stipulated that we couldn't inherit until after she died."

"But surely that would mean the solicitors were complicit in the deception. I mean, if they knew that some of the pools money was invested in this country, wouldn't it be their duty to inform her?"

"I'm not sure about the legal position on that one," Pete replied. "But Mum's dead now, and it's not as if she had spent the rest of her life in poverty. Clive was quite a wealthy man in his own right and he made sure she never wanted for anything. The fact is that you and I now stand to inherit £5 million and I for one don't want to pass up the opportunity."

"It seems to me that we have a lot of unanswered questions here," Mark added. "And I've got two more. Firstly, why did a man, who was living in Spain in 1984, choose a small firm of solicitors in Matlock to administer the trust fund? Secondly, what happens to the money should we fail any of the challenges?"

"Well, I can only guess at the answer to your first question. Father would have needed a British solicitor to administer the trust fund. Don't forget he had lived in Derbyshire all his life before he moved to Spain. It would only be natural for him to choose a Derbyshire solicitor to act on his behalf. I haven't got a clue why he should choose a firm from Matlock rather than one from Chesterfield. Maybe he knew Knight from when he lived in Derbyshire or perhaps Knight was already the family solicitor. I'm afraid I don't know the answer to that. As for your other point, I did ask Knight the same question and he said he had the discretion to give any surplus funds to charity. He told me about one specific charity which was mentioned in the details of the trust fund."

"Go on, surprise me," said Mark.

"It's Cats Protection," said Pete. "Yes, the man who has given us precisely nothing over the past forty years now has us about to jump through hoops and, if we fail, all our inheritance will go to bloody Cats Protection. If it wasn't so tragic, I'd find it funny."

"So are you going to go to Chesterfield?" asked Mark.

"Too bloody right I am," replied Pete. "And you?"

"I wouldn't miss it for the world," added Mark. "After all, what have I got to lose?"

"Only two and a half million pounds," replied Pete.

Chapter 4

Friday, August 30th, 2019

Six weeks later, Mark and Pete were both heading to Chesterfield with their families in tow. As she got into the car, Louise commented that the two brothers had spoken to each other more often in the past six weeks than they had in the past six years.

Despite this, most of their questions still remained unanswered and their attempts to get more information out of James Knight had proved fruitless. It seemed that his stock answer was to say he was only there to ensure the terms of the trust fund were carried out. He also said that he was not there to question any of the details behind the fund, nor did he have any desire to do so. As a consequence of this, they were still in the dark and could only hope that all their questions would be answered once they arrived at Striding Hall.

Pete and Mark's cars reflected their different personalities. Mark drove a Dacia Logan, a no-nonsense Romanian estate car that was practical, good value for money and not at all flashy. Mark's journey would take him about three hours providing there wasn't too much traffic on the M25 or M1.

Pete's choice of transport was completely different. He didn't have to buy his own car as he drove a company vehicle. He had free range to choose any car priced up to £25,000 and had plumped for a BMW 2 series coupe. It was not the most practical of cars for a man with two teenage children, as it only had two doors and a relatively small boot. Still, it looked great and was a BMW, which said everything you needed to know about Pete. He was an important executive on his way to the top. Mind you, Louise had a different view of BMW drivers. 'Flash gits with small penises' was how she described them.

Fortunately for Jack and Hannah, their journey from Stroud would take half an hour less than that of their uncle. Even so, they were pleased to be able to stretch their long legs when they finally arrived at the hotel at half past four.

Striding Hall was impressive. Originally built in 1752 for some junior member of the landed gentry, it had started to deteriorate after the Second World War. In fact, when the current owner bought it in 1983, it was barely fit for human occupation and only then if they possessed numerous large pans and buckets. The roof had so many holes in it back then that it resembled a colander.

The new owner spent thousands restoring the property to its former glory and that expenditure was matched by the government. They provided a grant to help save the Grade 2 listed pile from dereliction.

Nowadays, in common with so many similar buildings, it was serving a new purpose as a country house hotel with fifteen individually furnished bedrooms, a spa and a nine-hole golf course.

The hotel was set in landscaped gardens leading down to a man-made lake, which was located on the far side of a minor road. The setting was extremely peaceful, a rural idyll and yet only two miles from Chesterfield town centre.

Pete pulled his BMW into the guest car park and was surprised by the lack of cars parked there. There was a ten-year-old Jag, a Mazda MX5 and a nearly new Range Rover. Pete always noticed cars and was a little bit disappointed that his BMW was only the second-best car in the car park.

"That's a situation which won't change when Mark arrives," Pete thought to himself as he unloaded his family's bags from the boot.

The family entered the hotel and went up to reception. Pete was used to staying in hotels, usually Premier Inns and Travelodges. Or, if the company were pushing the boat out, a Marriott.

This hotel, however, was a cut above the type you would find in one of the major chains. In order to preserve the integrity of the interior, there wasn't a purpose-built reception. Instead, the receptionist sat behind an imposing antique desk, which was located in one corner of a large entrance hall.

Pete was immediately reminded of the time he'd been caught smoking behind the bike sheds at school and sent to see the headmaster. On that occasion, he'd received a severe reprimand and a detention. Mind you, if it had been twenty years earlier, his punishment would probably have been six of the best from the headmaster's slipper.

"I wouldn't mind being punished by her," he thought to himself whilst looking at the receptionist, before reminding himself that he was there with his family.

"I'd like to welcome you and your family to Striding Hall, Mr Bradbury," said the receptionist after Pete had announced their arrival. "I hope your stay with us will be a pleasant one. We have three rooms reserved for you, all on the first floor. You and your wife are in our Lathkill Suite, your son is in the Darley Room and your daughter is in the Beresford Room. Please feel free to make full use of the facilities at the hotel during your stay. We have a spa with a swimming pool and, if you like golf, we have a nine-hole course. I am instructed to inform you that all your expenses during your stay will be met by the firm of Knight and Son. So just charge everything to your room."

"Does that mean I can order anything I like," asked Jack, "a bottle of champagne, for example?"

"No, you can't," his father cut in. "You're only seventeen. Anything you order will have to be approved by me first and it certainly won't include any alcohol."

"Spoilsport," muttered Jack under his breath.

"Mr Knight has requested that you meet him in the bar at 6 o'clock this evening, so he can speak with you prior to dinner," added the receptionist as she handed Pete the room keys.

That was another way in which Striding Hall differed from most other hotels. These days the majority of modern hotels have a card entry system for their bedrooms, whereas Striding Hall still relied on good old-fashioned keys. Not any old keys, mind you. These keys had been made in the eighteenth century and were totally in keeping with the age of the building. Each key had a beautifully ornate brass fob attached.

"If you are ready, the porter will now show you to your rooms," the receptionist announced.

Pete smiled at her and took the keys. The porter picked up their bags and led them up the staircase to their rooms on the first floor.

The rooms were impressive, especially Pete and Wendy's suite. It was absolutely huge with a super king-sized bed and an area laid out as a lounge, complete with a sofa and a 50-inch flat screen TV. It was the type of room where you could have a blazing row with your partner, and you wouldn't need to sleep in separate rooms if you still hadn't made up by the time you went to bed. You wouldn't even need to sleep in separate beds for that matter. The super king-sized one in the room was so large.

In addition, the room had a fantastic view of the hotel grounds, a landscape that culminated with the boating lake in the distance. It was enough to make even Pete think it had been worthwhile coming to Striding Hall just for the experience. Well, it almost made him think that but then he remembered the trust fund.

Mark and Louise had set off before Pete but had decided to stop for an hour in Chesterfield before proceeding to Striding Hall. Mark had not been back to Derbyshire since he'd left when he was two years old and was embarrassed to admit he knew absolutely nothing about the town of his birth. Pete had been back, though. He came to Chesterfield once a month in order to visit a wholesaler who sold his company's cider. Mind you, his visits had never taken in any more of the town than the industrial estate where the wholesaler was based.

Their mother had never spoken about their time in Chesterfield and had shown absolutely no desire to return there. Mark, out of a sense of loyalty to her, had never thought of going back either. But now that she was dead, and with recent events throwing up all manner of questions about his father, he'd decided to explore the town a little.

They arrived at about half past three and parked in a multistorey car park close to the town centre. It was market day and the town was quite busy with shoppers and people who were just out to enjoy the late August sunshine. Mark had a preconception of what Chesterfield would look like. It was an image that was shaped by a lifetime spent in the Cotswolds and the Home Counties. In other words, he expected it to be a grim northern town still reeling from the loss of its heavy industry.

It came as a pleasant surprise to discover that it was, in fact, a relatively wealthy provincial market town. Many of Chesterfield's ancient buildings had been preserved, especially those around the market square and the shambles.

"I thought the shambles were in York," said Mark as they started to wander through the narrow alleyways that made up the Chesterfield shambles.

"No, it's a generic term for an area that used to house butchers," said Louise as they walked past the Royal Oak, one of England's oldest pubs dating back to the twelfth century. "Most towns would have had a shambles back in medieval times."

One thing that Mark had heard of was the Crooked Spire, Chesterfield's most famous landmark. But he was not prepared for such an impressive building. He thought about going inside for a quick look around, but he had business to attend to. So he left Louise, Noel and Josh in a local computer games shop, whilst he made his way to Chesterfield's public library. He wanted to look at the archives to try and do some research about his father.

He didn't know the exact date of his father's death, other than it was sometime in 1984. However, he was pretty certain that news of his death would have made it into the local newspaper. It was only a hunch, but it paid off. After a few minutes spent looking at the papers for that year, he found the *Derbyshire Times* dated May 17th, 1984. It carried the headline, 'Chesterfield pools winner dies in Costa del Sol car crash'.

It wasn't so much the headline that surprised Mark. It was what followed that caused him to catch his breath. The article provided the following information:

Controversial figure Mr Andrew Bradbury who, along with his family, won over a million pounds on the pools in 1979 and who subsequently absconded to Spain, has died in a head-on collision near Marbella last Friday. According to Spanish police, Mr Bradbury, who had previous convictions for speeding, lost control of his Porsche 911 whilst travelling at over 100 mph on the A7. His car ploughed into a Volkswagen Golf travelling in the opposite direction killing both Mr Bradbury and his partner Joanne Willis outright. The driver of the Golf was proclaimed dead at the scene and a fourth person, who we believe was a passenger in the Golf, was taken to hospital with critical injuries.

This was the first time Mark had ever read anything about his father's death and two things surprised him. The first was that his father had won so much money. After all, a million pounds back in 1979 was an absolute fortune, worth several millions in today's money. The second thing was that the paper said Mr Bradbury and his family had won the pools. It really brought home to him the fact that his father hadn't just run away. He had stolen from their mother and from him and his brother. In that respect, his father was no different from any of the other criminals on the Costa del Crime.

He also began to realise why his mother had moved back to Nailsworth. Everybody in Chesterfield must have thought she'd got half a million pounds in her bank account. She probably couldn't cope with the shame of what had happened, all that whispering behind her back by the local gossips.

Mark took a photocopy of the newspaper article and went back to join Louise and the boys. They were still in the computer games shop where Josh was pestering his mother to buy him the latest version of a Super Mario Brothers game. She looked flustered and was extremely relieved when Mark arrived and rescued her.

"If you really want the game, you will have to save up your pocket money in order to buy it," said Mark.

"That's so unfair," shouted Josh, stamping his foot.

Mark wasn't prepared to tolerate a tantrum from his son, especially when they were in a busy shop in the centre of town. So he crouched down and looked him in the face.

"Stop it, Josh," he said. "Otherwise, you won't be getting any pocket money this week."

Mark's firm stance had the desired effect and Josh stopped moaning immediately. Strop over, they all left the shop, returned to the car park and headed towards Striding Hall.

On their way to the hotel, Louise read the article Mark had photocopied. She didn't think it revealed anything they didn't know already.

"Okay, so you didn't know he'd won over a million pounds, but you did know he'd won a substantial amount of money. In addition, you knew he'd died in a car crash in Spain and he wasn't insured. I don't think this article helps you to understand anything about the trust fund."

"I guess you're right," Mark replied. "But I'm still glad I went and found it."

A few minutes later, he pulled into the car park at the hotel. They checked in and were given the same briefing by the receptionist as the one Pete and his family were given fifteen minutes earlier. All the rooms in Striding Hall were named after Derbyshire dales and Mark and Louise found themselves in the Dove Suite. Noel and Josh were in Millers Room, an adjoining twin. Being as though they had over an hour to kill before they were due to meet up downstairs, Mark and Louise decided that they would freshen up and have a shower.

Their en-suite bathroom was massive. In fact, it was bigger than their bedroom at home and almost as big as the entire upstairs of their house. It had a rolltop bath and a separate shower cubicle, as well as his-and-hers wash basins. Louise had her shower first, whilst Mark took advantage of the hotel's wi-fi and looked up some things on his tablet.

Just before six o'clock, they knocked on the boys' door and the four of them went downstairs together. The hotel bar was located in what must once have been the Hall's library. It still had bookcases filled with exquisitely bound volumes on three of the four walls. Pete and his family weren't down yet and the only other people in the room were a group of five, who were sitting by one of the Georgian sash windows. Mark went to the bar and ordered a gin and tonic, a small glass of merlot and two cokes, whilst Louise and the boys took a seat at one of the tables.

A little while later, Pete and his family joined them. Normally, Mark would have asked them what they wanted to drink and bought the first round. But on this occasion, there seemed little point, as everything was being paid for by the trust fund through its administrator, Mr Knight. Pete was disappointed that the hotel didn't sell his cider and, not wishing to support one of his competitors, he decided to have a bottle of Marston's Pedigree instead. Wendy opted for an orange juice, whilst Jack had a Red Bull and Hannah a lime and soda.

"It's not bad this hotel," said Pete as he went over to Mark. "Our room is the size of Liechtenstein, and the toilet's so posh it makes my prick look shabby."

Mark smiled but, in reality, he was used to his brother's jokes and had long since stopped finding them amusing. Once they were all seated, Mark showed Pete the article he had found in the library.

"Did you know?" he said. "If you had invested a million pounds in the FTSE100 back in 1979, it would be worth sixteen million today. I looked it up on the internet before we came down."

"That makes sense," replied Pete. "After all, we know Dad couldn't have invested all his winnings in the trust fund. For a start, he bought a house in Spain and a Porsche. However, it is perfectly feasible for him to have invested, say three hundred thousand, which would be worth about five million today."

"I wish you wouldn't refer to him as Dad," said Mark. "Clive is our dad, not him."

"Well, how do you want me to refer to him?" Pete asked. "How about biological dad, which would make Clive non-biological dad. It makes them sound like two packets of washing powder."

Even Mark thought that was funny, as did the rest of the group and they all started laughing. That was why they didn't notice a couple of smartly dressed gentlemen approaching them.

The two men had entered the room at about the same time as Pete and Wendy and immediately started talking to the group of people sitting by the window. But now they made their way over to where the Bradburys were sitting.

Clearing his throat, the older one of the two said, "Well, I'm glad you are all enjoying yourselves. Can I introduce myself? I am James Knight, and this is Simon, my son and business partner. We would both like to welcome you to Striding Hall. I hope you will enjoy your stay here and I trust that you will all be very comfortable. Are your rooms okay?"

"Fantastic, thank you," said Wendy. "It really is a wonderful hotel."

"If a little quiet for August," added Pete.

"There's a reason for that," James explained. "We have reserved the whole hotel for you this weekend. The only people staying here are potential beneficiaries of the trust fund."

"In which case, who are the people over there?" asked Pete, whilst pointing at the group of five at the other end of the room.

"How very rude of me," added James, whilst walking across to the other group. "Let me introduce you to them. Pete, Mark, I'd like you to meet Ben and Rosie, your brother and sister."

Chapter 5

Friday, August 30th, 2019

There was no mistaking the similarities in looks between Pete and Mark and their newly found brother and sister. For a start, both of them had the Bradbury conk, the prominent Roman nose common to all members of the family. Pete used to joke about it, saying that noses ran in his family.

Then there was the black hair and dark eyes. There was absolutely no disputing it. The people they were being introduced to were definitely related to them.

"Bloody hell," said Pete. "I bet your mother was the Boythorpe bike?"

"Just ignore him," said Mark. "He's in shock. It's the nickname our mother gave to your mother. She never met her, but she was very bitter about what happened, which was only natural."

"That's fine," said Rosie. "It's just as big a shock for us as it is for you. After all, it's not every day you discover a couple of half-brothers."

"Exactly," added Mark. "I suppose we ought to introduce ourselves properly. "I'm Mark Bradbury, and I'm 42 years old, two years younger than my brother Pete over there. This is my wife, Louise and our two sons, Noel and Josh. Louise and I are both teachers at St Boniface's Girls' School in Reigate. I teach Chemistry and Louise teaches Maths. No doubt we'll all have plenty of time to discover more about each other later. I'll hand over to Pete now."

"For fuck's sake," said Pete as he looked to the heavens. "This is just like the last management course I went on. You introduce yourself to a group of people you don't know from Adam and tell them what you do and where you live. They're not the slightest bit interested and you're not interested in what they've got to say either."

"Except these people are your relatives," added Louise, who was looking at him disapprovingly. "They've never met you before and are bound to be interested. Anyway, can I please remind you not to swear in front of our children?"

"I'm sorry," Pete replied. "I didn't know it was their turn first."

This time nobody thought he was being was funny.

"Yes, okay, I suppose you're right," he added. "I'm Pete Bradbury, Mark's elder brother and I live in Stroud with my wife Wendy and our two children, Jack and Hannah. I'm an area sales manager for the West Country Cider Company and I'm also a councillor on Stroud District Council."

"Oh really, which party do you represent?" asked Ben.

"There is only one party," replied Pete. "I mean, there's only one that believes in law and order and encouraging local businesses."

"I didn't know Stroud was a one-party state," said the man wearing a bandana who was to the left of Ben. "It must be like North Korea, with you as Kim Jong Un. In fact, you remind me of him a bit. It must be your hairstyle."

Pete decided to ignore the man in the bandana and continued.

"I'm referring to the Conservative Party, of course."

"Really," added the man in the bandana. "You do surprise me. I'd have thought you were a fully paid-up member of the Monster Raving Loony Party."

Undaunted by the man's comment, Pete turned to Rosie and said, "Anyway, that's us, how about you?"

"I'm Rosie Stephenson and this is my younger brother Ben," she replied. "This is my husband Frank, and my daughter Zara. Frank and I run Scallys, a pub in Weston-super-Mare."

Frank bore more than a passing resemblance to Boycie from *Only Fools and Horses*. He was quite a few years older than Rosie. Either that or he had had a tough paper round when he was a boy, as Pete was to say later that evening. It was obvious that Rosie wore the trousers in their house. She couldn't have been more than 38, but her face was criss-crossed by worry lines resulting from a hard life. Rosie was responsible for throwing troublemakers out of the pub. Frank, in contrast, always seemed to be changing a barrel whenever a disturbance broke out.

Their daughter Zara looked nothing like her parents. For a start, she was a very good-looking girl with delicate features, a wonderful complexion and beautiful teeth. She was only sixteen years old, but had a confident look about her, which indicated that she was mature beyond her years. Pete later commented about her, saying there must be a really handsome milkman in Weston, as he couldn't believe she was Frank's daughter. Jack had noticed her too. He hadn't taken his eyes off her since the two halves of the family were introduced to each other. She had that effect on boys, something she was aware of and which she used to her advantage whenever she could.

Zara had a very individual style of dress. Like the rest of the family, she had jet-black hair and eyes that resembled the sky at night. This was complimented by black lipstick and, if all you could see was her head, you'd have sworn she was a Goth. But, unlike a Goth, her dress wasn't black. Instead, it was made of white chiffon, which made her look like a young Miss Havisham from *Great Expectations.* Mind you, Miss Havisham wouldn't have had her dress made from see-through material like Zara's. It was no wonder Jack's eyes were transfixed. He couldn't stop himself from staring at her bra.

For a brief moment nobody spoke but then the peace was shattered.

"Which cider do you sell?" asked Pete, never one to miss out on a business opportunity.

"Thatcher's Gold and Traditional," replied Rosie.

"If you switch over to us, I'll make sure we give you a good deal," Pete continued. "You can have family rates. They're the best available, even better than mates' rates."

"He never ceases to amaze me," Mark whispered to Louise. "He starts off by calling her the daughter of the Boythorpe bike. Then as soon as he realises there might be an opportunity to flog some of his cider, he's referring to her as family."

"Unfortunately, Thatcher's is the local cider," replied Rosie. "We couldn't replace it even if we wanted to."

"Trust me," said Pete. "If you sell our cider for 10p lower than Thatcher's, none of your regulars will give a damn that you've replaced it."

"Thanks for the offer, but we're not going to change," added Rosie.

Once that was over, it was Rosie's younger brother Ben's turn to introduce himself.

"Hi, I'm Ben Bradbury," he started.

"Whoa," said Pete. "You mean you took Dad's name even though he wasn't married to your mother?"

"We didn't take any name," said Rosie. "It was the name we were both given at birth and we had no say in the matter. I was also a Bradbury before I married. Furthermore, our father is listed on my birth certificate, just as presumably he is on yours."

"But are you Spanish or British citizens?" asked Wendy.

"We are as British as you are," replied Rosie. "The fact that we were both born in Marbella has nothing to do with anything. Come to think of it, Prince Philip was born in Corfu, and nobody would say he isn't British."

"And I always thought he was a bloody Kraut," added Pete sarcastically. "I never realised he was a goat banger."

"If I could continue," said Ben, whilst turning towards the man in the bandana who was next to him. "This is my friend Phil."

"Is he your special friend?" Pete interrupted.

"If by that statement, you are asking if we are gay and in a relationship, the answer is yes," said Phil. "It shouldn't surprise anybody. It is the 21st century, for Christ's sake."

"Well, I'll be buggered," replied Pete.

He obviously thought he was being hilarious, but on looking around, he saw only Jack was sniggering, and even he stopped when he saw Zara was looking at him and frowning.

Ben cleared his throat and continued, "Phil and I live in Brighton."

"Typical," said Pete. "I heard that Brighton is the nancy boy capital of Britain."

It was Mark who cut in this time.

"Pete, will you shut the fuck up?" he yelled.

Now it was his turn to get a disapproving look from Louise, as he suddenly realised that he had just sworn in front of his children.

"Sorry," he added meekly.

"I'm an actor and I also work part-time in one of the antique shops in the Lanes," Ben went on.

"That must be interesting," said Wendy attempting to rebuild some of the bridges her husband had destroyed. "My husband likes acting. He likes acting like a prat."

Everybody thought that was funny, everybody except Pete.

"Phil works for British Airways," Ben continued.

"Are you cabin crew?" asked Pete.

On the face of it, it was an innocent enough question. But everyone knew what he was implying. He was suggesting that the only job a gay man could have with an airline was that of a flight attendant.

"Actually, I'm a pilot based at Gatwick Airport," Phil replied, putting Pete firmly in his place.

"Can I make a suggestion?" James interrupted. "Dinner is about to be served. If we move into the dining room, we can continue getting to know each other over our meal. Afterwards, Simon and I want to spend approximately fifteen minutes briefing you on what you can expect over the next five days."

Nobody objected, so James led the way into the dining room. But before they left the bar, Mark had a quiet word with Pete.

"Pete, there is absolutely no reason to be so hostile towards them. We are related to them. It's not their fault our father abandoned us. And don't forget, we only lost one parent. They lost both of theirs and were orphaned when they were very small children."

"Yippee do," replied Pete. "I'm more concerned that we now have to share our inheritance with the two of them, when previously it was just you and me."

"Can I just remind you that, two months ago, we didn't know we had any money to inherit in the first place?" added Mark.

Conversation over, they went to join the others in the dining room. It was a lovely oak-panelled room containing a large mahogany table covered in a white linen tablecloth with matching napkins. It was laid out with silver cutlery and lead crystal glassware. Completing the picture were three silver candelabras, one at each end of the table and one in the centre. They provided the only light in the room, which added to the overall ambiance of the occasion. The rest of the family were already seated around the dining table, which was set for fifteen.

"I've split up the two sides of the family," explained James. "In that way, you can get to know each other better."

"How wonderful!" added Pete sarcastically.

He was just pleased he wasn't sitting next to Phil. Instead, he was seated between Ben and Zara. James and Simon were at each end of the table and there were six settings down one side and seven down the other. Jack was happy as he was also sitting next to Zara.

"Have you been on TV, Ben?" asked Louise.

"Yes, I played the role of Richard Fielding in 'Fielding's Folly', an episode of *Midsomer Murders*," Ben replied.

"Hold on, I remember that episode," said Pete. "Wasn't Richard Fielding murdered before the opening credits?"

"There's no shame in playing the part of a body in *Midsomer Murders*," answered Ben defensively. "Some of the best actors in Britain were murdered in Midsomer."

"How many lines did you have?" asked Pete.

"In that particular episode, I only had to say, 'Oh my God' and look surprised as I was impaled by a Zulu spear. But it could well lead to bigger roles."

"Hamlet in the next production by the Royal Shakespeare Company in Stratford perhaps?" Pete queried, his sarcasm barely disguised.

"The role in *Midsomer Murders* also involved playing the part of a dead body in the mortuary and that's not easy, believe me. They had to shoot it twice as I started laughing the first time."

"I believe Lawrence Olivier had the same problem when he was playing Heathcliff in *Wuthering Heights*," said Pete whilst nodding in a show of mock sympathy.

"Do we all want wine?" James asked them. "If so, shall I order a couple of bottles of red and a couple of bottles of white?"

"Can I have a glass of sparkling wine, please?" asked Zara.

"Hold on, you can't be eighteen yet," challenged Pete.

"No, she's sixteen," said Rosie. "But the law states that you can have alcohol with a meal in a licensed premises if you are sixteen or over. That's as long as it's bought for you by a responsible adult. It is the one exception to the over eighteen law and something we had to learn on our licensee's course."

"In which case, I'll have a Jack Daniels and Coke," said Jack.

"Unfortunately, you aren't allowed to drink spirits," added Rosie primly, "only beer, cider or wine."

"Okay then, I'll have a glass of sparkling wine as well," Jack replied.

"No, you won't," said Pete whilst looking sternly at his son, "you can have a soft drink and like it."

"Didn't you hear what Rosie said, darling?" said Wendy, rolling her eyes at her son. "Alcohol has to be bought for you by a responsible adult, which rules out your father."

"But Dad's not buying the drinks," Jack replied. "It's Mr Knight who's paying. So he has the final say."

"I'm not going to go against your father's wishes," said James.

"No, but I am," added Wendy. "Let him have a glass. After all, he will be eighteen in six months' time, and I want him to learn how to drink responsibly. I'd rather he does it here with a glass of sparkling wine at a family meal, than by drinking fifteen Jägerbombs in a nightclub during freshers' week."

Pete knew there was no point in arguing with his wife. Nonetheless, he was convinced that drinking wine with them tonight would in no way stop Jack from binging on shots as soon as he got to university. So he held his tongue and let James order two bottles of French merlot, a bottle of New Zealand sauvignon blanc and a bottle of prosecco.

Hannah sulked a little because she was just two months short of her sixteenth birthday. But in the end, she consoled herself with the knowledge she'd just acquired about alcohol licensing laws in the UK. She was sure she'd be able to put that knowledge to good use once she'd turned sixteen.

Soon the starter of ham hock terrine was served and the room went quiet as everyone began eating. Zara wasn't having the same as all the others. She was having a mushroom risotto as she had declared herself to be a vegetarian the previous month. Jack thought she was very grown up.

When they had all finished their first course, Mark asked Rosie what had happened to her and Ben when their parents were killed.

"We were both very young when it happened," she replied. "I was three, and Ben was only eighteen months old. Neither of us remember anything about that night, but we were later told that our mother and father had gone out for a meal and that Ben and I had been left with a babysitter. I guess we were lucky. If they'd taken us along, the two of us would almost certainly have been killed as well."

"Unless your presence would have made Dad drive more carefully," said Mark, whilst realising he had just called his birth father 'Dad' for the first time.

"Two days after the accident, our grandparents flew out to Spain and took us back home to Swindon with them. Grandma and Granddad were really great despite the fact that they were both in their early fifties when the accident happened. They spoilt us rotten. I guess they were trying to make up for the fact our parents had both died. Those were happy times and I remember them trying desperately to keep up to date, so they could give us the same type of upbringing as our friends. They bought us a Sega Mega drive one Christmas when I was about ten and Granddad got quite proficient at Sonic the Hedgehog. Later, he even went to computer classes so he could help us both with our homework."

There was a little tear appearing in her eye.

"He got dementia and died in 2009," she added. "Grandma was totally lost without him, and she died of a heart attack two years later."

"I'm really sorry about that," said Mark. "As I said to Pete, in many ways your story is even more tragic than ours. At least, we had our mother to look after us. She was always so solid. I can't believe she has gone. She died of a stroke earlier this year."

"Well, I guess that makes us all orphans now," Rosie replied.

"Yes," said Mark, "but let's look on the bright side. We've now all got two extra siblings we never knew about."

The waiters were serving the main course by this stage, which was roast chicken in a white wine sauce served with vegetables and fondant potatoes. Zara was having a chickpea curry.

Jack felt something brushing his leg and, looking down, he discovered Zara had taken her shoe off and was rubbing her foot up and down his leg. He looked at her and she winked at him seductively.

"Wow," he thought. "Zara is really pretty and she obviously likes me, but she is also my cousin. What if we get married and have children with six fingers and webbed feet?"

Then he stopped himself, "Hold on a minute, you're getting ahead of yourself here."

But at the same time, he made a mental note to look up the legality of shagging your cousin.

"So how did you get on in your GCSEs, Zara?" asked Louise, who was trying to make small talk.

"I got two As, five Bs and a C," she replied. "I'm going to Weston College next term, where I've got a place on a BTEC course in Fabrics and Textiles. After that, I'm hoping to study for a BA in underwear design at De Montfort University in Leicester."

"And what's after that?" enquired Pete sarcastically, "a PhD in thong manufacturing, perhaps?"

Zara scowled, turned her back on him and started a conversation with Jack instead, much to his delight.

Whilst all this was going on, Wendy was chatting to Frank.

"How long have you and Rosie been in the pub trade then, Frank?" she asked him.

"I started doing bar work when I couldn't find another job after leaving university," he replied. "I studied History of Art at Exeter University. But my choice of degree didn't exactly give me a massive selection of career opportunities once I'd graduated. So I ended up getting a job in a pub back in my hometown of Plymouth. A couple of years later, I was recruited as a roadie by a local band, and I made a career out of it, working with numerous rock groups. Rock music has always been a passion of mine, you see."

"And did you work with any famous bands?" enquired Wendy.

"Well nobody as big as Blur or Oasis," Frank replied. "I worked mainly with medium-sized bands playing on the university circuit. I guess the biggest ones I was involved with were Elastica and Supergrass."

Frank could see Wendy had a blank expression on her face and he could tell she'd never heard of either of them. Undaunted, he continued his story.

"In 1998, I finally decided that I didn't want to be a roadie for the rest of my life. I applied for a trainee manager position with Chef and Brewer, and it was whilst working at a pub in Swindon that I met Rosie. She followed me to Bristol after I was offered the assistant manager's position at a pub in the city. Shortly after that, we got married and, one year later, Zara was born. The following year, the pub manager left, and I was promoted to take over from him. It was a good job and I enjoyed it a lot. However, I'd always wanted to run my own business, and my dream came true in 2013 when we bought the lease of Scallys, an Enterprise Inns pub."

"And is it a good pub?" asked Wendy.

"It's predominantly a boozer," Frank replied. "We don't serve food, but we do put on a lot of bands using my old contacts from my days as a roadie. So it's the ideal business for Rosie and me in that respect. We cater mainly for bikers and heavy metal fans. From my description of it, you might think that the pub is a powder keg. However, we rarely have any serious trouble, apart from one time when a man wielding a machete jumped over the bar. That was pretty frightening, I can tell you."

"It would have put the fear of God into me," said Wendy.

"Well, that's the worst thing that's happened in the past six years. There's the occasional drunk we have to eject, of course. There's even the odd fight, usually between locals and holidaymakers, but it's nothing that Rosie and I can't deal with. We both love the licensed trade, but I sometimes wonder how long we can keep working in a biker's pub. It's really a job for a young person and neither of us are getting any younger, I'm afraid."

By the time Frank had finished his story, the dessert was being served and he was pleased to see it was a rather nice chocolate fondant. Noel and Josh both devoured theirs in a matter of seconds, in sharp contrast to their first two courses, which they had barely touched. Meanwhile, Jack had noticed Zara was eating the same dessert as all the rest of them.

"Perhaps, I ought to become a vegetarian as well," he thought to himself. "It doesn't look too bad after all. I'd then have more in common with Zara than a shared grandfather."

After finishing her dessert, Louise started talking to Phil.

"So how did you and Ben meet?" she asked him.

"We met in an antique shop in Brighton," he replied. "Ben just happened to be working there when I went in one day."

"And are you originally from Brighton?"

"No, I was born and brought up in Isleworth, which is where my parents still live," he replied. "I moved to Brighton when I won a place at Sussex University to study geography. I've lived there ever since."

"So did you join British Airways straight from university?" she asked him.

"More or less," he replied. "After I graduated, I didn't have a clue what I was going to do. It was my dad who suggested that I apply for a job with British Airways, and I'll always be grateful to him for pointing me in the right direction. He'd worked for them himself for over twenty years, you see."

"Like father like son, then."

"He wasn't a pilot like me, though. He was in charge of one of the hangers at Heathrow. Dad knew I'd stand a good chance of getting a pilot's job because of my degree. Geography is considered to be a good subject for pilots, you see. More importantly than that though, was the fact that I already had a private pilot's licence. It was all thanks to my parents who had given me a course of flying lessons for my eighteenth birthday. As a result, I was the ideal candidate, and that was why they offered me a job. I began training as a commercial pilot later that year, and eighteen months later I qualified. Shortly after that, they offered me a permanent position based at Gatwick, which suited me down to the ground. It meant I could stay in Brighton and could afford to buy a flat close to where I'd lived when I was a student."

"It seems that everything worked out perfectly for you," added Louise.

"I was very fortunate. I've got a job I love and a wonderful apartment in a beautiful Georgian building close to the centre of Brighton. Ben says that it's the most immaculate flat he's ever lived in. But that's mainly down to my enthusiastic cleaner, Mrs Podgorski."

"And you say you met Ben in an antiques shop?"

"That's right, antiques are my passion. It was whilst I was out looking for a Regency clock to compliment my recently acquired period dresser that I first encountered Ben. He was working in one of the shops in the Lanes. Although it didn't have what I was looking for, the two of us got talking. I discovered we both frequented the same pub and we arranged to meet there the following evening. Several glasses of white wine later, the two of us ended up in bed together and we've been going out with each other ever since."

"You were lucky Ben was in the shop," added Louise. "After all, his acting career must take up a lot of his time."

Phil gave her a sideways look and said, "Ben's acting career hasn't exactly taken off as much as he would have hoped. Last year, he only had fifteen days' work. In reality, that makes him a full-time shop assistant and a part-time actor."

While he was speaking, the waiters started clearing away the dessert plates, after which coffee was served. It was time for James Knight to stand up and to address the assembled group. He banged his spoon on the table and cleared his throat.

"Ladies and gentlemen. It has been my privilege to administer quite a few trust funds in my career. But I have never been involved in one quite like the one Mr Bradbury asked our partnership to set up for him back in June 1984. The main difference between this trust fund and others I've been involved in is that you are required to complete three challenges in order to benefit from the fund and its proceeds. Every time you successfully complete one of these challenges, you will be rewarded."

"Oh, great," said Pete. "You make us sound like one of Pavlov's dogs."

James ignored him, while the others looked at him with disapproval.

"Having said that, I must inform you that if you fail to solve all these challenges, you will end up with nothing at all. We also have three excursions planned for you. These start tomorrow when I'll be taking you to a football match, but not to any old match. Your father was a big Chesterfield fan and back in May 1979, he was due to see Chesterfield play in their final game of the season. But he never made it. Tomorrow, we are going to see a rerun of the match your father missed back in 1979, Mansfield Town versus Chesterfield. It is an early kick-off at 1 pm, and after that, we will have the first challenge."

Pete was going to make a derogatory comment about football but changed his mind seeing that his comment about Pavlov's dogs didn't go down too well.

"On Sunday, I will be taking you all on a tour around the Peak District, taking in some of the places your father would have visited in his youth. It is important that you pay attention and be observant on this trip, as this will help you during the second challenge, which will take place on Monday. Then on Tuesday, I will take you to see various places where your ancestors lived and worked. Once again, it is important that you take note of everything you see and hear, as this will help you in your final challenge on Wednesday. Our last dinner together will be on Wednesday evening and the plan is for you all to leave after breakfast on Thursday. I hope that's clear. Now, are there any questions?"

"It's as clear as mud," said Pete. "I still want to know why we have to participate in these games in the first place."

"Okay," said James. "As I understand it from the terms of the trust fund, Mr Bradbury wanted you to find out more about your family and your roots here in Derbyshire."

"But we don't even come from Chesterfield," said Ben. "Both Rosie and I were born in Spain. Neither of us has ever been to Derbyshire before."

"Which is precisely why the terms of the trust fund are as they are. You know nothing about your family on your father's side, who all your relatives are or where they came from. Hopefully, by the end of the next few days, all that will have changed."

"What I don't understand," said Mark, "is why our father abandoned both his family and Derbyshire and moved to Spain if he was so enamoured with them?"

"For love, of course," added Rosie.

"Can I just say one thing?" said James. "Although I cannot answer most of your questions, I can promise you that you will find the answers yourselves over the next five days. Now, can I suggest that we all retire to the bar?"

Just as everyone was getting up from the table, he added, "Oh, there is one more thing I forgot to mention. Whilst the younger members of our group are more than welcome to come on any of the excursions and to participate in any of the challenges, I do recognise that they may wish to do something else. Consequently, we have arranged a variety of alternative days out hosted by Simon here and his wife Katie."

He added, "What have you got planned for tomorrow, Simon?"

"A trip to McDonald's followed by a visit to the cinema to see the new Star Wars movie," he replied.

"Good, so if any of your children want to participate in this, can you let us know after tomorrow's breakfast?"

James led the way back to the former library. Pete was the last to return. He approached Mark who was standing by himself at the bar deep in thought.

"I think I'd rather go to the cinema than watch a fourth division football match," he told him.

"It's called division two these days," Mark replied. "However, if you were brought up watching non-league football like I was, it will be a step up. That's despite the fact that Forest Green are in the same division as Chesterfield these days."

Something had been bothering Mark ever since James had started his speech. All of sudden, he realised what it was. He pulled the photocopied article from his pocket and showed it to Pete again.

"Pete," he said. "Read this article one more time and tell me what's wrong with it."

Pete studied the photocopy again and said, "You've got me. I haven't got a clue."

"It's the date," Mark added. "The paper is dated May 17th, 1984 and it says our father died the previous Friday, which would mean he died on May 11th."

"Your point being?" said Pete looking perplexed.

"Well," Mark went on. "James just said the trust fund was established in June 1984, which would be one month after the paper said he died. How on earth can that be correct?"

Chapter 6

Friday, August 30th, 2019

"Perhaps James has got the dates wrong?" suggested Pete.

"He's a bloody solicitor," Mark replied. "Everything he does has to be accurate."

"That's all very well and good, but it's not my experience of dealing with the legal profession," Pete continued. "What I think has happened here is that Dad instructed Knight just before he died, and it took him several weeks to set the whole thing up. It's a well-known fact that solicitors always take ages. It's how they justify their enormous bills. How else do you think he can afford to drive a Range Rover?"

"How do you know he drives a Range Rover?" enquired Mark.

"It's an educated guess," said Pete. "When we arrived, there were only three cars in the car park. The hairdresser's two-seater obviously belongs to Ben Doon and Phil MacCavity over there. Also, if you've dealt with as many publicans as I have over the years, you'd know that they all drive second-hand Jags. That leaves only the Range Rover, which, by a process of elimination, must belong to Knight."

"I'm not so sure that James did get the dates wrong," said Mark. "Perhaps our father didn't actually die in 1984. Think about it. He had already run away once. What's to say he didn't fake his own death and disappeared a second time? He could have had regrets about abandoning us. That was why he probably decided to set up the trust fund for us immediately after his second vanishing act."

"That doesn't make sense," replied Pete. "It would mean he'd have to have regrets about abandoning his first family at the same time as walking out on his second family. Also, what about Dozy and Bent's mother? Do you think she was in on it as well? In which case, you'd also have to believe she abandoned her children as part of a pact with Dad. Of course, there is another possibility. Dad killed her in order to get away from her."

"You've absolutely no evidence whatsoever to support that theory," Mark interjected. "Our father may have done some pretty despicable things in his life, but I cannot believe he was a murderer."

"Well, I may have no proof of that," Pete continued. "But I was only taking your theory that he didn't die back in 1984 one stage further. That theory isn't exactly built on rock-solid foundations either. It's all based on just a one month's discrepancy in Knight's briefing. Mind you, we could always clear it up by talking to him, asking him to clarify things."

"It would be waste of time," Mark went on. "You should know more than anybody that he will use the excuse that he is just here to implement the terms of the trust fund, not to question any of its detail. No, I think we should discuss it with Rosie and Ben. After all, they might have a totally different perspective on everything. Don't forget that all the information we have about our father has come from our mother. I may have loved her dearly, but I wouldn't expect her to be fair and impartial about him."

"That's not completely true," added Pete. "The article in the *Derbyshire Times* backs up everything she told us about his death.

But you are correct. Come on, let's go and have a word with Bet Lynch and the sugar plum fairy."

Rosie was deep in conversation with Louise when they approached her, but Louise wanted to put the boys to bed and was pleased for an excuse to leave. Pete and Mark explained that they wanted a word with both her and Ben and, a few minutes later, the four of them were sitting around a table in the corner of the room.

"I've noticed that there's a contradiction between the date on which the *Derbyshire Times* reported our father's death and the date the trust fund was established," said Mark.

"Perhaps the *Derbyshire Times* made a mistake," replied Rosie.

Mark showed them the photocopy he'd taken from the paper dated May 17th, 1984.

"The paper couldn't have made a mistake," he continued. "It says that Dad was killed on May 11th, six days before this edition was printed. Yet James said the trust fund wasn't established until June of that year. That was a month after he died."

"So perhaps James has made a mistake then," said Rosie.

"I doubt if he'd get something like that wrong."

"I think all it means is that Dad gave instructions about the trust fund before he died," added Pete. "But it wasn't set up until after his death."

"However, there could be a different reason," said Mark, "which is why we want to compare what we know about his death with what you were told."

Rosie had only been three when her parents were killed and Ben had been a toddler. So they obviously remembered absolutely nothing about that day. Everything they had learnt about the accident had come from their grandparents.

They compared what they knew about their father's death in order to identify any other discrepancies, but there weren't any. It seemed that Rosie and Ben had been told exactly the same story by their grandparents as Pete and Mark had heard from their mother. Except their grandparents had never mentioned the pools win or the fact that their father had another family in Chesterfield. But the conversation did help in another respect. Ben put forward an alternative explanation for what had happened.

"Our father might not have taken his entire winnings to Spain," he suggested. "Instead, he could have left some of the money in a deposit account in England. What if he also left instructions with James Knight, telling him to establish a trust fund for his children with this money in the event of his death? Not only that, but his instructions may have contained details of how he wanted the trust fund to be run."

"That would explain why the fund was set up after he died," said Mark. "But wouldn't it have compromised Mr Knight? If he knew that half the money belonged to our mother, wouldn't he have been breaking the law by not disclosing it?"

"You've hit the nail on the head by saying 'if'," added Ben. "What if he didn't know that some of the money belonged to your mother?"

"I don't believe that for one instance," said Pete. "He's a solicitor in Derbyshire and Mum and Dad's pools win must have been massive news in the county when it happened."

"Okay, but even if he did know the truth about it, I'm not at all sure he was breaking the law by not revealing it," Ben continued. "Surely, it's a solicitor's job to do the best for his clients irrespective of what crimes they have committed, not to question whether they are guilty or not."

"That's one way of interpreting the British judicial system," added Pete.

Mark was partially satisfied by this argument but still wasn't totally convinced. However, just like the rest of the group, he'd had enough of going around in circles for one day. Also, he'd noticed that all of their other halves were beginning to get a bit agitated with being left out of the conversation. Therefore, he suggested that they have another drink before retiring for the evening.

Later, as they were getting into bed, Louise turned to him and said, "You know, I never knew Pete was homophobic."

"He's not," said Mark. "He just thinks if he winds the others up, they will give up and leave the inheritance to the two of us."

"He's deluding himself," said Louise. "Who in their right minds would turn their backs on more than a million pounds just because of a few insults? Anyway, I think your new brother and sister are both very charming."

With that, she turned off the light and they both went to sleep.

"What do you think of your new relatives?" asked Frank once he and Rosie were safely back in their room.

"I can see us staying in touch with Mark and Louise," Rosie replied. "They both seem really nice and they've obviously done a good job bringing up their boys. To be fair, so have Pete and Wendy. However, I am not at all sure about the two of them. I don't like Pete. He reminds me of a business development executive I once met from Enterprise Inns, all mouth and no trousers, all show and no substance, thinks he's a comedian and God's gift to women. You know the type. But I do sympathise with him for being married to Wendy. I really don't like the way she keeps on putting him down in front of us. Not that he doesn't deserve it, mind you, after continuously making pathetic jokes about Ben and Phil."

Meanwhile, a similar conversation was going on in Ben and Phil's room.

"You know, I've always dreamt about having older brothers and now it's finally come true," said Ben.

"I thought it was always older men you dreamt about," replied Phil. "You've never mentioned anything about wanting brothers before. It's a pity one of them is a tin hat."

"A what?" asked Ben.

"A tin hat. It's Cockney rhyming slang for … Well, you can guess what it's rhyming slang for," replied Phil.

"I think you're wrong about Pete," added Ben. "It could just be the shock of what he's found out this evening that's making him say some of those things. He's probably fine when you get to know him."

Phil leant over and kissed him.

"You know, that's what I like about you," he said. "You always see the best in people."

The conversation in Pete and Wendy's room was slightly different.

"Can't you back me up for once?" said Pete, showing his frustration. "Why do you have to belittle me all the time?"

But Wendy had already turned her back on him and ignored his comments as she pretended to be asleep.

The one person who was really asleep was Jack. He was dreaming about Zara in a rerun of what had happened over dinner. Except this time, it wasn't his leg she was rubbing.

Chapter 7

Saturday, August 31st, 2019

The following morning, everybody met for breakfast in the hotel's dining room. This time Phil wasn't wearing his bandana, which revealed his perfectly bald head.

"Never trust a man with a bald head," said Pete. "If a man's head looks like his arse, then you know he talks shit."

He was getting his own back after Phil's Kim Jong Un and Monster Raving Loony comments from the previous evening.

"His head would be covered in spots if it looked like your arse," Wendy replied, which caused Pete to choke on his coffee.

At nine o'clock, James entered the room. Unlike the previous day when he'd been wearing a suit, he was dressed in casual trousers and a polo shirt.

"Hello, you can tell it's the weekend," sneered Pete.

"Have you all had a good night's sleep?" asked James.

"Great, thanks," replied Louise on behalf of all of them.

"Good," said James. "Now, have the younger members of the family decided to go to the football or to the cinema?"

The verdict amongst them was unanimous. They had all plumped for Star Wars. Noel and Josh both loved football but only went to matches involving Forest Green Rovers. Besides which, it was an opportunity for them to get some proper food at McDonald's. They both preferred happy meals to ham hock terrine any day of the week. Hannah and Zara didn't want to go with the adults because neither of them liked football and Jack had decided he was going wherever Zara went.

"In which case, I'll arrange for two minibuses to pick up both groups at 12 noon," James continued. "For those of you going to the football, I'm afraid you won't be able to have any lunch today since the match kicks off at 1 o'clock. However, there will be coffee and biscuits served in the bar at 11.15 and afternoon tea and sandwiches when you get back."

"Why is it an early kick-off anyway?" asked Pete.

"Because it's a local derby," Mark replied. "If they kicked off at 3 o'clock, most of the supporters would be as drunk as skunks and looking to kick seven bells out of each other."

"Since you've got more than two hours before morning coffee, you might as well make full use of the hotel's facilities," said James. "There's a golf course and a spa with an indoor swimming pool."

"Do you fancy a few holes?" Pete asked Wendy.

"If I must," she replied.

"I bet I know of one hole that's out of bounds," whispered Mark.

"Don't be so crude," replied Louise whilst at the same time trying not to laugh.

Whilst Pete and Wendy went off to play golf, the rest of the family decided to go swimming.

The hotel's pool was inside a large glass conservatory and there were members of the public using it. These were people who had all paid an annual membership allowing them to use Striding Hall's leisure and spa facilities. Mind you, that didn't mean they could use the hotel car park. They had to use the separate one reserved for people using only the leisure facilities instead.

Despite having more than 250 fully paid-up members, there were not many of them using the pool at 10 am on a Saturday morning, even though it was still the school holidays.

Shortly after diving in, Phil swam up to Mark and asked if he could have a quick word with him.

"I want to tell you something about Ben," he said. "Ben has always wanted an older brother. Now that he's discovered he's got two of you, it's a dream come true for him. Or rather it would have been if Pete wasn't being so horrible towards him. Can you please tell him to stop and think before he opens his big mouth again? Otherwise, I will be forced to shut it for him."

"Well, I'll try," said Mark. "But he doesn't usually pay any attention to what I say. He likes to wind people up, me included, and I don't think I can change that side of him. My advice would be to ignore him. He's not anti-gay. He just thinks he's being amusing with his constant jibes."

Mark didn't really want to reveal to Phil the main reason why Pete was doing it. How could he tell him that he was trying to piss them off, so they'd go home, leaving him and Mark with a larger share of the inheritance?

"Well, just see what you can do," added Phil before swimming over to join Ben.

On the far side of the pool, Jack was doing back flips off the diving board to try and impress Zara. She wasn't paying any attention to him, though. Instead, she was chatting to Hannah.

"Do you fancy my brother?" asked Hannah.

"Good God no, he's far too immature," Zara replied. "Anyway, I've got a boyfriend back home who's 22. He's called Brad and he drives a Moto Guzzi V85. I'll show you a photo of him if you like, he's a real hunk."

"So why are you leading Jack on?" Hannah continued.

"Because it's good fun," Zara replied. "Because it's what girls do. Boys play football; girls play at winding boys up. It's the way of the world, the way it's always been. You'll soon learn."

With that, Zara set off on another length of the pool. She was a good swimmer and had already told Hannah she'd been the under-sixteen county champion at the 100-metre freestyle event the previous summer. Hannah set off after her but was only halfway across by the time Zara reached the other side.

"Come on, slow coach," Zara shouted at her as she heaved herself out of the pool and headed for the changing area.

It was eleven o'clock and nearly time for coffee, although that was of little interest to Noel and Josh. Louise had great difficulty persuading them to get out of the pool and only succeeded after threatening to prevent them from going on the trip to McDonald's and the cinema.

Once they had all got changed, they made their way back to the bar where coffee was being served. Pete and Wendy soon joined them and Mark went straight across to the two of them. Out of the corner of his eye, he could see Phil watching him.

"Wendy, do you mind if I have a brief word with Pete?"

Wendy didn't say anything but merely took her cup and saucer over to where Louise was standing.

"Pete," he said, "you've got to stop winding up Ben and Phil. It's not clever and Ben is our brother, after all."

"Half-brother," Pete corrected him. "What's brought this on?"

"Phil's spoken to me. He told me Ben had always wanted an older brother and now you're ruining it all for him."

"What a bummer," added Pete.

"That's not funny," Mark replied. "Just think about it. You want Ben and Rosie to go home so we may benefit from a larger share of the cake. But even if you were successful, it probably wouldn't do us any good. Didn't you say any surplus funds would go to Cats Protection?"

Pete thought about it for a few seconds before admitting, "I've forgotten about that."

He took another pause and added reluctantly, "Okay, I'll try my best not to wind up the shirt lifters in future."

"Pete," said Mark, scowling at his brother, "just remember what you've promised."

"I said I'd try my best," Pete replied. "I never promised anything."

Their conversation was interrupted when James and Simon entered the room. They were accompanied by a pretty girl with curly blonde hair, no more than 25 years old.

"This is my wife, Katie," said Simon. "She'll be helping me with the trip to MacDonald's and the cinema."

Everybody introduced themselves and said hello to her.

Knowing that she would be leaving her boys in the hands of two virtual strangers, Louise asked, "And what do you do for a living, Katie?"

"I'm a teacher," she replied.

"That's a coincidence," said Louise. "Mark and I both teach. What subject do you specialise in?"

"I teach children with learning disabilities," she replied.

"That's admirable," said Wendy. "Personally, I wouldn't have the patience to look after children with special needs."

"It also makes her the ideal person to look after our lot," commented Pete.

Wendy was not impressed by Pete's interruption and mouthed the words, "Why did I ever marry him?" whilst at the same time looking towards the sky.

"Right," said James, "I hope you are all ready to go. Adults are with me in the white minibus. Teenagers are with Simon and Katie in the green one."

Noel and Josh weren't teenagers yet. But by referring to the group in this way, he at least avoided annoying Jack, Zara and Hannah by calling them children.

James led the way to the minibuses. The green one was the first to depart, with Simon driving. He headed off towards the entertainment complex in Chesterfield where MacDonald's and Cineworld were located.

A few minutes later, the adults were also on their way. Their minibus was driven by James, and he was heading towards Mansfield on the A617. It took him only half an hour to reach Field Mill, the home of Mansfield Town. Fortunately, he was able to park close to the stadium.

"We've got seats in the North Stand," said James as he handed out the tickets. "Just follow me."

He seemed to know where he was going, and it didn't take long for them to go through the turnstiles and take their seats.

"At least we've got seats," said Louise, who still remembered the first time she had been to the Lawn Ground with Mark to see Forest Green Rovers play. She had spent an uncomfortable two hours standing on the terraces watching them play out a dull 0-0 draw with Aldershot.

The North Stand at Field Mill was reserved for away fans and, being as though this was a local derby, it was going to be filled to capacity with its 1,800 supporters. However, the Chesterfield supporters were still outnumbered by the home fans of which there were approximately 6,000.

"Have you been to a professional game of football before?" Rosie asked Louise.

"A few times," said Louise. "Mark supports Forest Green Rovers, the local team from Nailsworth where he grew up. The last time I went with him was two years ago when we saw them promoted to the football league at Wembley."

"It was the proudest day of my life," Mark cut in. "Nailsworth only has a population of 5,000. That makes it smaller than the number of people in this stadium today. We are the only village team ever to make it into the football league."

Seeing the way Louise was looking at him, he added hurriedly, "What I meant to say was that it was the proudest day of my life other than our wedding day and the days when our two boys were born."

It turned out that Pete had also been to a few Forest Green matches. Clive had taken him when he was a youngster. But he'd never been as enthusiastic as Mark. Later on, he'd taken up rugby when he was a pupil at Marlings, the same school that Jack now attended.

Frank had been to a few Plymouth Argyle games over the years, even seeing them play against Chesterfield on one occasion. He still counted himself as a supporter although he hadn't seen them play in years, mainly because running the pub was so time-consuming.

Ben had seen Swindon Town play a couple of times when he was a teenager. Phil had been to a few Spurs games with his father, but neither Wendy nor Rosie had ever been to see a professional game of football before. Together they made up the unlikeliest group of spectators in the away end at Field Mill.

Their conversations were abruptly halted as a big cheer went up. The players were running out onto the pitch and their fellow supporters in the North Stand all started clapping in unison and chanting "Spireites," to which the Mansfield supporters replied saying "shit," every time the away fans shouted out the name of their team.

Anticipating this response, the Chesterfield fans taunted them back by shouting "Scabs, Scabs."

"What's that all about?" asked Wendy.

"Mansfield's nickname is the Stags," said James. "The Chesterfield fans started calling them the Scabs because of the miners' strike. Mansfield is in Nottinghamshire and the Nottinghamshire miners continued to work whereas the Derbyshire miners went on strike for a year."

"For Christ's sake," said Pete. "The miners' strike was 35 years ago. Don't these morons realise there aren't any pits in the UK anymore?"

At this point, a man behind them tapped Pete on the shoulder. He'd heard his comments and recognised his posh Gloucestershire accent.

"Oy yu southern poof," he said. "If yu don't shut yer fucking gob, I'll knock yer teeth so far down yer throat tha'll be eating yer next meal through yer fucking arse."

Most of the group wanted to curl up and die at this point, but not Pete who immediately replied.

"Here mate," he shouted, "don't call me a southern poof. I think you're confusing me with Ben Dover and Phil McCrackin over there. I'll have you know that I was born in Chesterfield."

Realising what he'd just said, he turned to Ben and Phil and said, "Sorry lads, I didn't mean it. It just came out."

Then he paused before adding, "A bit like you two. Do you get it? Came out? Out of the closet?"

Ben and Phil just scowled at him as did Mark.

In an attempt to change the subject, Rosie asked James which team they were supporting.

"Chesterfield, of course," he replied, "the team playing in red."

"So why are all the supporters wearing blue and white or blue and yellow?" asked Rosie.

"Blue and yellow are Mansfield's home colours whereas our home colours are blue and white," replied James. "Red is the colour of Chesterfield's away kit."

The game kicked off and it was a typical division two derby, high on passion and drama but low on skill. Pete set out to remain silent during the match but eventually couldn't resist. He joined in with the cheering when Chesterfield was awarded a corner or a free kick in a dangerous position. He also jeered whenever the referee gave a decision against the away team and even chanted "you don't know what you're doing" when he booked Chesterfield's Will Evans for a particularly bad challenge.

He was beginning to enjoy himself and even the guy behind him had forgiven him.

At half time, the score was still 0-0. Despite the lack of goals, there was no doubt that the group was having a good time. Even Wendy, Rosie and Ben were enjoying it, despite claiming they didn't like football. There was just something about a local derby in front of a capacity crowd that made the game far more intense than an ordinary football match.

James asked if any of them wanted anything to drink during the half-time break. None of them did though. They all remained in their seats whilst the Mansfield player of the month for August was announced.

Sammy the Stag, the Mansfield mascot, went berserk when it was revealed that the honour had gone to defender Hayden White. The Chesterfield fans immediately started taunting him, chanting "Hayden's shite" as he was presented with his award.

Once that was done, the rest of the players came out for the second half. Mansfield kicked off and were immediately camped in the Chesterfield half. They were obviously under instructions to take the game to the opposition and get an early goal. Chesterfield was defending manfully, but after ten minutes Mansfield's Andy Cook had a shot on goal, which Will Evans blocked with his hand.

"Handball," shouted the Mansfield fans.

If the referee had thought it was deliberate, he would have had no option but to send Evans off and to award Mansfield a penalty. Even if he'd only given him a yellow card, he still would have had to dismiss him, as he'd already been booked.

Depending on your point of view, either the referee was unsighted and therefore was unsure whether it was deliberate or not, or he bottled it. But either way, he waved play on and, as is so often the case, Chesterfield went straight up the other end and scored.

The North Stand erupted with joy, but the home fans were outraged.

"Dirty cheating bastards," they all chanted as one.

However, their main anger was targeted against the referee, and they began to chant, "You don't know what you're doing."

The situation was made worse by the Chesterfield fans who shouted out "handball" every time their side kicked the ball. They were mocking the home fans and the appeal they had made a few moments earlier.

The score remained at 1-0 until the final whistle. This was despite Chesterfield having to endure a final twenty minutes where Mansfield threw everything bar the kitchen sink at them.

It could have turned nasty outside the ground, but there were plenty of police on duty that day with all leave cancelled because of the local derby. Consequently, they managed to keep a lid on it.

"I really enjoyed that," said Ben as he climbed into the minibus. "The only thing I didn't enjoy was your outburst, Pete."

"I thought you'd forgotten about that," replied Pete. "Anyway, I did apologise, didn't I?"

"And I accept your apology," said Ben.

Even though Ben was prepared to forgive Pete, it was a very different story when it came to Phil. He certainly wasn't minded to forgive him.

"I didn't think it was particularly enjoyable," Pete continued, completely contradicting the fact that he'd been chanting and cheering along with everyone else. "I've never really liked football that much. Give me rugby any day of the week. There's no need for crowd segregation and the game's played by real men, not bloody ballerinas who fall over at the slightest hint of any contact."

That was the point when Phil saw his opportunity.

"It seems Ben and I aren't the only ones who bat for the other side," he said, looking at Pete. "After all, it's a well-known fact that guys who like rugby only watch it because they like to see grown men grabbing hold of each other's genitals in the scrum. That's why they're called rugger buggers, you know. It's also why it's called the scrum, it's short for scrotum. In fact, the whole game was dreamt up by a group of homosexuals from a boarding school, who liked nothing better than playing with odd-shaped balls."

"Don't talk rubbish," shouted Pete. "William Webb Ellis wasn't an arse bandit."

But Phil was far from finished.

"Anyway," he went on. "It's been proven that men who are the most vehemently opposed to homosexuality are gay themselves but are still in the closet. Truly heterosexual men don't have a problem with other men being gay."

"Are you implying that I'm a dung puncher?" said Pete, absolutely horrified.

"It takes one to know one," added Phil.

"I am not gay," screamed Pete going red in the face.

"No, but I bet you've slept with a few men who are," said Phil.

He was thoroughly enjoying winding Pete up and it was working. Pete went to grab hold of Phil but was stopped by Frank who was sitting between them in anticipation of trouble. Frank didn't like conflict and usually did his best to avoid it. In the tight confines of the minibus, he had little option but to act as peacemaker.

"Guys, guys," he said. "The rest of us are absolutely fed up with your bickering. Pete, can't you see Phil is just winding you up, in exactly the same way you've been winding him and Ben up ever since you met them yesterday? Can you please call a truce and agree not to discuss anyone's sexuality for the rest of the time we are here?"

Frank looked sternly at both of them before they nodded and settled back down in their seats again. With a potential crisis avoided, they set off for the hotel and half an hour later they were back.

"Okay, guys," said James. "The plan is that we will now have afternoon tea in the bar before starting the first challenge at 4 pm. And there's no need to worry about Noel and Josh. Simon and Katie will continue to look after them until we've finished."

"How long will the challenge take?" asked Mark.

"We should be finished by six o'clock," replied James.

Most of the conversation over tea was about the challenge, with everybody wondering what form it would take. Eventually, four o'clock arrived and James put them out of their misery.

"This particular challenge is designed to get you in the mood for the bigger challenges to come," he announced. "It's called the Red-Blue challenge and I am going to divide you into two teams. Pete, Wendy, Mark and Louise will be in one team. Ben, Phil, Rosie and Frank will be in the other. Both teams need to appoint a team leader who will act as their team's spokesperson. The two teams will be based in separate rooms, one in Wolfscote Room and one in Monsal Room. In each of the rooms, you will find sixteen Lego bricks, eight red and eight blue."

"What are you expecting us to do with them?" said Pete. "Make a model car?"

James just ignored him.

"Each team needs to decide which colour brick they are going to bring to me," he continued. "I am the scorer for this challenge, and I will be based here in the bar. If both teams bring a red brick to me then both teams will score one point. However, if one team brings a red brick and the other brings a blue brick, the team bringing the blue brick will score ten points and the team bringing the red brick will score minus ten points. Finally, if both teams bring me a blue brick, then both teams will receive minus two points. The challenge will take place over eight rounds and, in order to win the prize, you must not finish up with a negative score. Your team leaders will have the opportunity to negotiate with each other, but only after rounds four and rounds six. Now, do you have any questions?"

"Just go through the scoring one more time," said Pete.

"Two red bricks will give you one point each," James replied. "Two blue bricks will give you minus two points each. One red brick and one blue brick will give ten points for the team that played the blue brick and minus ten points for the team that played the red brick. Is everybody clear?"

"It certainly isn't the type of challenge I was expecting," said Mark.

"If that is all, let's get started," James continued. "I will be the adjudicator, as well as the scorer. After each round, I will write both teams' scores on this flipchart."

He pointed to an easel to his right.

"There will be no communication with the other team except by the team leaders after rounds four and six. Failure to adhere to this will lead to disqualification. In addition, there will be no further clarification of the rules. When the team leaders bring their brick to the bar, please conceal them until I ask you to reveal what colour it is."

Everybody thought he'd finished, but then he suddenly started speaking again.

"And finally, I nearly forgot to tell you the most important thing of all. The prize you are playing for is half a million pounds worth of National Lottery tickets."

There was an audible gasp from the assembled group, all of whom were shocked by James's announcement. Mark hadn't known what type of challenge to expect, but this caught him completely by surprise. He certainly wasn't expecting the prize to consist of lottery tickets, either.

"It's ten past four," James continued. "I'm going to give you half an hour to decide on the colour of your first brick, but the time gaps will get shorter as the challenge progresses. The team with Pete in it will use Wolfscote Room and the team with Ben in it will use Monsal Room. I will see each team's spokesperson back here at twenty to five."

Both teams started to make their way to their respective rooms. However, as they were walking, Mark turned to Pete and said, "Well, at least that knocks Ben's theory on the head."

"What theory?" asked Pete.

"The one where he said our father must have left written instructions about how the trust fund should be administered after his death," said Mark. "Don't forget that he died in 1984 and the National Lottery wasn't established until ten years later."

Chapter 8

Saturday, August 31st, 2019

"I think you're reading too much into it," said Pete, as he and Mark were walking down the hotel corridor. "After all, James told us he had discretion over any surplus money. Perhaps he also has discretion over how the trust fund monies are spent. Dad could have stipulated premium bonds in his original instructions and James could later have decided to update it for the modern era by buying lottery tickets instead. Anyway, how the bloody hell do you go about buying £500,000 worth of lottery tickets? I can just imagine James walking into his local corner shop and saying to the person behind the counter, 'I'll have a Mars Bar, a pint of milk and oh, I nearly forgot, can I also have half a million pounds worth of lucky dips, please?' This is a farce."

"I don't think it works quite like that," said Mark. "I presume you have to buy quantities like that directly from Camelot."

"It's not just Ben's theory that it knocks on the head, it knocks yours down as well," Pete continued.

"How's that?" asked Mark.

"Well, you said that if Ben and Rosie went home, their money would go to Cats Protection. Clearly, this particular challenge is a competition. Either we win half a million pounds or they do."

"Providing we don't both end up with a minus score in which case the money really would go to Cats Protection," added Mark.

"That's correct," Pete replied. "But now imagine if Rosie and Ben had gone home. Then the only option left open to James would be to place you and me on opposite sides, otherwise he couldn't run the challenge. In those circumstances, one of us would have won the prize. But if we'd agreed in advance to share the money irrespective of the outcome, we would each get £250,000. However, because those two are here, we can only get the money if we beat them."

"That's pure speculation," Mark replied. "We don't really know what would have happened if they had gone home. Perhaps in those circumstances, there would have been a totally different challenge for us to do."

However, Pete's comments had given Mark a thought, which he now shared with him.

"What if all four of us agreed to share the prize no matter what the outcome of the challenge was?" he asked.

"You're overlooking something," Pete replied, "we can't confer with them until after round four."

"Well, so be it. We will just have to wait until after round four before we discuss our proposal with them, won't we?"

Shortly afterwards, they walked into Wolfscote Room where Louise and Wendy were already waiting for them.

"Pete's had a wonderful idea," said Mark smiling. "He's suggested we share the prize with the others no matter what the outcome."

"I think that's a great idea," replied Louise.

"Are you sure it was Pete who suggested it?" asked Wendy incredulously.

Pete merely shrugged his shoulders.

"I also think it's an excellent idea," commented Mark. "So if we are all in agreement, that's what we'll do. Of course, we will have to wait until after round four before we can discuss it with Ben and Rosie. But it shouldn't be too late by then."

Louise and Wendy both nodded their approval.

"Now we have to nominate a team leader," Mark continued. "And I'd like to nominate Pete. After all, you did suggest our plan in the first place."

Mark hoped by giving Pete the kudos for coming up with the idea, he would actually buy into it. His tactic appeared to be working and, once again, Louise and Wendy nodded their approval.

"So what colour brick are we going to play first?" asked Pete.

"Isn't that obvious?" replied Mark. "We need to play red."

"Why?" asked Pete. "If we are going to share the money it doesn't matter what the score is. Unless we both end up with a negative number, which would be a total disaster."

"That's why we have to play red," said Mark. "Because if we play blue and they play blue both teams would start off with a score of minus two. Whereas, if we play red, at least one of the teams will have a positive score."

"Yes, and more likely than not it will be them," said Pete.

Mark just ignored him and continued.

"Then at the halfway stage, we tell them we want to share the prize. Obviously, the best result would be if we both choose red, because that way each team would start off with a positive score. In fact, the best of all worlds would be if both teams played red in every round."

"Personally, I'd rather hit them first and negotiate with them from a position of strength, rather than a position of weakness," added Pete.

"But you do understand why we have to go red," said Mark.

Pete gave a begrudging grunt before Mark added, "Red it is then."

Meanwhile, in Monsal Room, there was another discussion about tactics going on between Ben, Phil, Rosie and Frank. It was Phil who started it off.

"Obviously, this is a game of strategy," he said, "where the object is to beat the other team and finish the game with a positive score. Does everybody agree with that?"

"A score of zero could also win the prize," Frank reminded him.

This prompted a discussion whether zero was a positive number or not. But Phil realised that in the context of winning the game, it was a pointless exercise. So he changed the conversation to something that was far more relevant.

"I bet I know who their spokesperson will be," he said. "It's bound to be Pete. After all, he's got the biggest ego and the biggest gob."

"In which case, I think you should be our spokesperson as you're the only person who's stood up to him so far," said Rosie, totally ignoring the fact it had been Frank who had restrained Pete in the minibus.

They all agreed and set about deciding what their first move should be.

"Before we decide what we are going to do," said Phil, who was now taking the lead, "we first have to work out what the other team's tactics are going to be. I think I have a pretty good idea about that."

The others listened eagerly as Phil continued.

"I think they will start off by going red, red, blue. They can't win by playing blue on either of the first two rounds, as we could block them and ensure both teams ended the game with negative scores."

"Hang on a moment," said Ben, "if we did that, wouldn't we both lose?"

"That's a good point, Ben," replied Phil, "and that is precisely why they won't play blue in either of the first two rounds. What I think they will do, is to lure us into thinking they are going to play red in every round, tricking us into doing the same. In other words, they will try to make us believe they want to share the prize with us. Then in round three, they will play blue, as that way we won't be able to stop them from winning."

"So how do we counter that?" asked Rosie.

"Easy," replied Phil, "we play blue in round two."

"But you said you couldn't win by playing blue in round two," commented Ben.

"That's right," Phil continued. "But here's the clever bit. After four rounds, we have the opportunity to negotiate with them. That's when we offer to share the prize if they let us win."

"But what if Pete refuses," said Ben, "assuming that he's their spokesperson, of course?"

"He may well do, knowing him. But after two more rounds to think about it, I think even Pete would realise it is better to receive half the prize rather than getting no prize at all. So are we all agreed? We go red followed by blue."

The other three nodded.

It was now twenty to five and both Phil and Pete made their way to the bar.

"Right, gentlemen," said James. "Can I ask you both to reveal what colour brick you have brought with you?"

The two of them opened their fists to reveal two red bricks. There was a palpable sigh of relief from both Pete and Phil as they realised everything was going to plan.

"Thank you," said James who wrote +1 on the flipchart for both teams. "You now have ten minutes to make your next decision. I will see you back in the bar at ten to five."

Phil and Pete turned to go back to their respective rooms, but as they headed for the door, James realised he had another announcement to make.

"Sorry, guys," he said, "I nearly forgot to tell you that the children have returned from their visit to the cinema. Pete, can you tell Louise that Simon and Katie are keeping Noel and Josh amused by playing board games with them until you've finished the challenge? Oh, and Jack has asked if he could borrow your laptop. He says that he wants to go on Facebook but has forgotten to bring the charger for his iPhone."

"That's fine," said Pete. "Here, you'd better take our room key so that he can get it."

Pete and Phil went to join their teams. Naturally, they were all keen to discover what colour brick the other team had played. Pete's team were over the moon when he informed them it was red.

"It looks as if they are thinking along the same lines as us," said Mark. "All we have to do is to keep on playing red until we can confer with them after the fourth round."

"By the way," he added, "who have they chosen as their team captain?"

"Phil the fairy," Pete replied, which got him black looks from the others.

"I'm surprised they didn't choose Ben or Rosie," said Mark, "being as though they have the most to gain."

Back in Monsal Room, Phil addressed his teammates.

"They are so transparent," said Phil. "Not only were we right in our prediction that they would choose Pete as their team leader, but we were also right with our prediction that they would go with a red brick in the first round."

They agreed to continue with their strategy and Phil picked up a blue brick and returned to the bar.

Pete soon joined him, at which point James asked them for a second time to reveal the colour brick they had both brought with them.

This time there was no sigh of relief from Pete. Instead, there was outrage.

"You fucking bastard," he shouted as soon as he realised Phil had brought a blue brick with him.

"No conferring, gentlemen," said James sharply.

"I'm not conferring with him," Pete replied, shaking with rage. "I'm just telling him what I think of him."

James ignored his outburst and merely wrote Wolfscote -9 Monsal +11 on the flipchart, before sending Pete and Phil back to discuss their next moves with their respective teams.

As soon as Pete walked through the door, Louise, Wendy and Mark could tell things hadn't gone according to plan. If it wasn't the colour of his face that gave it away, it was certainly the way he slammed the door. The entire room shook.

"You and your bloody trusting liberal ideas," Pete shouted at Mark. "I told you we needed to hit them first and then to negotiate from a position of strength. But no, you thought they would be as rational and sharing as we are. Now look where that's got us!"

"I presume from your outburst that they have played blue?" said Mark.

"Too bloody right they did," Pete replied, "and the flying faggot just loved it. You could see from the look in his eyes he was saying 'up yours' to all four of us."

"Pete," said Wendy. "Firstly, there is no need to swear and, secondly, you promised not to talk about Phil's sexuality."

"It's not as if he can hear me," commented Pete.

"That's not the point, Pete," said Louise joining the conversation. "We can hear you."

Pete's anger was born out of sheer frustration, which wasn't helped when Wendy told him he needed to calm down or risk bursting a blood vessel.

"I don't understand why they played blue so early," he said in exasperation. Taking a deep breath, he continued, "We can still block them though. So they can't win the prize by the end of the challenge."

"If I can just get us back on track for one moment," Mark cut in. "When do we have to make our next move, Pete?"

Pete confirmed that James had given both teams another ten minutes to make their decisions.

"I have to be back in the bar by five o'clock," he said, "which gives us another four minutes to make our next decision."

"So come on guys," added Mark. "We need to decide which colour we are going to play next. I say we go red again as that will demonstrate to them that we want to share the prize."

"Hold on," said Pete. "They will almost certainly play blue. Why wouldn't they? I would if I were in their position. If we play red that will give us absolutely nothing to bargain with at the end of round four. In other words, they will already have won and it doesn't matter what we play. At least if we play blue for the next two rounds, they will still be in a position of not being able to win the prize without our help. That means they will be forced to negotiate with us."

It was clear that Louise and Wendy had been swayed by Pete's argument and so Mark dropped his objection. The team had decided they would play blue in the next two rounds.

Whilst all this was happening, the atmosphere in Monsal Room was far more upbeat.

"You should have seen the look on Pete's face," said Phil smiling. "'I thought his head was going to explode. He called me a fucking bastard."

"Don't knock him," added Frank. "He's making real progress. If it had happened this morning, he probably would have called you a fucking queer."

They all thought that was highly amusing and after the laughter had died down, Phil continued.

"It's obvious they are going to try and block us by playing blue in the next two rounds," he said. "We need to play blue as well, before we negotiate with them."

The others nodded their agreement.

As a result, there was no surprise in either room when Pete and Phil returned and told their teams that both of them had played blue in round three. The scores were Wolfscote -11 Monsal +9.

"Okay, so what is our negotiating position going to be?" asked Mark.

"Easy," Pete replied. "Assuming we both play blue in the next round, the score will be -13 to us and +7 to them. So we tell them we want to share the prize with them. We then say that if they play red in the next round and we play blue, we will both be on -3 points. Then if we both play red in the following three rounds, both of us will end the challenge with a score of zero. According to James, zero will be enough for us to share the prize because neither team will have a negative score."

A similar discussion was going on in Monsal Room. Their proposed solution was totally different.

"We are obviously in the driving seat," said Phil, "although I do accept that we need the help of the other team in order to win the prize. What I'm going to say to Pete is that we share the prize with them providing they let us win. I'll also tell him that in order to do that, both teams must play red in the remaining four rounds."

"Sounds good to me," said Ben.

"And me," added Rosie.

Frank merely nodded.

A few minutes later, Pete and Phil reappeared in the bar and both of them were carrying blue bricks again.

"Right that's Wolfscote on -13 and Monsal on +7," said James. "Now gentlemen, you have five minutes in which to discuss tactics, before returning to your teams."

"What were you thinking?" said Pete, starting the negotiation. "We were going to play red in every round, anticipating you'd do the same. That way we would both have finished on plus eight and shared the prize."

"You say that now," said Phil. "But that's not the Pete Bradbury I've come to know and love over the past 24 hours."

The thought of Phil loving him was not one Pete wanted to dwell on. But he didn't have too long to think about it as Phil continued talking.

"We believe you wanted us to think that," he added. "However, we thought you would play blue in round three and then there would have been no coming back for us. You would have won and I bet all talk of us sharing the prize would have gone out of the window. That was the reason we decided to play blue in round two."

Pete secretly wished he had thought of that, but realised it wouldn't make any difference to the situation they now found themselves in. He had to be pragmatic.

"You forget there are three others in the team and I am merely the team's spokesperson," he said. "It is not only my decision which brick we play. It is a consensus decision made by the four of us and we decided that playing red in every round would result in the best possible outcome for both teams. You can believe it or not, but the fact is we are where we are and you know as well as I do that neither of us can win the prize unless we come to an agreement."

Pete put his plan on the table, but Phil's response was not favourable.

"That's not acceptable to us," he said. "I know James said that we would win the prize as long as we didn't end up with a negative score, which I presume includes a score of zero. But I'm not completely sure, and I wouldn't want to risk it. Also, what's to stop you from shafting us by playing blue in round eight? No, I've got a far better idea."

Phil outlined his position and this time it was Pete's turn to be unhappy.

"I don't like it," he said." Under my proposal, we would automatically share the prize. Under yours, we have to rely on your generosity."

"It's not our generosity," Phil said angrily. "It's the only solution that ensures we all come out of this with some money."

"So does my proposal," countered Pete.

"Yes, but this solution is the only one that doesn't allow you to shaft us."

"Talk about the pot calling the kettle black," Pete replied.

James cut their conversation short.

"Time's up, gentlemen," he said. "Please return to your respective rooms and discuss your negotiation with your teammates. I will see both of you again in another ten minutes."

Phil returned to Monsal Room where Ben, Rosie and Frank were keen to discover the outcome of the discussion.

"He didn't accept it," said Phil.

"Why not?" said Rosie. "Is he thick?"

"You know? I think he is," Phil went on. "When James asked him to discuss tactics with me, I was sure he was going to say, 'well they're really small mints that come in a plastic container with a flip top'."

Ben supressed a giggle.

"What he wanted was for us to give them their ten points back and then each of us to play red in the last three rounds. His argument was that both teams would have ended on zero points and therefore would automatically share the prize. The trouble was, I don't trust him and therefore I rejected it. He rejected my proposal and, as a result, I am afraid we are at an impasse. But it's not all bad news, because we have a second opportunity to negotiate with them after two more rounds. By that time, they will be on -17 points whilst we will be on +3. Therefore, his proposal won't work anymore, but ours will. Consequently, he will have no option but to fall in with our plans. All we have to do is sit tight and wait."

Meanwhile, in Wolfscote Room, Mark couldn't believe what Pete was telling him.

"Why didn't you agree to his proposal?" he asked. "After all, he was proposing to share the prize with us, which is exactly what we wanted."

"Yes, but he wanted it on his terms," blustered Pete. "We have to trust him to keep his word and I, for one, don't trust him at all."

"But it's not just him, it's all four of them," Mark went on. "They are our relatives and even if they weren't, we still have another two challenges to go after this one. We need to trust them."

"OK," said Pete, "I will agree to his proposal at the next negotiation, but in the meantime, we have to keep playing blue. Don't forget that I rejected his proposal. So why should he make the same proposal again unless he is forced to?"

The others reluctantly agreed and, as a result, both teams played blue in the next two rounds. As predicted, the score was at -17 to +3 when James told Pete and Phil that they had another five minutes to discuss tactics for the following two rounds.

"So," said Phil looking smug, "let's hear your proposal this time."

"I don't have one," answered Pete. "The only thing I will say is that unless we come to an agreement, neither of us will win."

"I understand that," Phil replied, "which is why I am going to make you the same offer as I did last time. If we both play red for the next two rounds and you let us win, we will share the prize with you."

"My teammates have instructed me to accept your offer so that is what I am going to do," Pete replied through gritted teeth.

"Gentlemen," said James. "Your five minutes of negotiation are now at an end, and I must instruct you to go back to your teams. However, before you do that, there are a couple of things I have to tell you. Firstly, in the final two rounds, you will only have five minutes to discuss the colour of the brick you are going to play. Secondly, the number of points on offer will double during rounds seven and eight."

Having listened to the new rules, Phil and Pete returned once more to their respective rooms.

"They've made us the same offer as they did before, and I've accepted it," said Pete.

"Good," said Mark.

"There are also some rule changes. We only have five minutes to discuss which brick to take, and it's double points for the final two rounds."

"That shouldn't make any difference," said Mark. "We continue as agreed. We let them win and share the prize."

The conversation in Monsal Room was going along similar lines with Phil telling the team that Pete had agreed to their proposal and that the rule change shouldn't alter the final outcome.

A few moments later, Phil and Pete returned to face James, both clutching a red brick.

"Right, that's round seven completed, just one round to go" said James as he wrote the latest score onto the flipchart. It now read Wolfscote -15 Monsal +5.

Phil and Pete went back to their teams to collect the Lego pieces for the last time and to assure their teammates that the other team was sticking to their side of the bargain.

"Well, thank goodness it is nearly over," said Mark. "This must be the most intense thing I've done in a long time."

Pete merely shrugged his shoulders, picked up a red brick and left the room.

"I can see why this challenge was designed," commented Mark. "It was meant to teach us that we should trust our relatives and show us we can only succeed if we cooperate with them."

Then he went quiet as something caught his eye.

"Hold on a minute," he finally said. "We went red in rounds one and two, blue in rounds three to six and red in rounds seven and eight. That means there should be four red bricks and four blue bricks left on the table. So why are there four red bricks but only three blue ones?"

Chapter 9

Saturday, August 31st, 2019

Pete returned to the room triumphantly.

"That wiped the smirk from his face," he announced as he walked through the door.

"Pete, what have you done?" said Mark. Although he suspected he already knew.

"That'll teach that balding bum boy not to mess with me again," Pete replied before explaining. "I played blue in the last round, which means we've won with a score of +5 to their -15."

"Oh no," said Wendy. "Please tell me you're joking."

"I knew you wouldn't agree with my plan, which was why I put a blue brick in my pocket as soon as I returned from round seven. I then swapped it with the red brick once I left the room. It means we don't have to share the prize with them. After all, we only agreed to do that if we let them win. We never agreed what we would do if we won."

"You cannot be serious?" said Mark with a look of total astonishment on his face.

"Of course, we are going to share it with them," added Louise looking at Wendy.

"Pete, you've done some pretty dreadful things in your life," said Wendy. "But this time you've excelled yourself. I'm in total agreement with Mark and Louise. We will share the prize with Rosie and Ben."

After having had her say, Wendy gave Pete a look of disgust. It wasn't the first time he had been on the receiving end of such a look, and he suspected it wouldn't be the last.

"Err … well no," spluttered Pete. "I must have misspoken. What I actually meant to say was that it is at our discretion whether we share the prize with them. It goes without saying that we will. But now it will be us giving them half rather than the other way around."

Having at least partially extricated himself, he changed the subject.

"Anyway," he continued, "we need to return to the bar as James is going to tell us what happens next."

When Louise, Mark, Wendy and Pete walked into the bar, Phil, Ben, Rosie and Frank were already there, looking decidedly angry.

"If looks could kill," whispered Louise.

"I want to apologise for my husband's behaviour," said Wendy. "He went against the wishes of the rest of the team when he played that blue brick in the final round."

"It doesn't really matter who won," added Mark. "The prize will be shared between us as we agreed."

Whilst all this was going on, Pete stood by himself in the background looking sheepish.

After a few minutes, James addressed them all.

"Thank you everybody," he said. "I hope you found that challenge interesting. The purpose behind it was to show that, even though the two sides of the family have never met each other before, nor even knew about each other until yesterday, you are all part of the same family. It was also designed to demonstrate that you can trust your family members and that cooperating with them will help you achieve your goals."

At this point, seven pairs of eyes stared accusingly at Pete.

"I said the purpose was to demonstrate you are all one family," James continued. "Therefore, it should come as no surprise when I tell you that you made a serious error at the start of the challenge. When I said you had to finish with a score of zero or higher, you assumed I meant the score for your individual team. I did not. What I meant was the combined score for the whole family. As a result, your total score of minus ten points means you have failed this particular challenge. I'm very sorry."

You could have heard a pin drop. The family were shell-shocked by the news. Eventually, it was Rosie who spoke.

"Can you tell us why you didn't make it clear that we needed to achieve a combined score?" she asked.

"Well, the whole purpose of the exercise was for you to work that out for yourselves," James replied. "After all, if I had told you at the start what the purpose of the exercise was, there wouldn't have been any point to this particular challenge. It would have been obvious that all you needed to do, was to play red every time. Believe me, this task was not designed for you to fail. Indeed, neither are the other two challenges. All I can say, is please learn from it as it will help you to be successful next time. Now, try to relax and I will join you for dinner in about an hour."

James left the room, which was when the recriminations started.

"Well, I hope you are satisfied, Pete," spat Phil. "If you had accepted our offer when it was made after round four, we would have finished with a combined score of plus six. In which case, we would have won the challenge and the prize."

Pete was not going to take this lying down.

"Whilst I fully recognise that my actions in round eight were not conducive to family harmony," he replied, "at least they didn't affect the final outcome. Because even if I'd played a red brick in round eight, the final score would still have been negative."

"That's not the point," said Phil. "You should have accepted our offer when it was originally made to you."

"Well, I think that there's only one person responsible for this mess," Pete continued. "And that's the one person in this room who is neither a Bradbury nor married to one. In other words, it's you, Phil. Because if you had trusted us, both teams would have gone red every time and we would now be sharing the half a million pound prize. After all, that was our team's plan right from the start."

Pete looked at Mark, Louise and Wendy and, subconsciously, they nodded in agreement.

"Right," said Phil, visibly angry. "I've had enough of this. I am out of here. I am not part of this family. You've made that perfectly clear. I have absolutely nothing to gain by staying in this hotel. I have been insulted and humiliated ever since I arrived. I am going to go home right now."

With that, Phil stormed out of the room.

"I'd better go after him," said Ben.

"Bloody drama queen," Pete commented, adding, "don't worry Ben, I'm sure he will come to his senses."

Which was ironic really, being as though Pete's plan had all along been to insult Phil in the hope that he and Ben would get fed up and go home. But with half of his plan having worked, Pete was finally starting to realise that his actions were not helping the situation. Or so it appeared. Things were never clear-cut in Pete's case.

Before anyone had the chance to ask Pete about his newfound concern for his half-brother, Jack, Hannah and Zara entered the bar. They looked far happier than their parents.

"Did you enjoy the film, guys?" asked Wendy.

"It was great," replied Jack. "But what we really want to know is how did you get on with the challenge?"

"Don't talk about it," said Wendy.

"You mean you failed," added Jack. "Go on, tell us what happened."

"Well, it was called the Red-Blue challenge," Wendy continued. "We were divided into two teams and each team was given eight red bricks and eight blue bricks. We had eight rounds and, in each round ..."

"I know it," interrupted Jack.

"What?" said Pete in disbelief.

"I know it," repeated Jack, "it's a team-building exercise. We played it at scout camp back in May. Its purpose is to show that we are all part of the same team. Or, in this case, I presume its purpose was to show we are all part of the same family."

"And what was the result when you played it?" asked Pete.

"Well, once you have worked out you aren't playing against the other team, but you are all on the same side, there is really only one colour to play each time and that's red. Red is the positive choice because you can never have a combined negative score if you play red. Even if the other team doesn't realise what the objective of the game is and play blue every time, you would still end up winning because the final score would be zero. Blue, however, is the negative choice because you can never have a positive score in a round if you choose it. When we played, both teams worked out what the real challenge was right from the start. So both played red in every round and we ended the game with the maximum score possible. Tell me, did they change the scoring part way through the game?"

"Yes," replied Wendy.

"The reason they do that is to reflect real life," Jack continued. "In other words, the goals keep changing in real life. But the objective always remains the same. It's to take the other team with you and to finish the game in a win:win situation. If you try to win and make the other team lose, ultimately everybody loses. That's the whole point of the game."

Whilst Jack was speaking, Pete's jaw was dropping lower and lower. When he finally spoke, he was obviously upset.

"I don't bloody well believe it," he said. "Jack was the only person in our family who knew what the challenge was about, and he was watching Jabba the fucking Hutt instead of being here with us."

"Hey, don't blame me, numpty boy," Jack replied. "It's not my fault you are too thick to work out what the game is about."

"Jack," shouted Wendy, "you do not refer to your father as numpty boy, no matter how thick he is. Now apologise at once."

Jack went red. He wasn't used to being told off by his mother in front of others, especially not in front of the girl he fancied.

Mind you, he wasn't as shocked as Pete was at being called numpty boy by his son.

"Sorry, Dad," Jack mumbled whilst looking at his feet.

"And as for you," said Wendy looking at Pete, "this is the last time I am going to warn you about swearing."

"Okay," said Pete, "I apologise."

But there was no sincerity in his voice. In fact, Pete didn't have a sincere bone in his body. That was why nobody really believed his apology was genuine.

At this point, Simon and Katie entered the room with Noel and Josh.

"Did you enjoy yourselves today, boys?" Louise asked them.

"Oh yes," they said in unison. Then Noel continued, "We had a Big Mac Meal and the largest bucket of popcorn ever."

"That sounds great," said Louise, secretly thinking they wouldn't want their supper after all that junk.

"We have to leave now," said Simon, "and, unfortunately, Katie and I won't be joining you for dinner this evening as we are going to a friend's house. It's a long-standing invitation, I'm afraid. But before we go, we need to know whether the children are going to accompany the rest of you on your trip around Derbyshire tomorrow. If not, do you want us to plan another day out for them?"

"Can you just give us a few minutes to discuss that?" asked Pete.

"No problem," Simon replied.

"I think they should come with us from now on," said Pete to the others. "After all, if Jack had come with us today, we would now be sharing half a million pounds worth of lottery tickets."

"That's true," said Louise. "However, Noel and Josh are probably too young to contribute. That's unless the next challenge involves Sonic the Hedgehog or Donkey Kong. In reality, they might even get in the way. So why don't we let Simon and Katie take the two of them out for the day and let the other three come with us?"

"I'm happy with that," said Zara. "The only reason I didn't want to come with you today was because it involved football."

"I agree," said Hannah.

"Me too," added Jack.

Jack's decision had never really been in doubt once Zara had announced her intention to participate.

"If we are all agreed," said Mark, "Noel and Josh will go with Simon and Katie, and Jack, Hannah and Zara will come with us."

Nobody objected.

"That's decided then," said Simon. "Katie and I have to take our leave. But we will see you tomorrow at breakfast and, afterwards, we'll take Noel and Josh to Gulliver's Kingdom in Matlock Bath."

Shortly after they left, Ben reappeared looking upset.

"I'm afraid I couldn't persuade Phil to change his mind," he said. "He's gone home."

"Oh, Ben, I am sorry," said Louise. "Tell me, was it Phil's car you came in?"

Ben nodded and said, "But don't worry, I can always get the train home."

"Nonsense," said Mark. "Reigate's not very far from Brighton. We will take you home, won't we, Louise? We've got a large estate car, so there will be no problem fitting you in."

"Are you sure?" Ben replied. "You'll be going out of your way. You can always drop me at Redhill station and I can get a train back from there."

"If I hadn't meant it, I wouldn't have offered," Mark replied.

"Right everybody," James announced. "If we could all move through to the dining room, please? Dinner is served. Afterwards, could I ask you to stay behind for ten minutes? I want to tell you what we are going to do tomorrow."

Without further ado, they all went into the dining room and took their seats at the table. Unlike the previous day, there was no seating plan. Everybody sat where they wanted. There was still a reasonable amount of integration between the two sides of the family and not just because Jack wanted to sit next to Zara.

But there was a downbeat air in the whole room as everybody was coming to terms with the fact that they had failed the challenge.

"Well, I hope the cats are happy," commented Pete. "With half a million pounds worth of lottery tickets coming their way, they should be licking their chops. Perhaps they'll win the jackpot."

"Unfortunately, you have to be sixteen before you can play the lottery, which rules out most cats," James replied. "We just plan to give them a cheque instead. I hear they've got an account with Cat West Bank."

"That's all we need," sighed Pete, "a solicitor who thinks he's a fucking comedian."

Realising he had sworn again, he apologised before Wendy had the chance to chastise him.

Wendy was ignoring him, however, and had instead started a conversation with James.

"So James," she said, "tell me, are you married? And if so, why haven't we met your wife yet?"

"Divorced," James replied. "It was quite amicable. I handled the divorce settlement myself."

"Never one to miss out on a business opportunity," commented Pete.

"Look who's talking," replied Wendy.

"My wife had quite a lot in common with your father, Pete," James continued. "She was never happy with her life here in Derbyshire. She wanted to expand her horizons and explore the world. The last I heard was that she was living in a commune in Goa."

"All sun, sex, and samosas, I'll bet," commented Pete.

On the other side of the table, Louise still felt sorry for Ben, and she started a conversation with him.

"What did you do between leaving Spain and getting a job on TV, Ben?" she asked him.

Ben took a sip of wine before replying.

"You have to remember that I was very young when my mother and father were killed. I've got no memories of Spain or of them. However, I do have a photo of the four of us, which was taken shortly before the accident. Our parents looked so happy and tanned. Rosie and I are both smiling. It was a photo full of hope for the future, a future that was destined never to happen."

For a second, Louise wondered if it had been the right decision to question Ben about his past, when he was already upset about Phil's departure. But Ben soon composed himself and continued.

"I had a happy childhood in Swindon with Rosie and my grandparents," he told her. "But that happy child turned into a troubled teenager as I grappled to understand my sexuality. I was bullied at school and didn't do well academically, leaving at sixteen with only two GCSEs in Art and English. I had a series of jobs, none of them lasting that long. But I also gained a love of the theatre, which became my escape. I joined Swindon amateur dramatic society when I was seventeen and my various acting roles with them helped me to get a few parts as an extra on TV. When I was eighteen, I came out, which was something my grandparents never understood."

"That's often the case with people from an older generation," said Louise. "You have to bear in mind that homosexuality was illegal when they were growing up."

"'You just haven't met the right girl yet,' was one of the many comments they made, whilst trying to persuade me that I wasn't gay. However, I always knew in my heart that I was. Rosie had already moved to Bristol with Frank when I came out, so I was their only grandchild still living at home. What was hardest, was that my grandparents refused point blank to let me bring any of my boyfriends home. Eventually, the situation got too much for me. So I moved in with a guy I met whilst buying a takeaway pizza. He was an accountant at the headquarters of the Nationwide Building Society, and we got on really well to start off with. At the time, I was working in WH Smith's and was managing to fit in the odd job as an extra. Then I met Justin."

A smile came across Ben's face as he mentioned his former lover.

"Justin originally came from Swindon," he continued. "But he was running a guest house in Brighton when I met him. He was back visiting his parents and he wandered into the shop where I was working to buy a newspaper. The sparks began to fly immediately. I realised it was Justin who I really loved and, two days later, I gave up my job and moved to Brighton with him. Suddenly, I was serving breakfasts to miserable pensioners, people who had nothing better to do than moan about the weather and the fact their eggs hadn't been boiled for long enough. I knew it wouldn't last. Justin was a drinker, and his personality would change after he'd had a few. It was a tempestuous three years but I knew I'd eventually have to leave, and that was when I met Roger."

"Really," said Louise wondering how long this story was going to go on for and, at the same time, thanking her lucky stars her love life had never been as complicated as Ben's.

"After Roger there was Neil," he added, "and then Antonio, a Spanish waiter, before I finally met and moved in with Phil last October."

"And are you and Phil happy together?" asked Louise.

"Well, we were until we came here," came the dejected reply.

Louise could tell that Ben was upset. So she decided to ask Rosie about her early life instead.

"I was a bit of a rebel when I was a teenager," Rosie told her. "I fell in with a bad crowd when I was only fifteen. We'd drink vodka, smoke dope and do other things that I'd rather not tell you about. Looking back on it now, I feel really sorry for my poor grandparents who were only trying to do their best for me. Just like Ben, I left school at sixteen with minimal qualifications. Also like him, I had a variety of jobs until I was eighteen, when I got a job as a barmaid at the Boot and Shoe in Swindon. Frank was a shift manager at the time, and he was the person who interviewed me."

"And was it love at first sight?"

"Well, he must have liked what he'd seen," she replied. "Because I got the job, and he ended up with me. Four weeks later we were going out together. Frank's ten years older than me, but that's never concerned me because he provided the steadying influence I needed. Six months later, he was offered an assistant manager's job at another pub. This one was in Bristol and it came with its own flat. He asked me to go with him. I accepted and the rest is history. We got married, had Zara and then took on the lease of Scallys."

By the time Rosie had finished her story, everyone had completed their meal and coffee had been served. That was James's cue to address the group once more.

"As you are all aware, there is no challenge tomorrow, because we are going for a tour around Derbyshire. It is a pretty full day and, for that reason, breakfast will be served at 7.30. I want us to leave here at 8.20. Please don't forget that you need to pay attention as this will help when you face your next task. I will be your guide tomorrow, and I will be very disappointed if you miss anything that could help you. I know you are all upset by the outcome of this afternoon's task and I suspect some of you may even question whether or not every challenge has been specifically designed to trip you up. Can I say here and now, this is not the case. Both Mr Bradbury and I thought you would succeed with all three challenges. But we did worry about what you would think if you failed today, which is why Mr Bradbury made a tape that I am now going to play for you."

"Good God, will the surprises never end?" said Pete as James took a cassette out of its box and put it into the cassette player. A few seconds later, the disembodied voice of a man was talking to them.

> *Hello everybody and many apologies that I cannot be with you in person tonight. The reason you are listening to this tape is because you have failed the first challenge. If it is any consolation, the fact that you failed today makes it more likely that you will achieve the remaining two challenges. That is because challenge one was designed to demonstrate that you need to work together and trust each other. Now you know that, I am confident you will put this into practice and will succeed with the remaining two tasks.*
>
> *You will discover more about the nature of the other challenges in due course. But what I will tell you is that one*

is all about Derbyshire and the other is all about family, two things that are very close to my heart.

Pete and Mark, you were both born in Derbyshire. But when your mother took you to Gloucestershire, you lost contact with both the county of your birth and with my side of the family. It is now time to rectify this.

Rosie and Ben, you were born in Spain and know very little about the county your ancestors called home. By the end of the next four days, all this will have changed.

You may be wondering why you have to go through these challenges in order to get your inheritance, perhaps wondering why I couldn't just have told you about your family history. Or indeed merely have written you a letter. Well, the answer is quite simple.

Ask yourself how much you would have recalled if I'd done either of those things. You wouldn't even have paid attention. Instead, you would have been too busy thinking about how you were going to spend the money. But, by doing things this way, it will become something that will stay in your memories forever.

Now, farewell everybody, have fun and make damn certain you don't cock it up again.

Everybody was pretty shocked after listening to the cassette. But before anybody had the chance to discuss it, James announced that he would leave them to talk in private.

"I'll see all of you at breakfast tomorrow morning," he said before walking through the door.

The room was silent as he left. Everybody was taking in all the things they'd just heard.

"What a load of crap," said Pete.

He was the first to break the silence.

"How dare he say that Derbyshire and his family are close to his heart. He abandoned both of them back in 1979."

"It was weird hearing him like that," said Mark, "a voice from beyond the grave."

"That's if it was from beyond the grave," added Frank.

The others all turned around and looked at him. He got up and marched over to the cassette recorder and pressed the eject button.

"I thought so," he said. "You know, I've always loved my music and I've always been a bit of a hifi geek. Well, when I went to university, I didn't have room for my stereo or my vinyl collection. That was why I taped all of my favourite LPs. It was so I could listen to them on cassette."

"Your point being?" queried Pete.

"Well, this cassette is a Maxell Metal Vertex, the same type as the ones I used all those years ago. I remember them distinctly because they had only just been put on the market when I bought them. The quality was far better than anything that was available at the time. However, that was back in 1990 and that's why I have a problem. You see, your father couldn't have recorded that message back in 1984. This brand of cassette didn't exist back then."

Chapter 10

Sunday, September 1st, 2019

There was only one topic of conversation over breakfast the next day and that was the recording they had heard the previous night.

"I think there's a simple answer to the cassette mystery," said Pete. "It could be a later copy. Dad could have recorded it on an old reel-to-reel tape machine and James could have transferred it onto a cassette at a later date."

He gave James a quick glance, but he showed no reaction.

"I don't think he recorded it on a reel-to-reel machine," said Frank. "They started to disappear in the early 1970s."

"Well, he might have originally recorded it on a Dictaphone," replied Pete more in hope than anything else.

"He might have done," said Mark. "But aren't we falling into the same trap that bad scientists fall into? In other words, are we trying to make the facts fit the theory rather than the other way around? No, it is time we faced up to the reality of the situation, which is that Dad didn't die in 1984. He must have been alive at least ten years later and may still be alive today for all we know. Perhaps all this trust fund stuff is a precursor to him reappearing in our lives. After all, why shouldn't he now that Mum's dead?"

"That's a load of rubbish," said Rosie, who was getting quite angry by this stage. "That means he must have abandoned Ben and me in Spain."

"Well, you have to admit that he's got form when it comes to abandoning his children," added Pete.

"'But when he abandoned you, he at least left you with your mother," Rosie replied. "If he'd abandoned us in Spain, it would mean that our mother must have colluded with him, and she would never have done that."

"How do you know that?" asked Pete, who was quite irritated by Rosie's stance. "You were only three when it happened. How do you know that she wouldn't have gone along with him?"

"Because Granddad and Grandma told me all about her. She was a wonderful person."

"The type of person who would run off with another woman's husband and money?" Pete continued. "At the same time leaving her to bring up her children by herself whilst she was sipping piña coladas on the Costa del Sol?"

"There is another possibility," said Mark. "Your mother may have died in a car crash in 1984. But our father didn't."

"What are you saying?" asked Rosie.

"We don't know if they were even recognisable after the crash," said Mark. "Pete suggested to me that your mother may have been murdered by our father. However, I don't buy that. But what if it was somebody else in the car with her?"

"She was a tart after all," added Pete.

Rosie just gave him a glare. She didn't like the hostility in Pete's voice.

"Sorry, I don't believe it," she added. "Dad isn't still alive. He and Mum died in a car crash back in 1984."

"Well, okay," said Mark. "If the whole thing isn't answered by Wednesday, we will have the rest of our lives in which to work it out. In the meantime, we've got more pressing matters to attend to. We need to be a hundred percent focused today if we want to avoid another slip-up tomorrow."

They all knew Mark was right. Despite this, Pete promised himself he would Google everything about his father and the crash as soon as they returned to the hotel later that day.

"Right, everybody," said James as he rose from the table. "We need to be outside and ready to leave in ten minutes' time."

It turned out that this didn't apply to Noel and Josh. Gulliver's Kingdom didn't open until 10.30, and Simon and Katie had decided to keep the boys amused in the meantime with a Harry Potter DVD.

Soon the group was heading towards the centre of Chesterfield in a minibus. Since there were eleven of them traveling that day, James had hired a seventeen-seater Mercedes Traveliner this time. It came with a driver named Stan, which left James free to concentrate on his job as their tour guide.

"First up is the Crooked Spire," he said. "I've made a special arrangement with the verger. Morning service is at 9.30 and he is going to meet us at 8.30 to give us a quick private tour."

A few minutes later, the minibus pulled into Church Way and everybody got out. The verger was already waiting for them in front of the main entrance.

"Good morning, everybody, and welcome to the church of St Mary's and All Saints Chesterfield," he said whilst shaking James firmly by the hand. "Or as it is more commonly known, the Crooked Spire. It is the largest church in Derbyshire and the only Grade I listed building in Chesterfield. I will be your guide this morning and if you have any questions, please feel free to ask them."

"If it's the largest church in Derbyshire, then why isn't it a cathedral?" asked Jack.

"The answer is simple, young man," said the verger. "This church may be larger, older and taller than the cathedral in Derby, but it is not the seat of the bishop. As a result, it remains a parish church."

"I think that's ridiculous," added Jack.

"Ridiculous or not, it's the way things are, I'm afraid," the verger replied. "Now, if you would all like to follow me, we will begin the tour in the nave."

The party entered the church through the main doorway and the verger began by showing them the north and south aisles. He pointed out the transepts and the chancel with the four gilded chapels surrounding it. After that, he took the group to the high altar with its Jacobean pulpit and striking altar screen. They were able to look back from this vantage point at the massive west gallery, under which they had entered the nave. Even if it hadn't possessed the crowning glory of the spire itself, the church was still a lovely building, with some fantastic stained-glass windows.

"You know, it's only by chance that this fine old building is still standing," the verger informed them. "No doubt you will remember the fire that devastated Notre-Dame Cathedral earlier this year. It destroyed much of the interior including the roof and an 800-year-old spire. Well, we are extremely lucky that the same thing didn't happen here. The Crooked Spire has suffered two major fires during the past 160 years. In 1861, the tower was struck by lightning, which severed a gas pipe. The resulting fire smouldered for three and a half hours before it was discovered by the sexton. Then in 1961, a devastating fire destroyed many of the fixtures including an eighteenth century Snetzier organ. Fortunately, the fire brigade was able to bring the blaze under control before it spread to the rest of the building. As a result, the spire and most of the interior were saved."

"Do you know what this all means?" he asked them. His voice had risen dramatically.

Nobody answered.

"Well … it means that whoever is trying to burn down the church will probably try again in 2061. So I wouldn't visit during that year if I were you. In fact, there are strong rumours doing the rounds that God himself is responsible. After all, he wouldn't be the first person who's tried to burn down his own house for the insurance money. Don't forget that he's gotten away with it twice before at Notre-Dame and York Minster."

There was a ripple of laughter from the group, who hadn't expected the verger's commentary to be so light-hearted.

Moving on, the verger pointed out various other features, some of which dated back to medieval times. Finally, they arrived at the door to the tower.

"Now for the bit of the tour that is not for the fainthearted," he said. "These stairs will enable us to climb to the top of the spire."

The entire party looked shocked.

"Only joking," said the verger. "They will actually take us to the top of the tower on which the spire sits. Even so, it is 152 steps and we are going to do it in three stages. If you would like to follow me, we are going to start by ascending the spiral staircase to the bellringers' room. But just before we do that, does anyone know what the correct name for a group of bellringers is?"

"Campanologists," replied Ben.

"Very good, young man," replied the verger, as he led the way up the first set of stairs.

"And I always thought that campanologist was the collective noun for a group of homosexuals," muttered Pete.

But Ben didn't hear him. He was just elated that he was still being referred to as a young man even though he was in his mid-thirties.

Once they had reached the small room located directly below the church bells, the verger started to tell them the history of the spire.

"The spire was added to the church in the fourteenth century," he said, "and I know what you're going to ask me."

"Why is it bent?" said Ben.

"I'd have thought that you'd know the answer to that one," said Pete.

He knew that his statement would cause renewed hostility towards him from the rest of the group, and he wasn't wrong. However, the temptation to say something in reply to Ben's comment was just too great this time. However, before any of the party had the opportunity to chastise Pete, the verger was answering Ben's question.

"We don't say that the spire is bent or twisted," he said. "We only say 'crooked'. And why do you think it's crooked?"

"Because the builders were drunk," replied Pete.

"No," said the verger firmly. "The spire was added just after the Black Death when there was a lack of skilled craftsmen. It was built using unseasoned timber and the builders did not put in enough crossbeams. The whole structure was then clad in lead, and it was the weight of the lead, coupled with the lack of internal support that caused the spire to twist and bend as the timber dried out. But there is an alternative theory. Local legend has it that, once upon a time, a beautiful virgin got married in the church and the spire bent down to salute her. The legend claims that it will straighten up again the next time a virgin marries in the church."

"There's no chance of that happening if you get married here then, Zara," joked Pete.

Jack was the only person who thought that was funny. But he tried hard not to laugh, as he knew it wouldn't go down well with his cousin.

The tour continued as the party climbed up through the bell tower and into the spire itself.

"How the hell does it manage to stay up?" asked Louise as the group all stared incredulously at the crossbeams above their heads.

They had already been told there weren't enough of them, but what they weren't prepared for was just how randomly the small number of crossbeams were arranged.

Finally, they had to climb a short ladder and go through a door where they found themselves on a small viewing platform at the top of the tower. The whole of Chesterfield was laid out before them and they could even see Striding Hall in the distance. It looked a bit like a doll's house surrounded by a miniature landscaped garden.

A few minutes later, they were back down at the base of the tower, thanking the verger for giving them such an informative tour. They had a bit of time to visit the gift shop and to wander through the church grounds before getting back into the minibus.

"I hope you enjoyed that," said James. "We are now off to Castleton, but on the way there, I want to show you Ladybower and Derwent Reservoirs."

"And then the local sewage works, no doubt," muttered Pete.

The minibus headed out of Chesterfield towards Owler Bar and the Peak District. The scenery began to change as lush green fields eventually gave way to open moorland covered in purple heather. This part of the national park looked bleak and desolate. The few buildings they passed all had thick walls and small windows designed to protect the inhabitants from long cold winters. This was especially the case for Fox House, a pub located on the edge of the moors. Even though it was only the beginning of September, it already looked as if it was prepared for hard times ahead.

"If you look to your left, you will see Surprise View in a few seconds," said James. "The reason it's called that is because there's nothing to see until we go around the corner and begin our descent into Hathersage."

The village of Hathersage was down in the valley and had a totally different feel to it when compared with the sparse settlements higher up on the moors. It was bustling with tourists, many of whom were enjoying the shops in the village after visiting Little John's grave, the main tourist attraction in the area.

They soon left Hathersage behind, turning off the main road and going through Bamford towards Ladybower Reservoir.

"I'm afraid we don't have time to stop here," said James as they approached the massive grass bank holding back the water. "However, I wanted to show you these reservoirs, as they are just off the main road to Castleton. There are three reservoirs in total on the River Derwent. They were built to serve the growing populations of Sheffield and the East Midlands in the first half of the twentieth century. The first to be completed was Howden, which opened in 1912, and this was followed by Derwent, which opened two years later. Both these reservoirs have massive stone walls over which water flows when the reservoirs are full. It's a truly spectacular sight for anybody lucky enough to be here at the right time."

As they were approaching Derwent Reservoir, they noted that they were out of luck. There wasn't any water cascading over the dam wall. Indeed, it was only three-quarters full, which was to be expected as they were visiting during late summer when the water level was usually at its lowest.

"During the Second World War, the RAF used to practise here for the famous dambusters raid," James added. "This dam is virtually identical to the Möhne and Edersee dams in the Ruhr Valley."

While he was speaking, Stan slowed the minibus down so that everybody could get a good look, before turning around and heading back towards the main road again. Pretty soon they were alongside Ladybower Reservoir, which once more prompted James to resume his role as tour guide.

"Ladybower Reservoir was built after the other two and is much larger," he announced. "It was built between 1935 and 1945 and, unlike the other reservoirs in the valley, its construction involved the demolition of two villages, Derwent and Ashopton. Their remains can still be seen when the water level is low."

After seeing the reservoirs, they headed back to the A625 and went through the village of Hope.

"That's something I lost when I married you," said Pete, who'd noticed the village sign.

"You also lost your charm at the same time," replied Wendy.

Nobody bothered to react. By now the others were used to Pete and Wendy having a go at each other in public. That included Ben, Frank and Rosie who'd only met them two days before.

Their journey continued through the Hope Valley towards Castleton. Peveril Castle had just come into view when Rosie leant across to Mark.

"Did you really mean it when you said you thought our father is still alive?" she asked him.

"I don't really know what to think," he replied. "All my life, I've been told he died in 1984 and you say that both you and Ben were told the same story. So there shouldn't be any doubt in my mind that this was indeed what happened. Yet, some of the things we have learnt over the past two days have led me to question this version of events. That's why I'm now convinced that he was still alive until at least 1994 and maybe much longer. As to what happened in Spain and whether or not your mother is still alive, I really don't know."

"I bet there's one person on this bus who knows the truth," said Rosie nodding towards James.

"We've tried to get more out of him, but he always says the terms of the trust fund have limited what he can and cannot reveal," replied Mark.

"That's a pretty lame excuse if you ask me," said Rosie. "I'm going to get him by himself when we're in Castleton. I'm going to tell him that we all believe our father didn't die in 1984 and he needs to be straight with us, irrespective of the terms of the trust fund. I might even have to resort to a few tears in order to get him to talk, but even if I don't, I still intend discovering the truth."

Mark noted the determined look on her face and didn't doubt for one moment that she meant what she said.

A few minutes later, they arrived in the centre of Castleton, where Stan parked the minibus in the main car park.

"Right, everybody," said James. "Welcome to Castleton, which is famous for three things, one of them being the eleventh century Peveril Castle that stands high above the village. There are also numerous caverns in the area, four of which are open to the public and, finally, it is the only place in the world where the semi-precious stone known as Blue John is found. Some of you probably noticed the shops as we came into the village, many of which sell jewellery using Blue John. You will have time to do a bit of shopping later, but first we are going to go and do a tour of the Devil's Arse."

In the past, Pete would have made a comment that involved Ben. But by now, he was beginning to realise that any snide remark about his sexuality would get him in trouble with the others.

As a result, he just said, "Devil's Arse, eh? It sounds like a description of me the morning after a chicken vindaloo."

Pete looked around to see if there was any response from the others to his comment. But he was disappointed to discover that the only person who showed any reaction was Zara.

"God, how gross," she muttered.

"The Devil's Arse was the name of one of the caverns in Castleton," explained James. "They changed its name in 1880 to Peak Cavern so that it wouldn't offend Queen Victoria when she visited that year. The cavern is on the far side of the village, so you all need to stick together and follow my lead. I don't want to lose any of you."

They disembarked and made their way through the village, following a small stream, which they later discovered originated from the mouth of the cavern. When they reached their destination, James paid the entrance fee, and their guide joined them a short while later.

The tour was enjoyable, and the guide was particularly pleased that the entire group was paying attention to his every word. He didn't realise that the reason they were so attentive was because they didn't want to miss anything that might help them in the next day's challenge.

They took in all the details about the troglodytes who used to live in the cave entrance and who earned their living by making rope. They also made a mental note of all the famous visitors to the cavern over the centuries, including Lord Byron and Daniel Defoe, as well as Queen Victoria.

Louise began to regret not bringing the boys as she felt they would have loved Castleton and particularly Peak Cavern with its stalactites and stalagmites.

"You know how to remember which is which?" queried Pete.

They were about to find out even if they didn't want to.

"Tights come down and mights go up. Just like me and Wendy when we first started courting."

"That was a long time ago," replied Wendy without smiling. "There isn't much of that going on these days."

As they progressed through the cavern, Louise told Mark that she thought the boys would really love Castleton.

"Perhaps I ought to suggest to Simon that he and Katie bring them here tomorrow," she said.

"That's a good idea," Mark agreed.

Once they had reappeared from the cavern, James began setting out what would happen next.

"We are going to leave the village at 11.30," he told them. "That gives you just over half an hour either to grab a coffee or to visit the shops. So I'll see you all back in the car park."

Whilst James made his way back to the minibus, the rest of the group headed towards the centre of the village. All of them except Rosie.

"I'm going to have a word with James," she told Frank. "I'll catch up with you after I've spoken to him."

James meanwhile had arrived at the minibus and settled in his seat ready to read his paper, which was where Rosie found him.

"Could I have a word with you, James?" she asked.

"Of course you can, Rosie," he replied.

"Look," she said. "Mark and I have been talking and both of us have serious doubts whether our father died in 1984. We think that you are using the terms of the trust fund as something to hide behind. We want to know the truth and you're the only person who can tell us what really happened. For a start, you must know if our father is still alive, or at least if he survived the crash. After all, you're his solicitor."

James looked at her in exasperation and said, "Rosie, how old do you think I am?"

This caught Rosie by surprise. It was not the reply she was expecting.

"On second thoughts, don't answer that as it might upset me," he continued. "Let me tell you. I am 55 and if you work it out, it means I was only fifteen when your father went to Spain and, more importantly, I was only twenty when he had the crash. Although I am the solicitor responsible for your family's trust fund, I was never your father's solicitor. I was still at university back in 1984."

Chapter 11

Sunday, September 1st, 2019

Rosie caught up with the rest of the group in a nearby tearoom. They were all sitting together at a corner table, chatting and enjoying morning coffee. Frank had already told the others what Rosie had been doing and they were keen to discover the outcome of her conversation with James.

"Well, the first thing is that we all wrongly assumed the name Knight and Son refers to James and Simon," she informed them. "It doesn't. The firm was actually established by James's father and it's James who is the son. Also, he is only 55 years old and didn't even join the family firm until 1986."

"I'd have said he was at least sixty," added Pete, who was genuinely surprised that James was as young as that.

"That's as maybe," Rosie continued, "but the truth is he wasn't part of the firm in 1984 and he didn't draw up the trust fund. His father did. In fact, he didn't take over as a trustee of the fund until shortly before his father retired in 1997. Unfortunately, we can't ask his father anything about the establishment of the fund because he died in 2013."

"So all this means is that James might not be holding back on us like we thought," added Mark. "It's quite possible that he knows nothing about our father, other than what he's been told."

"It would appear that way," replied Rosie.

She looked at her watch and added, "We need to get back to the car park as it's nearly time to move on."

They were all finished anyway, and after a short walk along the main street, they arrived back at the minibus where James and Stan were waiting for them.

"We've got one more stop to make before we have lunch," said James. "We are going to visit the village of Eyam. It should take us approximately twenty minutes to get there. Eyam is known as the plague village because of an outbreak of the disease that occurred there in 1665. The villagers volunteered to isolate themselves and this selfless act stopped the plague from spreading elsewhere. But they paid a terrible price, with at least 260 of the inhabitants perishing from the infection. We are very fortunate to be going there at this time of the year as we will also be able to see Eyam's well-dressings."

The journey took them through the villages of Bradwell and Foolow before they finally arrived at their destination. Eyam was extremely busy but despite this, they were lucky and managed to find a space in the car park.

"Well-dressing is a Derbyshire tradition practised by most villages in the Peak District," explained James. "Historically, a well was crucial to the survival of a village. The fact that it didn't dry up in times of drought was literally a matter of life and death. That's why people in villages around here decided to celebrate another year with fresh water by dressing their wells with scenes made from flowers. Well-dressings in Derbyshire take place throughout the summer months and this one is always at the end of August or the beginning of September."

Eyam had three wells that had been dressed, and the group visited them all. One was the children's well, which was particularly poignant. James had just told the group about the

Riley graves, which were located a short distance outside the village. In August 1666, Elizabeth Hancock buried her husband and all six of her children there, within eight days of one another. They had succumbed to the plague. The National Trust now maintained the lonely spot on the edge of Eyam Moor where the graves are situated.

After they had visited the three wells, the party stopped at Plague Cottage. It was the place where the outbreak of the disease had started after a local tailor had received a roll of flea-infested cloth from London. Finally, they took in the Saxon Cross in the churchyard before returning to the car park.

"I've booked lunch in the Devonshire Arms in Beeley at one o'clock," said James once they were all safely back on board the minibus.

A few minutes later, they had left Eyam behind and had gone through the villages of Stoney Middleton, Calver and Baslow, before taking the B6012 to Beeley.

"We are soon going to go past one of the jewels of the Peak District," announced James as Stan slowed down for a cattle grid. "If you look out of the window on your left, you will shortly see Chatsworth House, the ancestral home of the Dukes of Devonshire. Chatsworth Park, which surrounds the house, was laid out by the famous landscape gardener Capability Brown in the eighteenth century."

As they looked out of the window, they could clearly see the magnificent house and its Emperor fountain, built for a visit of Tsar Nicholas I of Russia. In the end, the Tsar cancelled his trip, so he never saw the fountain, with its water rising to a height of 296 feet. Back in 1844, it was the tallest fountain in the world.

Five minutes later, they arrived in the village of Beeley where they were due to stop for lunch. Beeley was originally one of the many estate villages owned by the Duke of Devonshire and the Duke still owned most of the houses there. He also owned the village pub, which was named after him.

The pub was a fine-looking building built from Derbyshire stone. It was located in a picture-postcard setting with a crystal-clear stream running past the front of the building.

"Well, thank God for that," said Pete. "After visiting the Devil's Arse and the plague village, I could do with a pint in a traditional English pub. I wonder whose cider they sell?"

He eyed the bar and soon discovered that it was Strongbow. Not wanting to support one of his competitors, he ordered a pint of Bakewell Best Bitter from the Peak Brewery instead.

James had booked a table for them in the restaurant where they had a fine view of the stream before it disappeared into a culvert under the road. It subsequently reappeared in a field on the other side of the village, where it continued its journey before eventually joining the River Derwent.

Most of the party opted for one of the Sunday roasts on offer, except for Zara who chose a truffle and wild mushroom open lasagne. Her T-shirt displayed her disdain for what the others were eating as it proudly proclaimed 'Meat is Murder' in bold letters across her chest.

However, it didn't put Pete off from tucking into his prime rib of beef. This was despite the fact that he was seated directly opposite her.

Mindful of the fact that they were all due to eat another three-course meal at seven o'clock that evening, nobody opted for a dessert. Some of them paid a quick visit to the toilet before they all got back on the minibus to continue their tour.

"Our next stop is Haddon Hall," said James as they pulled out of the village.

Their destination was only a couple of miles away and five minutes later they pulled into the car park.

"Okay, guys," said James. "In a moment, we will be having a look around Haddon Hall. It is the most complete medieval manor house in the country, with a large part of it dating back to the twelfth century. The plan is for everyone to wander around the house and gardens on your own. There are guides throughout the hall who will be happy to answer your questions."

He looked at his watch.

"It's 2.15 at the moment," he continued. "So can you all be back here by a 3.45, please?"

The group disembarked from the minibus and proceeded through the main entrance to the ticket booth, where James paid the entrance fee. They walked over the bridge spanning the River Wye, before ascending the stairs to the lower courtyard of the Hall. That was where Rosie caught up with Mark again.

"Let's think about it logically," she said.

She was not going to let go of her suspicions.

"If Dad didn't die in 1984, where has he been all this time?"

"He probably disappeared with the remainder of his fortune and could have reinvented himself anywhere?" replied Mark.

"But why?" she asked, frustrated by Mark's response.

"Because he'd killed one person and crippled another in a car crash whilst he was disqualified from driving," he replied.

"But think about it," Rosie continued. "All the reports say there were two bodies in Dad's car. Anyway, we are talking about Spain not some third-world country. Surely, they would know whether or not it was him who was driving? Somebody must have identified his body. Either that, or they would have been able to prove it was him through his dental records."

Mark thought about what Rosie was saying for a minute.

"Okay," he replied. "If he did die in the crash, why the discrepancies with the dates?"

"Well, I think Dad left a proportion of his winnings with James's father when he left the UK. He also probably left instructions that the money wasn't to come to us until after your mother died."

"But you weren't even born when he left the UK," added Mark. "Therefore, he couldn't have done that. You and Ben wouldn't be beneficiaries of the trust fund if he had."

"That wouldn't matter if he stipulated that the money should go to his children rather than specifically to you and Pete. I'll give you an example of what I mean. A close friend of mine and her sister were left £6,000 in her grandfather's will, which they were to inherit when they turned eighteen. But then her parents had another child which resulted in the two girls getting less money than their grandfather had intended. You see, the will said that the money was to be divided between his grandchildren and now there were three of them rather than two."

"Thinking about it, the wording of the trust fund was very similar to that," added Mark. "When Pete spoke to James on the day he received his letter, he was told that the beneficiaries of the trust fund were the children of AS Bradbury. We only assumed that it meant Pete and me because we didn't know about you and Ben at the time."

"Mind you," said Rosie, "even if he had originally mentioned you and Pete by name, he could still have altered the wording later to encompass all his children. He probably kept in contact with his solicitor all the time he was in Spain. Dad wouldn't have had much to do on the Costa del Sol, which is why he'd have had time to dream up these challenges. He probably drew up an outline of his plan and left James and his father to put the meat on the bones. That would explain why the trust fund was established a month after he died and would also explain why certain other things happened later. It was purely because they weren't added into the mix until later."

"Aren't you forgetting the tape, which Dad couldn't have recorded until 1990?" asked Mark.

"How do you know it was Dad?" Rosie replied. "It could have been anyone who recorded it, and why record it on cassette? Surely, if he had recorded it on video, it would have had even more impact and left us in no doubt whether it was him or not?"

Mark began to see the point she was making, but Rosie wasn't finished yet.

"Don't you think there is something strange about James?" she asked.

Mark admitted that it had never crossed his mind.

"Aren't you even a little bit curious to find out how he fits in with all of this?"

"He's just the administrator of the trust fund, Rosie," Mark replied.

"When did you ever know a solicitor who works on a Saturday and a Sunday?" Rosie continued. "Or act as a tour guide? And one who ropes his son and daughter-in-law in as child minders? Or one who's so evasive about answering questions? Actually, forget the last one. All solicitors are evasive by nature. But don't you see my point? James appears far too closely involved in this whole trust fund thing. It's like its personal."

"Well, you don't know how much he's being paid," said James. "Anybody would work at the weekend if they were being paid enough."

But Rosie wasn't listening as she continued, "And anyway, there's his car."

"What? The Range Rover?" replied Mark. "I know they are quite expensive, but it's the type of car I would expect a country solicitor to have."

"But it's not a Range Rover," replied Rosie. "It's an Overfinch. Frank pointed it out to me the other day. He's a petrolhead, as well as being a hifi geek."

"What the hell is an Overfinch?" asked Mark. "I've never heard of that make before."

"An Overfinch is a customised Range Rover," Rosie replied. "Prices start at £160,000 and they are bought by people who have money to burn, people for whom a standard Range Rover isn't expensive enough. It is the type of car you would expect an Arab sheik to drive, not a country solicitor, and it's not just him. Have you seen what Simon drives?"

Mark admitted he hadn't. On the first day they'd met, he'd obviously come with his father. Subsequently, he and Katie had arrived in their own car, but Mark hadn't clocked what it was. Rosie had, however, and she was about to tell him.

"It's a one-year-old Porsche Cayenne Turbo," she said. "The starting price for one of those little beauties is a mere £96,000."

Chapter 12

Sunday, September 1st, 2019

Mark went looking for Pete and found him in Haddon's banqueting hall alongside Wendy and Louise. He wanted to tell him about the conversation he'd just had with Rosie.

"James and Simon must be either pimps or drug dealers in order to afford cars like that," said Pete once Mark had told him. He quickly added, "I wonder whether James would let me drive his Overfinch."

"I don't want to worry you, Pete," said Mark. "But it's far more likely that James has got his fingers in our trust fund rather than being involved in either drugs or prostitution."

"Well, I fully intend to quiz him about his car as soon as we get back to the hotel," added Pete.

Mark and Pete joined Louise and Wendy and continued looking around the magnificent medieval manor house. They moved through the parlour into the Long Gallery before continuing into the anteroom and the state bedroom. From there, they went back to the banqueting hall and into the fourteenth century kitchen, where the stone steps were spectacularly worn down after hundreds of years of use. Pretty soon, they found themselves back outside again, this time in the garden where they met up with the others.

"It's 3.40," said Louise. "We'd better get back to the minibus."

They made their way through the grounds back to the car park where James and Stan were waiting for them.

"Right," said James once they were all back on board, "we have only one more stop to make and that's in Ashbourne. After that, we will return to Striding Hall."

The next part of the excursion took them on a route through the market town of Bakewell.

"Home of the tarts," announced Pete. "You'll feel right at home here, Zara."

Zara responded by pulling a face at him.

"In Bakewell, they aren't known as tarts, they are called Bakewell puddings," said James. "Also, they never have icing on top or a cherry for that matter."

"Well, there you go," added Pete. "You learn something new every day. It's a pity nobody ever told Mr Kipling."

James just smiled. They were now on the main road heading towards Ashford in the Water. From there, they took a minor road leading to Monyash, after which they joined the A515 to Ashbourne. They were travelling through the southern part of the Peak District where the rolling hills of the Derbyshire Dales had taken over from the bleak moorland of the Dark Peak. A short while later, they arrived at their destination.

"This is the historic town of Ashbourne," said James. "It's a small market town close to the southern tip of the Peak District National Park. The town is famous for football, but not football as you would know it. A version of the game has been played here for over 1,000 years. It takes place every Shrove Tuesday between two teams known as the Up'ards and the Down'ards. The whole of the town is the pitch and the goals are three miles apart. People from the town play for one of the teams depending on whether they were born north or south of

Henmore Brook, a stream that runs through the centre of town. There are hundreds of players in both teams and the game can be extremely violent, with many owners of premises in the town boarding up their windows on the day it is played. It's where the term 'local derby' originated."

"Is there anything specific that we need to see?" asked Ben.

"No, I've just brought you here to look around the town centre," James replied. "The minibus will leave at 5 pm sharp. So you have just over 45 minutes to do whatever you wish."

"I'd like to suggest that we go somewhere for a cup of tea," said Mark. "We can discuss the conversations some of us have been having."

They headed off to Bramhall's Deli and Café in the Market Place.

Nothing new came out of their impromptu meeting. However, Pete revealed that he intended to search the internet as soon as he got back to Striding Hall. He wanted to look for anything it might tell him about their father's death. It was Zara, though, who brought them down to earth.

"I thought we'd agreed that the main thing we had to do today was to pay attention to everything we saw and heard," she reminded them. "James told us that it would help with tomorrow's challenge. However, we've spent so much time talking about what had happened back in 1984 that I think we've lost sight of what the day is about."

All of them realised what she was saying was true but, at the same time, they hoped that between them they would have managed to notice most things.

A few minutes later, the party were back outside again. They had only a short time left to look around the shops before it was time to head back to Striding Hall.

Stan took the road to Belper where he joined the A6 towards Cromford and Matlock. As they travelled through the Derwent Valley, James explained that this was the only UNESCO World Heritage Site in Derbyshire. One of the main reasons for this accolade was the fact that Sir Richard Arkwright's Cromford Mill was the first factory to be built anywhere in the world. Its construction changed Britain forever as it signalled the start of the Industrial Revolution.

"Unfortunately, we don't have time to visit the village of Cromford itself," he told them. "But it is well worth looking around if you come back to Derbyshire again. In particular, the Cromford Canal and the Cromford and High Peak Railway, both of which terminate in the village, are two outstanding pieces of industrial engineering. Not only that, but Cromford also has many examples of workers' cottages in the village. Most of these were built in the eighteenth century by Sir Richard Arkwright in order to house the factory workers."

They continued past Masson Mill built in 1783. After that, it was on to Matlock Bath with its high cliffs and cable car before they arrived in the town of Matlock itself.

"Matlock is the county town of Derbyshire," said James. "It once had a tramway similar to the one in San Francisco, which used to go up and down the steep hill on which the town is built."

"What does county town mean?" asked Jack.

"Well, if Derbyshire was a country, then Matlock would be the capital," explained James. "It's the administrative centre for the county and is where the county council is based."

Once they had travelled through Matlock, they headed back towards Chesterfield and by the time they arrived at Striding Hall, it was nearly a quarter to six.

"Shall we all meet in the bar at 6.30?" asked James.

After everybody agreed, James set off towards his car to swap his newspaper for a magazine he wanted to read. This was the opportunity Pete had been waiting for and he went over and engaged James in conversation. The conversation only lasted a few minutes before Pete joined the others as they were collecting their keys from reception.

"Well," said Mark. "What did he say?"

"I told him I was a big fan of super cars, and I couldn't help but notice he drove an Overfinch. I asked him what it was like to drive and how long he had owned it. He told me it was absolutely superb, the best car he'd ever driven. He said that he'd bought it last summer in a proceeds of crime auction for a fraction of the price it would have cost when new. He told me that Simon had done exactly the same when he bought the Porsche a couple of months ago. Knowing about these auctions is one of the perks of being a solicitor, I suppose. He said the original owner of the Overfinch is now serving twelve years for armed robbery."

"He didn't buy it out of his client account then," said Mark.

"It would appear not and, furthermore, I believed him. Not only that, but he's invited me to take it for a spin on Tuesday," Pete replied.

"Lucky old you," said Mark.

He didn't mean it, of course. He was being sarcastic.

Having finished their conversation, they retired to their rooms to freshen up before dinner. Well, at least that was what Mark did. Pete, however, wanted to search the internet to see if he could find out anything about their father's crash. As soon as he was back in their room, he sat down with his laptop.

"For crying out loud," shouted Pete as he opened it up.

"What is it now?" replied Wendy wearily.

"I am going to have to have serious words with that son of ours," Pete continued. "Jack was the last person to use my computer and he's forgotten to delete his browser history. Look at the final search he made on Google," he said whilst showing Wendy his computer screen. "Is it legal to shag your cousin?"

"Well, at least he's being sensible. And there's a big difference between looking up about sex on the internet and actually having sex," she replied. "But then again, you should know all about that. Your browser history has loads of porno sites on it."

"Bloody hell," thought Pete to himself. "Is there no privacy in this world anymore?"

By half past six, Pete was still not finished on his laptop and when Wendy threatened to go to the bar without him, he merely told her that he was busy and would join them all as soon as he had finished. Consequently, Wendy collected Jack and Hannah and the three of them went downstairs together. When they arrived in the bar, they discovered that Louise, Mark, Noel and Josh were already there. Josh was telling his parents all about their day out at Gulliver's Kingdom. He'd really enjoyed it. Noel, however, wasn't as keen. He thought it was geared towards younger children.

"Well, we visited a fantastic cavern in Castleton," said Louise. "I think you'd both love it there. I'm going to ask Simon and Katie if they can take you tomorrow."

It was at this point that Wendy interrupted her.

"I've got a suggestion to make," she announced. "But I want to discuss it with the four of you first."

By the four of you, Wendy meant Rosie, Zara, Hannah and Louise.

"Do you think we could sit down together somewhere for a few minutes before dinner?"

Louise hadn't the faintest idea what Wendy wanted to discuss but had no objection. She asked Noel to keep an eye on his younger brother whilst they joined Wendy in order to hear what she had to say.

They sat down at one of the tables in the corner of the bar, out of earshot of the men.

"Tomorrow, we face the second challenge," said Wendy, "and I, for one, don't want it to be another cock-up like the first one. The question we have to ask ourselves is why do we think it went so badly?"

She wasn't expecting an answer to that particular question because she continued without a break.

"Testosterone," she announced. "It was caused by Pete and Phil trying to show us who the alpha male is. It was all about egos and who could be the most macho. Now, I don't know what form tomorrow's challenge is going to take but I do know one thing. We need one person to take charge of the whole thing and that person has to be one of us."

They all agreed with the suggestion.

"Good," Wendy continued. "I want Rosie to take charge of tomorrow's challenge with Louise taking over on Wednesday. Is everyone happy with that?"

She sounded determined and none of the others would have dared to disagree.

"Right," she added, "I will tell the boys after dinner."

Mind you, by the time dinner was due to start, Pete still hadn't appeared.

"We shouldn't wait for him," said Wendy. "He knows what time dinner is served. It's his fault if he is late."

The conversation over dinner was the usual mixture of small talk and speculation about the next challenge. Louise asked Simon if he and Katie could take the boys to Castleton the next day and was pleased to discover that he thought it was an excellent idea.

After dinner, James told the group that tomorrow's breakfast would be at 8 am and they were to meet in the bar where he would tell them what to expect. Following his announcement, James took his leave along with Simon and Katie whilst everyone else made their way back to the bar.

That was Wendy's cue to make her announcement.

"Can I have one minute of everybody's time before we all go to bed?" she said.

She told Mark, Ben and Jack what the girls had decided. The person she really wanted to tell was Pete. But since he hadn't appeared yet, she had to be satisfied with just the three of them.

"I think it's a great idea," said Ben.

Mark was just about to agree with him when Pete finally entered the room.

"Where the hell have you been?" asked Wendy. "You've missed dinner. Oh, and whilst you were absent, we voted that Rosie will be the team leader for tomorrow's challenge and Louise for the challenge on Wednesday."

"How do you know that we won't be in two teams again?" Pete replied.

"We don't," said Wendy, "but even if we are in two teams, it would still be better if one person was ultimately in charge. Anyway, you haven't answered my question. Where have you been all this time?"

"Well, I got so engrossed in trying to find out about Dad, that I completely forgot about the time," Pete replied. "When I saw it was eight o'clock, I decided to order a sandwich from room service as I wanted to carry on with my research."

"What did you discover?" asked Mark.

"Very little regarding the pools win, or the accident in Spain," Pete replied. "Don't get me wrong, there was plenty in the papers about both of them but nothing we don't know already, even in the Spanish papers. Mind you, that was as far as I could tell using Google Translate. However, there was one thing I discovered in the *Derbyshire Times*, and I got the hotel reception to print it off for me. The paper's entire archive has just been made available online, by the way."

Pete handed the piece of paper to Mark. The first thing he noticed was the date, which was Thursday March 5th, 1987. The article was by the paper's deputy editor, Howard Hill, and had the headline, 'Whatever happened to Chesterfield pools winner's missing millions?'

It was clear that the deputy editor was being a bit economical with the truth as far as his headline was concerned. According to the article, only a part of their father's fortune had gone missing. However, the headline had impact and no doubt the deputy editor would have hoped it would be picked up by one of the national newspapers. The fact that Pete had been unable to discover a similar story anywhere else suggested it hadn't.

Mark read on and discovered that Howard Hill's suspicions had been raised when probate was granted for their father's estate. The total amount he'd left once the villa in Spain had been sold was £314,000. The court had awarded £300,000 to the passenger of the Golf and the relatives of the driver, which left a residual amount of £14,000. Since their father hadn't made a will and had never bothered to get divorced, this money went to his wife, Mark and Pete's mother.

"She never told us about that," said Mark. "That's why we could afford to go to Disney World on holiday in 1987. It's all making sense now."

"But carry on reading," said Pete. "You haven't got to the main part of the article yet."

Mark continued and discovered it was the size of their father's estate that had made Hill curious. After all, why should a man who had won over a million pounds only leave an estate worth £314,000 six years later? Surely, even the most feckless of people would find it difficult to spend over £100,000 a year in the 1980s and not have anything to show for it?

It was at this point in the article that Hill produced his trump card. He'd managed to obtain a copy of their father's bank statement from May 1979. He didn't say how he'd managed to get hold of it, although Mark suspected it involved a backhander to somebody from the bank.

However, it wasn't the way the paper had managed to obtain it that interested Mark. It was the detail in the bank statement that fascinated him. For on Thursday May 24th, 1979 the pools company had deposited £551,086.24 into their father's bank account. The same day, a similar amount had been transferred to an account at the Banco Caixa Geral in Marbella. The question that Howard Hill had posed back in 1987, and Mark was now asking in 2019, was if his father had won over £1 million in 1979, where was the other £450,000. Also, why wasn't it paid into his bank account?

Chapter 13

Monday, September 2nd, 2019

"I thought one of the reasons for us coming here was to answer some of the questions we have about our family," said Mark to Pete at the breakfast table the next morning.

"It seems to me that the longer we are here, the more questions we have," replied Pete.

"That's true," added Louise who had overheard the conversation. "But can you just put those questions on the back burner for a few hours? We need to be a hundred percent focused on today's task."

Whilst the three of them were talking, Jack was looking decidedly nonplussed. He'd received a telling off from his father over the Google search and he'd been told to stay away from Zara in future.

"Watch it, young man," Pete told him. "I'm keeping an eye on both you and the wicked witch of Weston over there."

Bang on nine o'clock, Simon and Katie collected Noel and Josh and set off for Castleton. It was now time for the second challenge to begin.

"Good morning, everybody," said James. "I hope you are all looking forward to today's challenge, which is a picture challenge. In this folder are six old photographs of Derbyshire and all you have to do is to reproduce them by taking a modern-day photo from approximately the same spot.

Obviously, the first part of the exercise is to identify where each photo was taken. To help you, I am providing you with several Ordnance Survey maps. In addition, you will have the use of four iPads, each of which has a built-in camera. The iPads have the six photographs downloaded onto them. One further thing is that the modern photos must contain a shot of one of you in each of them. This is just to prove you've actually been there and haven't merely downloaded the photos from the internet. Now I said you needed to pay attention yesterday and the reason for that was because all these photos were taken within a mile of where we went during our trip around Derbyshire."

"So what's the prize this time?" asked Pete. "Half a million pounds worth of scratch cards, perhaps?"

"You'll be pleased to hear that it isn't," James replied. "If you are successful in this challenge, each of the four beneficiaries of the trust will receive a freehold property. Are there any questions?"

"Yes," said Pete. "Do we get to choose where our property is located? If so, I'd like mine to be in Belgravia."

"I think that is the type of question best left until after you've been successful," replied James succinctly.

"Can I ask what your definition of approximately the same spot is?" asked Mark.

"By all means," James replied. "Some of the scenes have changed dramatically since the original photograph was taken. As long as you have correctly identified what the subject of each photo is, where it was taken, and have made a genuine attempt to take a modern-day photo from the same spot, that will be acceptable."

"How long have we got?" asked Louise.

"Good point," said James. "You need to present the six photographs to me back in this room at 6 pm. As well as telling me where each one was taken, you will also need to tell me why any of the new photos are completely different from the original. Is that everything?"

Nobody reacted.

"In which case, the challenge has now started," announced James. "And I'd like to wish you all the best."

"Said with complete sincerity," muttered Pete.

Rosie immediately took charge.

"Right, let's all gather round and have a look at these photos and see if anybody recognises anything."

She took hold of the folder and took out the six images. The first one was a picture of a church.

"We must have passed it yesterday," she said. "Does anyone recognise it?"

Initially nobody replied, but then Frank said, "It could be in any one of the villages we visited yesterday. If one of us were to retrace the route, I bet we would be able to find it."

"Good idea, Frank," Rosie replied. "Somebody can do that as soon as we've identified exactly where we went yesterday. In the meantime, let's continue with the photos."

The second photo was one of a boat in a tunnel.

"That doesn't look like anywhere we went yesterday," said Jack.

"No, but we did drive alongside the Cromford Canal," Rosie replied, "and if there is a tunnel, it could have been taken there. Let's move on to number three."

The third photograph was of a well-dressing, just like the ones they had seen in Eyam the previous day. However, there was no clue which village it was taken in.

Rosie took photo number four out. This depicted an old scene of a group of men outside a village pub. But which pub and in which village was a mystery.

Photo number five showed a grand country house but, once again, nobody recognised it or had the slightest idea where it was located.

Mind you, it was photo number six that caused the most raised eyebrows.

"It reminds me of the gents' toilets in our pub," said Rosie.

"That's because it's a gents' urinal," said Pete. "All of us went for a pee at some point yesterday. Does any of us recognise it?"

"Surprisingly enough, I don't recognise it at all," replied Wendy.

"I meant the men," added Pete.

When none of the men replied, Rosie said, "So nobody recognises any of the pictures? In which case, we all need to put our thinking caps on. Are there any quick wins?"

Ben, who had already opened the Ordnance Survey maps and was studying them in great detail, looked up and said, "Photo number two could be a quick win. The Cromford Canal actually has three tunnels on it but only one of them was close to the route we took yesterday. It's Gregory Tunnel and it's alongside the A6 we took between Belper and Cromford."

"Excellent," said Rosie, "we are starting to make progress. I'd like Pete and Wendy to go and check out Gregory Tunnel. The first thing you have to do is to confirm that it is the tunnel in the photo. If it is, then you need to take a modern shot of it using the iPad. But before you go, let's make sure we all have each other's phone numbers. We need to ensure that we can stay in contact all the time."

"Why do we have to go?" moaned Pete.

"Because somebody has to and I've nominated you," Rosie replied curtly. "Just thank your lucky stars that somebody has to be in the photo, otherwise I'd have asked Wendy to stay here, and you could have gone by yourself."

"He could always take a selfie," added Wendy, which Pete was clearly not very happy about.

"You'd better both go," said Rosie. "You're less likely to make a mistake if there are two of you."

Pete knew there was no point in arguing with her. He picked up one of the iPads and an Ordnance Survey map. A few minutes later, his BMW was throwing up stones in the car park as he and Wendy set off for Cromford at breakneck speed.

"You only sent him in order to get him out of our hair," commented Mark.

"Whatever makes you think that?" replied Rosie.

The twinkle in Rosie's eye told him he was right.

"Ben, you seem to be good with maps," Rosie continued. "Do you think you can mark out the route we took yesterday on one of those Ordnance Survey maps?"

"I should be able to as long as I can have somebody with me to check for mistakes," came the reply.

Rosie decided to delegate that particular job to Frank.

"The Ordnance Survey maps we've been given all have a scale of one and a quarter inches to one mile," she continued. "So after you've marked out the route in pencil, I want you to draw two further lines at a distance of one and a quarter inches on either side. In that way, we can identify the search area in which all our photos are located."

Whilst Jack and Frank were working on the map, the rest of the group took a more detailed look at the photos.

One of the things that nobody had mentioned when they'd looked at them the first time around was photo one and photo six were in colour, whereas the other four were in black and white. Mark now pointed this out.

"I guess photos one and six are more recent than the other four," he announced. "Although I don't know if that helps us."

"Except it probably means that photos two to five are the ones most likely to have changed since they were originally taken," added Zara.

On closer inspection, the photos did throw up a few of their secrets. The well-dressing had a date written above a scene depicting Jesus taking the Sermon on the Mount. The date was 1898.

"It still doesn't help us to identify where it was taken though," said Mark.

Also, they realised the picture of the church in photograph one was that of a church with a spire.

"Now that will help us," said Mark. "Churches with spires are marked on Ordnance Survey maps as a circle with a cross on top. Churches with towers, on the other hand, are marked as a square with a cross on top. Therefore, we will be able to narrow the field down a little."

The discovery they made regarding the photograph of the pub was also promising. The photo was pretty faded but, even so, they could just make out the words on the pub's sign. It said Devonshire Arms.

"That must be the Devonshire Arms we went to yesterday," said Hannah, who was pleased to be able to join in the conversation.

As the youngest person who'd been allowed to participate in the challenge, she was understandably nervous about sharing her ideas. She had no desire to be shot down to earth by her father and that was why she had decided to remain quiet so far. Now he had gone, she felt as if a weight had been lifted from her shoulders and she was able to speak her mind.

"It looks nothing like it," said Zara with such vigour that Hannah wished she'd remained silent.

Recognising what had happened, Mark came to her aid.

"You don't know that, Zara," he said. "The photo is very old and the pub could have changed quite a bit over the years. In addition, the pub we ate in was located on the corner of two roads. We only saw it from the front. How do you know that this photo wasn't taken from the side?"

Hannah heaved a sigh of relief and decided to continue contributing, well, at least whilst her parents weren't there.

"It may or may not be the Devonshire Arms in Beeley," said Rosie. "It's almost certain that there are other pubs called the Devonshire Arms in Derbyshire. What we need to do, is to identify all of them that are in our search area. Jack, can you take one of the iPads and compile a list of every pub in Derbyshire called Devonshire Arms? That will help us to find those that are inside our target area."

Next, Ben and Frank announced that they had finished plotting the search area on one of the Ordnance Survey maps.

"Can you please identify all the churches with spires in the target area?" said Rosie.

After a moment's thought, she added, "Let's just see where we've got to so far, shall we? Ben and Frank are identifying possible churches that could be in photo one. We've identified where picture two was taken and Pete and Wendy have gone to photograph it. We don't know where the well-dressing is yet. However, we have identified that the pub in picture four is called the Devonshire Arms and Jack is looking for all the likely candidates on the internet. We haven't identified where the country house is yet. However, there can't be too many in the area where we are looking. Ben and Frank can look for possible candidates once they've finished looking for churches. As for photo six, I have no idea where that was taken. It could be absolutely anywhere."

"Can I make a suggestion?" said Mark. "Why don't I take the photos to the local tourist office and ask the staff if they recognise any of them."

"That's a really good idea, Mark," Rosie replied. "Do you know where it is?"

"It's near the Crooked Spire," he replied. "I noticed it when I was in town with Louise and the boys on Friday afternoon."

He picked up one of the iPads and headed for his car. Shortly afterwards, Ben and Frank announced that they had identified 21 churches with spires that were located inside their search area. In reality, it was only twenty, since one of the churches was the Crooked Spire and it was obvious that the church in the picture was not Chesterfield's parish church.

"I need two volunteers to visit all twenty of them," said Rosie. "They need to discover which one it is and take a photograph of it."

"No, there's a much quicker way of doing it," Ben interrupted her. "We can use Google Earth instead."

It was an obvious thing to do and Rosie wondered why she hadn't thought of it herself. But there was no point wasting time worrying about it. They had six photos to identify, and the clock was ticking.

"That's a great idea, Ben," said Rosie, who realised she'd better delegate some more of the tasks. "I want Zara and

Hannah to look for the church on Google Earth and, whilst they are doing that, I want Ben and Frank to identify large country houses inside our search area. At last, we seem to be getting somewhere."

As soon as Rosie had said it, her phone began to ring. It was Pete.

"Rosie," he said, "Gregory Tunnel has a towpath running down one side whereas the tunnel in photograph two doesn't. I don't know where this photo was taken, but it definitely wasn't here."

"Fuck," she replied, which was both succinct and summed up precisely the way everybody in the room felt at that moment.

Chapter 14

Monday, September 2nd, 2019

"You might as well come back," said Rosie. "After all, there's no point in staying out there as we haven't identified any of the other photos yet."

"Will do," replied Wendy.

Once the phone call had ended, Rosie looked at her watch.

"That's one and a half hours gone and seven and a half remaining and we haven't identified a single photo yet," she said "Jack, can you give us an update of where you are with identifying pubs called the Devonshire Arms?"

"Well," he replied. "I've been on a website called Beer in the Evening and, according to that, there are nine pubs called the Devonshire Arms in Derbyshire. That's if you include one in Belper that is just called the Devonshire. I've included it because it may well have been called the Devonshire Arms at some point in the past. Of those, four of them are in our search area. They are the pubs in Belper, Baslow, Beeley and Pilsley. I've just started looking at them on Google Earth and I'll let you know when I spot it."

Ben and Frank were not finding it easy to locate grand country houses in the search area. Churches with spires had been far easier because they were all clearly marked on the Ordnance Survey map. They could tell that the photo of the country house was taken quite a few years ago, as it was in black and white. It was almost certainly taken before the war, possibly even before the First World War. A lot of things could have happened to it since then. It could now be another country house hotel like Striding Hall, or a youth hostel or a conference centre. It could have been converted into flats or it might even have been demolished. There was all manner of things that could have happened since the original photo was taken. As a consequence, it was proving extremely difficult to identify.

Rosie was getting depressed. They were now over two hours into the search and still nothing. In fact, she was seriously beginning to wonder whether or not it had been a good idea to volunteer to be the leader for this task. Then she remembered she hadn't actually volunteered. It had been Wendy who'd nominated her.

"Got it," came a cry from the corner of the room. It was Zara who was ecstatic because she and Hannah had just identified the church in photo one. It was the parish church in Edensor, a village on the Chatsworth estate, which they had driven past the previous day.

After being at rock bottom, they were all suddenly lifted.

Rosie, Louise, Ben, Frank and Jack all went over to have a look at Zara and Hannah's iPad. There was no doubt that the girls were correct, they had discovered the location of the first photograph.

"How did we miss it?" asked Ben. "We drove right past it yesterday. Surely, at least one of us must have seen it?"

"I think I know the reason for that," said Louise. "Look where Edensor is on the map."

"Right next to Chatsworth House," replied Ben.

"Precisely and, more importantly, the church is located on the other side of the road from Chatsworth House," noted Rosie.

"If you remember, James had us all looking out of the windows on the left-hand side of the minibus, so we wouldn't miss the view of the house. That's why nobody remembers it. None of us actually saw it. We were all looking in the opposite direction."

"Do you think he did it deliberately?" enquired Ben.

"Does the pope have a balcony?" Rosie replied. "Of course he bloody well did."

Rosie phoned Pete and Wendy to find out where they were as she wanted to redirect them to Edensor. It was Wendy who answered.

"We're halfway between Matlock and Chesterfield," she said.

"Well, we've identified the church in the photo as being the one in Edensor," Rosie told her. "You need to put Edensor into the car's satnav and head there immediately."

"Will do," Wendy replied.

If Rosie was happy that they had identified the first photo, she was positively overjoyed when Mark phoned her a few minutes later. It was to tell her that the people in the tourist information bureau had positively identified two of the photos. In addition, they were 95% certain about the identity of a third.

"The one photo they identified immediately was the picture of the boat in the tunnel," said Mark. "That's because it was taken in one of Derbyshire's main tourist attractions, Speedwell Cavern in Castleton."

Unlike Peak Cavern, which they had visited the previous day, Speedwell Cavern was discovered by lead miners. They had stumbled across it by accident whilst digging their mineshaft. The shaft was subsequently flooded and nowadays tourists entered the cavern by boat.

"Pete and Wendy need to go and take a photo there," said Rosie.

"The second photo the staff identified was the church in Edensor," Mark continued.

"That's a disappointment," said Rosie. "We'd already worked that one out. In fact, Pete and Wendy are now on their way to photograph it. What was the one that they were 95% sure about?"

"That's the one of the well-dressing," Mark replied. "They were pretty sure it was taken in Tissington, due to it being dated 1898. One of the staff members told me that, although most villages in the Peak District have a well-dressing these days, the custom started in Tissington. Back in the 19th century, however, well-dressing nearly died out and Tissington was virtually the only village that persisted with it. That's why they think it was taken there."

"Well done, Mark," said Wendy. "Did they have any suggestions about the other three photos?"

"No one knew where the photo of the urinal was taken. All they could suggest was that it could be either a public toilet or the gents in a large pub. None of them recognised the photo of the Devonshire Arms, which makes me wonder if it's a pub anymore. There were conflicting views about the photo of the country house. One of the staff members suggested that it could be Longshaw Hall near Hathersage. But she was far from certain and one of the other staff members said she had been there recently and thought it definitely wasn't."

"Thanks again, Mark," said Rosie.

"There's nothing more that I can do here, so I'm coming back," he replied. "I'll see you shortly."

"Zara and Hannah, I want you to check out Longshaw Hall on Google Earth," said Rosie. "Jack, do you have an update for me on your search for the illusive Devonshire Arms?"

"The photo is definitely not of one of the four existing Devonshire Arms that we've identified in our search area," he told her. "I've checked them all on Google Earth and none of them bears even the slightest resemblance to the pub in the photo. And yes, I have checked out the side view of the pub in Beeley and got no joy there."

"Mark's shown the photo to the staff in the tourist information centre, and they think that it probably isn't a pub anymore," said Rosie.

"And I agree with them. That's why I'm now looking on a website called closedpubs.co.uk in order to identify any former pubs that were previously called the Devonshire Arms."

Rosie's next task was to phone Pete and Wendy to ask them to visit Tissington, before moving on to Speedwell Cavern. She sent them in that order because the staff at the tourist information centre hadn't been completely sure that the photo of the well-dressing had been taken in Tissington. She decided that it would be prudent to sort out whether they were correct or not, before going to Castleton where they were a hundred percent certain.

Zara and Hannah's internet search for Longshaw Hall confirmed that it was not the house in the photo.

"Okay, at least we've ruled it out," said Rosie. "Can you try and identify all the public toilets in the search zone next?"

This was both a difficult task and a long shot. After all, public toilets aren't shown on Ordnance Survey maps, and even if they could identify where they were all located, they would still have to carry out an internal inspection in order to find the correct one. Google Earth was not going to help them this time.

Ben and Frank, meanwhile, had given up looking for grand country houses on the Ordnance Survey map, as it was proving to be an impossible task. Instead, they had done a search for 'Derbyshire country houses' on Google. This had thrown up a list of sixteen, including Chatsworth House and Haddon Hall. All of them were far grander than the house in the picture and none of them bore even a passing resemblance to it.

Next, they tried 'Derbyshire country house hotels', which took them to a website featuring eleven buildings including Striding Hall. Most of them appeared to be of a similar size to the house in the photo, but that was where the similarities ended.

They thought they'd finally identified it when a search of Derbyshire youth hostels threw up Losehill Hall. But a closer inspection revealed several differences. Therefore, they continued their search, trawling the internet for the identity of the mysterious house.

Jack's search for closed pubs called the Devonshire Arms had thrown up four possibilities. But only one of them was in the search area. This was the Devonshire Arms in Holywell Street in Chesterfield, which closed in 1957 and was demolished in 1960 in order to make way for a car park. Closedpubs.co.uk had a picture of the long-demolished pub on its website and, unfortunately, it looked nothing like the pub in the picture.

"Next, I'm going to try to identify any pub that might have changed its name from the Devonshire Arms over the years," said Jack. "In order to do that I'm going to have to look at all the village websites within one mile of yesterday's route. Don't forget that our initial feeling was that it was a picture of a village pub, rather than one in a town and I think we should go with our gut feeling."

"It's amazing what you can find on the internet," announced Zara, who had discovered a complete list of public toilets on the Derbyshire Dales council website.

In total, there were 22 of them, with sixteen located within their search area.

"I need somebody to go and visit them all," Rosie announced, just as Mark returned from his trip into town.

That was why Mark and Louise found themselves heading out into Derbyshire at just after twelve noon in order to visit sixteen public toilets. It was not a task Louise would normally have relished. However, she felt she hadn't been of much help so far and she was glad to be involved in one of the searches.

Then there was another breakthrough, although this one wasn't particularly unexpected. It was a message from Pete to say that the photograph of the well-dressing had definitely been shot in Tissington. All the wells in the village were clearly marked, which had helped him and Wendy identify possible locations from where the photograph could have been taken. In the end, it was obvious that the well in the picture was the main village well opposite Tissington Hall. It may have been taken over 120 years ago but the scene had hardly changed at all.

Pete quickly took a photo of Wendy standing in front of the well, before they headed off to Castleton, where they arrived just after half past one. Speedwell Cavern was about half a mile out of the village and since it was clearly marked on the Ordnance Survey map, they easily found it. After paying the £11.50 per person admission fee, they descended the 105 steps down to the flooded mine.

Once at the bottom, they had to stand in line for one of the boats that would take them through the flooded shaft to the cavern itself. They didn't notice that Noel, Josh, Simon and Katie were also in the queue. Noel, however, was far more observant.

"Hello, Uncle Pete, what are you doing here?" he shouted out.

Pete wandered over to where they were standing and told them the reason for their visit to Speedwell Cavern. He looked at Simon hoping that his face would give something away. It didn't, but it was immaterial in the end. When their boat reached the cavern at the end of the tunnel, it was obvious that the photo had been taken there.

"Stand over there and you can be in the photo," said Pete to Noel and Josh once they'd gotten out of the boat.

Both boys dutifully obliged.

"We've had a fantastic day so far, Uncle Pete," said Noel. "We've been down the Devil's Arse."

He shouted the word 'arse' far louder than was really necessary, as he knew he normally wasn't allowed to say a word like that.

"It's called Peak Cavern these days," said Wendy.

"The guide told us that Devil's Arse is the correct name," said Noel. "It was only renamed Peak Cavern so that its name didn't appear rude to Queen Victoria when she visited it."

He had obviously been paying attention to the guide's running commentary.

"We also climbed the hill above Castleton to Peveril Castle," added Josh. "I bet you didn't know there was a pit in the basement of the castle that went straight down to the Devil's Arse below. In olden days, they used to throw people down it and if the fall didn't kill them, they would die in agony in the pitch black of the cavern."

He painted a gruesome story, just the type that was bound to enthral a ten-year-old boy.

"How lovely," replied Wendy.

Five minutes later, it was time to climb aboard the boat in order to return to the entrance. When the six of them re-emerged from the depths, Pete's phone started to bleep. Rosie had left a message as she couldn't get through whilst they were underground. The reason for her call was to tell them that Zara and Hannah had identified another four public toilets that needed visiting. These were in the north of the county in the area administered by High Peak District Council. It made sense to give that particular task to them, as two of these were in Castleton, one in Hope and one in Bamford.

"Great," said Pete. "If we find the right one, I hope nobody's in it. After all, they are going to think I'm some kind of pervert, taking photos inside a gents' toilet."

"Haven't you forgotten something?" asked Wendy. "You will need to take a photo of me inside the gents' loo. Who do you imagine they will think is the biggest weirdo, you for taking the photo, or me for being inside a gents' toilet having my photograph taken?"

"In which case, I really will have to take a selfie," added Pete.

"Which will definitely prove you're a pervert," replied Wendy. "Just in case anybody was still in doubt."

Pete and Wendy decided that they would make up their minds about how to take the photo if and when the occasion arrived. In the meantime, they said farewell to Noel, Josh, Simon and Katie and went in search of the two toilets in Castleton.

Mark and Louise had already had a similar conversation earlier that afternoon, wondering how they were going to take a photo in a gents' toilet when one of them was a woman.

Fortunately, none of the public toilets they'd visited so far had been very busy. If there was someone already using them,

Mark always felt obliged to use the facilities himself. But by the third visit, he was finding it increasingly difficult to pee.

"I hope nobody notices I can't pee," he said to Louise. "They'll probably think I'm one of those people with a nervous condition, preventing them from peeing in front of other people."

"If I were you, I'd be more worried about what the guy next to you was looking at if he noticed you weren't peeing," she replied.

Back at Striding Hall, Ben and Frank had discovered a website called lostheritage.org and they were looking at grand country houses in Derbyshire that had been demolished. It was a big job as there were 137 of them. Mind you, some could be discounted, as they had been demolished before the invention of photography. The website contained images of most of the houses that had been pulled down in the recent past and Ben and Frank were beginning to trawl through them all.

Meanwhile, Rosie was beginning to get frustrated with the lack of progress that Jack was making in his search for the Devonshire Arms.

"It's the only photo where we had the name of the building right from the start and yet, we still haven't been able to identify it," she said to Jack.

"Do you know how many websites I've had to look at and I'm nowhere near finished yet?" he said.

He was pretty pissed off by her attitude.

"In total, there are 31 of them and I can't just glance at them. I have to read them all. Okay, some of them have got a 'history of the village page' and I can get away with just reading that. But these aren't professional websites and there is often no logic to their order. I've lost count of how many mother and toddler groups I've read about."

"If the job is too big for one person, you should have asked for some help," Rosie replied curtly.

She shouted at Zara and Hannah for one of them to come over and help Jack in his search for the illusive pub. Jack was hoping it would be Zara who'd volunteer but was disappointed when he discovered it was his sister.

Meanwhile, Zara had identified another three public toilets in their target area. These were maintained by the Peak District National Park Authority rather than by the local council.

Mark wasn't too impressed at being given another three gents' toilets to visit when Rosie phoned to break the news to him. He'd already visited fourteen so far that afternoon.

After the rapid progress they'd made earlier in the day, things were definitely starting to slow down again. They needed another breakthrough. It soon came when Ben shouted, "That's it!" which was an indication that he and Frank had finally identified the grand country house.

"It's called Derwent Hall and it was demolished in 1944," Ben continued. "We were fortunate it began with the letter D as it was only the tenth one we'd looked at on lostheritage.org."

"Where is it, or rather where was it?" asked Rosie.

"Its ruins are now under Ladybower Reservoir," Ben replied, "which is why it was demolished. It was located in the village of Derwent that was flooded when the reservoir was built."

Rosie looked on the map and saw that a small part of Derwent village still existed on the banks of Ladybower Reservoir. Having identified the location of the original photo, she phoned Pete in order to get him to take a modern photo from approximately the same spot.

It was Wendy who answered this time, as Pete was exploring the inside of the public toilets in Bamford.

"He's doing a sterling job," she told her. "Pete really loves acting like a pervert. I think he's finally found his vocation in life."

Mind you, the fact that Pete and Wendy were in Bamford was good news, as it meant they were only a mile away from the former location of Derwent Hall.

"Once Pete has taken the photo of the reservoir, it will be four down, two to go and a little over three and a half hours left," said Rosie. "Jack, Hannah, have you made any more progress yet?"

"Not yet," came the reply.

"I've had an idea," said Frank. "There's something about the route we took yesterday that has been bugging me. Firstly, why take the detour off the main road to go and visit Ladybower Reservoir. Okay, it's a beautiful place, but when all is said and done it's just a reservoir. If you wanted to show somebody the best parts of Derbyshire, you'd choose to take them to see Dove Dale. But even though Dove Dale is only two minutes away from the main road we took when going to Ashbourne, we didn't visit it. However, we did go five miles out of our way in order to see Ladybower Reservoir and we now know the reason for that. It was to take us to within a mile of where Derwent Hall was located."

"Following on from that, I wondered if there were any other odd choices of route and I think I've found one. When we left Bakewell, we went to Monyash via Ashford in the Water. That involved taking this minor road, which took us past the village of Sheldon. You have to ask yourself why we went that way when the B5055 goes straight from Bakewell to Monyash. I reckon it's for the same reason we went to Ladybower Reservoir. In other words, it was a detour to take us within one mile of where one of the photos was taken. Therefore, I'll bet you anything you like that the site of either the pub or the urinal is in Ashford in the Water or Sheldon."

Chapter 15

Monday, September 2nd, 2019

"That is a brilliant deduction," said Rosie. "You and Ben take a village each and see what you can find out. I suppose it's too much to hope that the urinal belongs to the pub, in which case we can kill two birds with one stone."

"I hope so too, because I've discovered that some of the villages in the Peak District are responsible for their own toilets," said Zara. "I've found three so far, two in Youlgrave and one in Darley Dale. Both of them are outside our search area, but who knows how many more there are. We're not even sure it is a picture of a public toilet. It could be a urinal in a pub or a visitor attraction or even a railway station."

"Let's have another look at that photo," said Rosie. "It's been taken in colour and looks relatively recent. But the urinal itself looks quite old. I wouldn't claim to be an expert on gents' toilets, but I know a little about them from cleaning the ones in the pub. Modern urinals tend to have individual bowls whereas old ones tend to have a long trough. This one looks pre-war, as it's got an earthenware trough on three sides of the room. It looks like the type of outside urinal you might find in a large old-fashioned pub."

"Get in there." Ben shouted, interrupting her. "I think I've found our illusive Devonshire Arms. I was looking on the Sheldon page of a website entitled Discover Derbyshire and the Peak District and look what I've found."

Rosie leant over his shoulder and read the following:

> *The village is recorded in the Doomsday Book. But most dwellings were built when lead mining was enjoying a prosperous time in the locality. The stone houses in the village date from the 18th century, but not the pub. The Cock and Pullet was built in 1995, and must be one of the Peak District's newest pubs. It is named after the cockerels and pullets that used to run around in front of a barn where the pub is now situated. The village's previous pub, the Devonshire Arms, which stood next door, closed in 1971, and is now a private house.*

Google Earth confirmed that the house next door to the Cock and Pullet was indeed the mystery pub in the photo. Everybody in the room was overjoyed. They had now solved the location of five out of the six photos. Everybody that was, except for Jack who was pretty pissed off. After all, he'd just spent over five hours looking for the Devonshire Arms on the internet, only for Ben to identify its location correctly in ten minutes flat.

"Why isn't it on the list of closed pubs?" he asked unable to hide his frustration. "It isn't mentioned on the official Sheldon village site either."

"Well, I guess we should never take anything we find on the internet as being gospel," answered Rosie.

In an attempt to lighten the mood she added, "Last week, I got a friend request from Vlad the Impaler and saw a video of Hitler dancing to the Birdie song on TikTok."

But Jack was not in the mood for jokes. Rosie could tell he was pissed off by the whole thing, so she continued in a more serious vein.

"After all, the content is only as good as the person who put it there," she said. "You shouldn't be surprised if things are omitted sometimes."

Despite her efforts, it was obvious that Jack was still annoyed.

"Anyway, it's a team effort that has led to five of the six photographs being identified," she added. "So you're not to feel bad that you weren't the person who identified the photo of the pub."

After trying to placate Jack, Rosie phoned Pete and Wendy.

"We've identified where our mysterious Devonshire Arms is located," she told them. "It's the old pub in Sheldon and it's located next door to the current village pub. Once you've taken a photo of it, you can come back here."

By this time, Mark and Louise had finished visiting all the public toilets on their list. So they phoned Rosie to ask her what she wanted them to do next.

"You need to return to Striding Hall," she said. "We could do with all the help we can get in trying to solve the mystery of the sixth photo."

They got back just after Pete and Wendy and went to join the others in the hotel bar, where Rosie addressed everyone.

"Guys, we have one and a half hours left in which to identify the sixth photo. Does anyone have any ideas?"

"Well, I now consider myself a world expert on gents' loos having visited nineteen of them this afternoon," said Mark. "And I can tell you that none of them looked anything like the urinal in the picture. Those maintained by local authorities are all far more modern than the one in the picture. I believe that even if we have missed one or two, it doesn't matter. I do not believe this is a photo of a public toilet. I believe it is far more likely to be a photo of one in a pub."

"That's exactly what I was saying before you came back," said Rosie. "But if it is a photo of a pub toilet, how are we going to identify which one? The urinal looks pretty large and old fashioned. So if it is a pub toilet, it must be one in a big pub that hadn't been modernised when the photo was taken. But where do we start?"

"We could try Google Images," said Ben. "If the exact same photo is anywhere on the internet, Google Images should locate it. It's the same way people find out that the picture of the Spanish villa they were thinking of renting was lifted by conmen from a real estate site in California. Or the photo of the good-looking girl you've been chatting to on a dating site has been taken from Facebook and she's really a 65-year-old man with no teeth. I know it's a long shot but it has to be worth a go."

"Do it," replied Rosie, although deep down she was sceptical.

"After all," she thought to herself, "when have you ever seen a pub post a picture of their gents' urinals on the internet? Let alone a picture of really awful, old-fashioned ones?"

Still, she kept her fingers crossed. In the end, it was to no avail. According to Google Images, the picture wasn't anywhere on the internet. Neither were any of the other five photos, as Ben was pleased to discover a few minutes later. He realised he should have thought of looking on Google Images a few hours earlier. At least he knew now that it wouldn't have made any difference if he had.

Then came the breakthrough they were all hoping for.

"I think I've solved it," said Jack looking extremely pleased with himself. "I think it's a lateral thinking problem."

The whole room looked at him.

"Go on," said Rosie.

"All the photos are connected with what we did yesterday," he continued. "Mr Knight told us we had to pay attention to what we saw and heard on Sunday and I think I know why. Also, it explains why we didn't get off the bus at either Ladybower Reservoir or in Bakewell."

"You've lost me," said Pete.

"The reason we didn't get off was because those locations weren't connected with any of the photos," Jack continued.

"But that's not true," replied his father. "There was a connection between Ladybower Reservoir and Derwent Hall. The Hall was demolished when the reservoir was built."

"We went to Ladybower Reservoir because we needed to be within a mile of the site of Derwent Hall," Jack added. "But that's not what I mean."

Jack was frustrated that nobody understood him.

"Let me explain," he said. "On Sunday, we made six stops where we got off the minibus. Each one of those stops correlates with one of the photographs. Not only that, but they correlate in exactly the same order in which the photos were presented to us."

Jack checked quickly to see if everyone was listening to him.

"Our first stop was at the Crooked Spire and the first photo we had to identify was a church with a spire. But it wasn't the one we went to. It was a different church. Our second stop was in Castleton where we went down a cavern. The second photo was also of a cavern in Castleton, but not the one we went into. Our third stop was in Eyam where the main purpose was to see and hear about the village well-dressing. The third photo was also of a well-dressing, but not the one we'd been to. Our fourth stop was at the Devonshire

Arms in Beeley and the fourth photo we had to identify was also a Devonshire Arms. However, it wasn't the one we had lunch in. Then our fifth stop was at Haddon Hall and the fifth photo we had to identify was one of Derwent Hall, a different Derbyshire hall. Which brings me onto the sixth stop and the sixth photo."

Jack loved this. After the frustration of his failed attempt to identify the location of the Devonshire Arms, he now had the entire room hanging on his every word.

"Our sixth stop was in Ashbourne," he continued, "where we were told that the whole town becomes a football ground every Shrove Tuesday. That is why I believe photo six was also taken at a football ground. Only, it's a different one to the one used for the Shrove Tuesday match in Ashbourne."

"That's brilliant," said Louise.

"See? I was right to insist you joined the adults rather than the children," added Pete.

"Well, it's got to be at Chesterfield's ground," said Mark who was getting increasingly worried that they were starting to run out of time. "Otherwise, why would we go to a Chesterfield match yesterday and why would James tell us our father was a big Chesterfield fan? It wouldn't make sense if it was anywhere else."

"Mind you, Matlock Town's ground is also within our target area," said Ben looking at the map.

After deciding there was no point in just assuming it was Chesterfield's ground, only to find out later that they had guessed wrong, they decided to visit both of them. Mark and Louise were tasked with visiting the Proact Stadium, the home of Chesterfield Football Club, whilst Pete and Wendy headed for Matlock Town's Causeway Lane ground.

Although it was on the other side of town, it only took Mark and Louise ten minutes to reach Chesterfield's stadium. It was located next to Tesco just off the A61 dual carriageway.

"This can't be right," said an exasperated Louise as they approached the shiny new stadium. "It's far too modern."

But Mark followed lower league football and he knew that many clubs had moved to new grounds in recent years. Forest Green Rovers was one such club. They had moved from their original home at the Lawn Ground to the New Lawn Ground next door. He wasn't at all sure if Chesterfield was another club that had moved grounds recently, but the only hope he had left, rested on them having done so.

They pulled up outside the stadium and made their way to reception. Mark hoped the receptionist would be male. After all, a female was hardly likely to recognise a gents' urinal. Unfortunately, he was out of luck.

"Leave it to me," said Louise as she walked up to the receptionist.

"I do hope you can help us," she said to the woman behind the desk. "Only I've got a rather strange request. My husband and I are taking part in a treasure hunt, and I wonder if there is anybody here who can identify this photo? We think it was taken at a local football ground, either here in Chesterfield or in Matlock."

The woman took one look at the photo of the urinal and immediately started laughing. She walked over to where a small stack of coffee table books was located and picked one up.

"Now, I don't want you to think I'm strange," she said. "Because you have to believe me when I say I've never been in a gents' urinal in my life. But I know exactly where that photo was taken."

She opened the book at a page near the middle and showed it to Mark and Louise.

"Snap," she said.

The book contained the same picture that Louise had on her iPad.

"This book came out just after we moved to our new stadium in 2010," she added. "It's a series of photographs of the old ground and is called *So Long Saltergate*. The photos reflect every aspect of Chesterfield's previous stadium and, as you can see, there are even pictures of the gents' urinals."

"What happened to the old ground?" asked Mark.

"It was demolished and houses were built on it," the receptionist replied.

"And you wouldn't happen to know which house now occupies the plot where this toilet block used to stand?" Mark continued.

"Well, this particular gents' was located next to the kop," she said, getting out a street map of Chesterfield, "which means it was here, where number 39 Spire Heights now stands."

Mark couldn't thank the lady in reception enough. He considered having a chat about the previous Saturday's match with her, but then decided that they didn't have enough time for such pleasantries. Therefore, he merely thanked her one more time before he and Louise left.

Back in the car, Louise phoned Pete to tell them to cancel their search of Matlock Town's ground. Pete was relieved because there was nobody at the stadium, which had been locked up when he and Wendy got there.

It didn't take long for Mark and Louise to arrive at the new housing estate built on the old football ground. They found number 39 Spire Heights straight away. Fortunately, there was nobody around as Mark didn't want to have to explain why he was taking a photo of his wife outside a stranger's house.

Once the photo was taken, they dashed back to Striding Hall. It was twenty to six and they realised that they had successfully achieved the challenge with just twenty minutes to spare.

Well, at least they thought they'd successfully achieved the challenge. But they wouldn't know for certain until James confirmed they had correctly identified all the photos.

They didn't have long to wait. First, Simon and Katie arrived back with Noel and Josh and then James appeared.

"I guess all the happy smiling faces means you've got six photographs to show me," he said.

"We certainly do," replied Rosie. "Although I have to say, it has taken us all day and was a lot more difficult than the first challenge."

"And don't forget that you failed the first challenge," James replied. "But you all seem pretty confident that you've achieved this one. Which says a lot about how you've all managed to work together this time."

"That's probably because Phil wasn't here," said Pete, which drew a disapproving look from Ben.

"Anyway, the proof of the pudding is in the eating," James continued. "So can you show me the photos one at a time and tell me where they were taken?"

Rosie got to her feet and started her presentation.

"Photo one was of the church in Edensor and here's Pete's reproduction of it with Wendy standing in the foreground."

"That was probably the easiest one of the six to identify and, of course, you are correct," said James.

"Picture two was taken in Speedwell Cavern and here's Pete's version with Noel and Josh."

"That one was also pretty easy as Speedwell Cavern is such a large tourist attraction," added James.

"You speak for yourself," whispered Louise.

"Picture three was of Tissington well-dressing and here is a picture of Wendy at the well."

"And you've even managed to identify the correct well. So well done for that," said James.

"Picture four was of the Devonshire Arms in Sheldon, which is now a private house. Here is a photo of Wendy outside the house."

"This one was far more difficult because the pub closed down in 1971 and there is very little evidence today that it ever was a pub," said James. "Well done everybody for identifying it."

"Photo five was of Derwent Hall, which was demolished when Ladybower Reservoir was built," Rosie continued. "The photo Pete took is of Wendy standing by the reservoir close to where the Hall used to be."

"Well done," said James. "This one was not easy at all. Although there are far more photos around that feature Derwent Hall than there are of the Devonshire Arms at Sheldon, you at least had the pub's name to help you with that one. This photo could have been any one of numerous country houses in the Peak District. It could have been an existing one or one of those that have been demolished. Congratulations on finding it."

"And finally," said Rosie, "picture six was taken inside the gents' urinal next to the kop at Chesterfield Football Club's old ground. After the football club moved into the new stadium, the old ground was redeveloped as housing, with Spire Heights built on the site. Number 39 Spire Heights was built where the urinal used to be and here is a picture of Louise standing outside the house."

Rosie was quite triumphant as she revealed the last photo. She was a hundred percent confident it was correct.

"Actually, the site of the old urinal is now the garage of number 39," said James, which drew a hushed response from the room. "But that's just me being pedantic and, anyway, the garage is in the photo alongside the house. A brilliant achievement everybody, you've got all six right. By the way, photo six was by far the most difficult one to identify and not just because it has been demolished. It's also because the photo you had to identify is the only photo of the old urinal known to exist. After all, who takes photos of the inside of a toilet? Personally, I thought the best way of identifying it was just to take it out onto the streets of Chesterfield and ask as many men as possible if they recognised it. That photo was only taken nine years ago and most of the local football supporters would have used this urinal over the years. But I guess you'd have had to know it was taken at the football ground in Chesterfield in order to do that."

By the time he'd finished speaking, none of the others were listening to him. Everybody was too busy talking to each other about the day they had just had. They were all elated and Pete suggested they get some champagne to celebrate.

"Might as well make it my favourite Laurent Perrier Pink being as though we are not paying," he said.

Then he remembered that James hadn't given them any details about the properties they had just won.

"So what we all want to know," he added, "is what properties have we won and where are they located?"

"That's a good point and I'll be telling you later," James replied. "The plan for the rest of the evening is that we will have dinner first and after that I am going to tell you a little bit about the next two days. Then I will reveal your prizes for successfully solving today's challenge."

There was plenty of chatter over dinner fuelled by a heady mix of adrenalin and champagne. Pete proposed a toast to Rosie for doing such an excellent job leading them during the challenge.

"In marked contrast to the disastrous leadership during the previous challenge," Mark whispered in Louise's ear.

But all that was forgotten as everybody toasted Rosie for leading the challenge. They also toasted Jack for solving the puzzle that enabled them to complete the task. Finally, when the meal was over, James rose in order to address the group.

"Once again, may I take the opportunity of congratulating you for successfully solving today's challenge," he began. "Now I know you still have many unanswered questions. All I can say is keep going and your questions will be answered over the next two days. The reason I say that is because the emphasis is now changing. The previous two days have been about Derbyshire, the county where your father was born and brought up. The next two days will be about your family. Tomorrow, I have a business meeting that I need to attend. So it will be Simon who will take you to see where your ancestors lived, worked, got married and ultimately died. Once again, I will ask you to pay close attention to everything you see and hear as this will help you with the final challenge on Wednesday."

He then looked at Mark and Louise and added, "Don't worry about Noel and Josh. Katie will still be able to look after them whilst you're with Simon."

"Thanks," said Louise. "But Mark and I would prefer it if the boys came with us on this occasion, so that they can also learn about our family history."

"And what do you want to do about the third challenge on Wednesday?" asked James.

"We've agreed that they would be better off going with Simon and Katie again," Louise replied. "It's only tomorrow that we think they'd be better off going with us."

"That's no problem," said James. "If that's what you want then that's what we'll do. So tomorrow, breakfast will be at eight o'clock and the minibus will again leave at nine o'clock."

Finally, he came to the bit they had all been waiting for.

"As you are already aware," he continued, "your success today means that every beneficiary of the trust fund is going to receive a freehold property. Pete asked earlier if you could choose the location of your property and I have to tell you that you cannot. That's because all four of the houses have already been purchased and they are located within half a mile of each other. Pete also expressed his wish that his house should be situated in Belgravia. The answer to that is also no, as these properties have a far better location. They are all situated on the St Augustines estate."

"Where's that?" asked Ben.

"It's the bloody council estate in Chesterfield where Mark and I were both born," replied Pete.

Chapter 16

Tuesday, September 3rd, 2019

"Well, I'm going to sell my house as soon as possible," Pete announced at breakfast the following morning. "In fact, I plan to instruct a local estate agent before we go back on Thursday. There's no way I'm going to keep a house on the St Augustines estate. It's full of council tenants and single mothers on benefits."

"They are people just like you," said Louise. "There's no need to look down on them."

"They are nothing like me," replied Pete. "I haven't got a tattoo and I don't do all my shopping in Poundland."

"If I can just interrupt you for a minute," said James. "I have to tell you that you cannot actually sell the properties. That's because they all have restrictive covenants on them that forbids any of you from reselling the houses for a period of twenty years."

All of a sudden, the room went very quiet.

"Your only option is either to rent the houses out or to live in them yourselves," he continued.

Having told them that, he casually started to butter another piece of toast.

"There is a third option," said Pete. "We could always try to get the court to overturn the covenant."

"Ooh," said James with a sharp intake of breath. It was as if he was a car mechanic about to give some bad news regarding the price of a repair. "I'm not your solicitor, but if I was, I would strongly advise against it. It can be very expensive with no guarantee of success. I recently had a client who tried to get a restrictive covenant removed from a pub he was buying. The process took ages, it cost him £35,000 in fees, and his appeal still failed."

"That explains where he got the money from to buy the Overfinch," said Mark under his breath.

"Now, you're going to have to excuse me, I'm afraid," added James. "I've got to be in my office in Matlock in thirty minutes' time. So I'll leave you in Simon's capable hands."

Once he was out of earshot, Louise addressed the rest of the group.

"It's time to focus," she said. "I don't want us to miss anything that might be important for tomorrow's challenge. Can I therefore suggest that we all bring a pen and some paper with us so that we can make notes? Don't forget, it was a wise man who said that the bluntest pencil is still sharper than the sharpest mind."

"Jesus Christ," muttered Pete as he looked to the heavens. "She thinks she's talking to her year tens."

In spite of his comment, Pete did as he was told.

Stan had arrived in the minibus by this stage and was waiting for them in the car park. It was time to get on board and set off on their next adventure. That's if you could call it that.

Jack went to sit next to Zara, who was looking even more lovely than usual. But after a stern look from his father, he decided he'd better move. So he sat next to his sister instead.

Once they were on their way, Simon told them where they were heading.

"To start off, we are going to visit the Derbyshire village of Parwich," he said. "I will tell you why once we get there."

The journey took them through Darley Dale and Winster before they eventually found themselves on the road to Ashbourne. Shortly afterwards, Parwich was signposted on their right and they turned off the main road towards the village.

Parwich is the type of place you could easily miss as it isn't on a main road. Actually, it isn't on a road to anywhere in particular. Despite this, it was quite a large village with more than its fair share of fine old stone houses. It had a duck pond and a church. Opposite the church was a pub called the Sycamore Inn, which doubled up as a village shop and post office. The minibus pulled up outside and Simon began to speak again.

"The reason we've come to Parwich today is because this is where your grandfather was born, right here in this pub in 1915. Your family were tenants of the Sycamore Inn for four generations and your grandfather's grandparents and great-grandparents are all buried in the village churchyard as we are now about to see."

"Hey, Rosie," said Ben mischievously. "It looks like you aren't the first publican in the family. We must all have beer in our veins. Except for Pete, of course, he's got cider."

"And Wendy," muttered Pete. "She's got vinegar in hers."

Fortunately for Pete, Wendy didn't hear him as she would undoubtedly have replied with some acerbic comment. Instead, she was already getting off the minibus and was following Simon's lead into the graveyard of St Peter's Church. The rest of the party followed close behind.

"There we are," said Simon pointing at two graves that were next to each other. "These are the graves of your two times and three times great-grandparents. Please take some time to look at them."

The graves were in an old part of the graveyard and both looked somewhat forlorn. The gravestones were covered in lichen, and it was obvious that nobody was taking care of them. It was a long time since anybody had brought flowers to either of these graves. Despite this, it was still easy to make out the writing on the gravestones. The first read:

In Loving Memory of
Herbert Ebenezer Bradbury
Died 12.2.1931
Aged 65

And his wife
Mona Doris Bradbury
Died 15.1.1924
Aged 57
Reunited in death

The second said:

Cherished memories of
Herbert Ebenezer Bradbury
Died 11.12.1912
Aged 72

And his wife
Rachel Emily Bradbury
Died 31.8.1915
Aged 71
Blessed are the pure in heart
For they shall see God

"That's interesting," said Mark, whilst taking a photograph of the gravestones. "Father and son were both called Herbert Ebenezer Bradbury. It's weird to think we are looking at the graves of our ancestors. I had no idea they were here or that our family had a connection to this village."

"I understand that it was the tradition in your family always to call the first-born son Herbert Ebenezer," said Simon. "Your great-grandfather was also called Herbert Ebenezer although he isn't buried in this churchyard. Instead, he's buried in Chesterfield, and we will be visiting his grave later on."

"It's a pity the tradition didn't carry on because I think the name Herbert Ebenezer would have suited you, Pete," joked Mark.

"Mind you, nobody would ever put the inscription, 'Blessed are the pure in heart' on Pete's gravestone," added Wendy. "'Beneath this sod lies another', would be far more appropriate."

Pete didn't find his wife's comment particularly amusing. He was quick to reply.

"And it's a pity your parents didn't call you Mona, darling. Then your name could have matched your personality."

Simon could sense that another argument was brewing, so he cut in.

"The reason that the tradition hasn't continued was actually because your grandfather wasn't the eldest son," he told them. "His name was Robert and he had two older brothers, the eldest of whom was called Herbert Ebenezer. So there's no need to be worried, Pete. There was never any chance of you being called Herbert Ebenezer. Now if you would all like to follow me to the Sycamore Inn. I've arranged for them to open early in order to serve us morning coffee."

The Sycamore Inn was a fine country pub with a mixture of tiled and flagstone floors, an eclectic collection of wooden furniture and a fireplace with a wood-burning stove. The sign outside proclaimed it was a Robinsons brewery house and indeed, the beers on the hand pumps were all from Robinsons of Stockport. The pub also doubled up as a shop and had done so ever since the village post office closed a few years before. As a result, you could now buy a newspaper or a loaf of bread whenever you popped in for a pint.

Jenny, the landlady, had laid out cups and saucers on the bar together with two pots, one with tea and one with coffee. There was also a jug of milk and a bowl of sugar cubes.

"Would the boys like orange juice, instead?" she asked.

"That would be nice, thank you," replied Louise.

Jenny went and fetched the orange juice whilst the others began helping themselves to tea and coffee.

"Let me know if you need anything else," said Jenny when she got back.

"How long have you and your husband been in the pub?" asked Rosie.

"Alan and I have been here for twelve years," Jenny replied. "Unfortunately, Alan couldn't be here today because he's got a rent review meeting this morning."

"And we know just how difficult they can be, don't we, Frank?" said Rosie.

"We had to get independent adjudicators involved the last time we had one," added Frank.

"Frank and I are also publicans," Rosie explained.

Jenny smiled before disappearing back into the kitchen.

"I want to show this to all of you," said Simon pointing at a small frame on the wall of the bar.

The frame contained a list of all the licensees of the pub dating back to 1725. However, it was those in the second half of the nineteenth century and first half of the twentieth century that interested everybody. The names were as follows:

1865 – 1906 Herbert Ebenezer Bradbury
1906 – 1929 Herbert Ebenezer Bradbury
1929 – 1949 Herbert Ebenezer Bradbury
1949 – 1952 Arthur Gordon Bradbury

"I don't understand," said Mark. "Who is Arthur Gordon Bradbury?"

"Let me explain," said Simon. "Arthur Gordon Bradbury was your great-uncle, the second son of Herbert Ebenezer Bradbury, the one who was the licensee between 1929 and 1949."

"So Arthur Bradbury was our great-uncle and his father, the publican before him, was our great-grandfather," said Mark.

"That's correct," Simon replied. "Then the two before him are your two times and three times great-grandfathers, whose graves we've just seen."

"So why did the second son take over the pub in 1949?" asked Pete.

"That was because Robert's elder brother, whom I mentioned earlier, was captured by the Japanese during the Second World War. He was one of the POWs who were used as forced labour whilst building the Burma-Thai railway and he died out there in 1943. He is buried in the Commonwealth War Cemetery in Kanchanaburi in Thailand. As a result, it was the middle son who became the next licensee. He was the final member of your family to do so. Don't forget that it was customary in those days to have large families, especially since infant mortality was so high. Of course, only one son could take over the pub from his father. Any other sons had to find alternative occupations."

"I'd imagine that wouldn't have been very easy in a remote village like this," said Louise.

"You'd be surprised at how many jobs there were in the countryside back then," Simon continued. "After all, everything was very labour-intensive in those days. As well as farmhands, there were quarrymen, miners and all sorts of craftsmen. Alsop-en-le-Dale station was also just up the road and, despite being very small, it still had a staff of seven."

"So they would have had plenty of choice then?" added Louise.

"That's true. But none of the younger sons would have been as lucky as the eldest, because not only was he destined to inherit a business, but that business came with accommodation for his family to live in. Back then it was an unwritten rule that once a licensee became too old or infirm to continue in the role, his eldest son would take over from him. After taking over, he would allow his parents to remain with him in the pub's accommodation for the rest of their lives. As you are no doubt aware, there was no such thing as an old-age pension or retirement homes back in those days. Instead, families would be expected to take care of their own."

"I hope you are paying attention, Jack," added Pete. "I might have to move in with you when I get old and incontinent."

"I'll have murdered you long before that," muttered Wendy.

"Now, your grandfather was the third son," Simon continued. "So he presumed there was no chance of him ever inheriting the pub. That was why he got himself a job as a trainee mechanic with Silver Service buses based in Darley Dale. He later obtained a public service vehicle licence after deciding that he preferred driving buses to repairing them, and it was whilst he was working in Darley Dale that he met your grandmother. The two of them fell in love and wanted to get married. But the problem was that your grandfather was only living in digs at the time, and they couldn't afford to rent a house on his meagre wages. Then he saw an article in the local paper. It said that Chesterfield Corporation had a shortage of bus drivers and was offering good rates of pay, far higher than he was earning with Silver Service."

"Was that why he moved to Chesterfield?" asked Rosie.

"It was, and it wasn't just the higher pay that appealed to your grandfather. Chesterfield Corporation was also dangling a carrot that was particularly appealing in your grandfather's circumstances. The corporation guaranteed that any employees could move straight into a council house. So your grandfather and grandmother got married and moved to Chesterfield in 1938. And apart from a time in the Royal Engineers during the war, he continued to work for Chesterfield Corporation until he retired in 1980. Meanwhile back in Parwich, your great-uncle took over the pub in 1949. Arthur had never married, which would normally have been a problem for the brewery. But your family had run the pub for nearly 75 years by then and they decided to make an exception for him. Unfortunately, he only lived for another three years. In 1952, he contracted pneumonia and died, and that caused a major problem for your great-grandparents. You see, they were still living in the pub at the time."

"Why didn't our grandfather move back to Parwich and take over the pub then?" asked Mark.

"Your grandfather and grandmother were very happy in Chesterfield. They had a modern house and your grandfather had a well-paid job with a pension. There was no way he wanted to give it up in order to run a pub and work twice as many hours for less money and no provision for his retirement. In the end, the compromise they came to was that the family would give up the pub and your great-grandparents would move to Chesterfield to live with their son and daughter-in-law. As you can imagine, it wasn't the solution that your great-grandparents really wanted, and they were both dead within a year. They are buried in Boythorpe Cemetery, which we are planning to visit later."

"Thanks for that, Simon," said Mark. "It's been a real eye-opener learning all about our family history. I knew nothing at all about any of these people, or our connection to this village. But tell me, how come you and your father know so much about our family?"

"There's really nothing to it," he replied. "We are just very thorough in our research."

"Well, I think it's a very sad story," added Wendy, "especially thinking about your great-grandfather. After all, two of his three sons died before him and he had to give up the family business, the place where he was born and had lived all his life. This is such a beautiful village and he had to leave it and go and live on a council estate in Chesterfield."

"It is a sad tale," said Rosie. "But you have to bear in mind that children predeceasing their parents was a common occurrence in the first half of the twentieth century, especially when you consider the two world wars. Also, living in the countryside was nowhere near as idyllic as it is now. Houses often didn't have electricity or running water and the toilet facilities would have been very basic. Granddad's house in Chesterfield must have seemed like paradise on earth in comparison."

"People often didn't live very long after retiring back then," added Simon. "The fact that your great-grandfather died four years after he stopped working was actually pretty good by the standards of the 1950s."

Everyone had finished their drinks by that stage and were ready to move on.

"We have to leave Parwich at 11 o'clock," said Simon. "That will give you about twenty minutes to look around the village before we depart."

It seemed a bit unreal as they wandered around. None of them had ever been to this village in the Peak District before and yet, after learning the story of their family, it felt as if they had come home. Louise was particularly happy that she and Mark had decided to bring the boys with them. She hoped they would remember the story of their ancestors and maybe one day they would return here. Perhaps they would bring their own children to see the family graves in the churchyard and the list of former licensees on the wall of the pub.

The village was picture-perfect and looked even more so in the bright sunlight of a late summer morning. Pete and Mark were walking together, with Louise and Wendy a couple of paces behind them.

"I've been thinking about the missing £450,000," said Pete as they were wandering past Parwich Memorial Hall. "That must have been the money Dad used to set up the trust fund. Perhaps he asked for it to be paid into a different account."

"Why would he do that?" replied Mark. "More importantly, why would the pools company agree to a request like that? I'm pretty sure it would only agree to split the payment if the prize is won by a syndicate. It would never do it for a single winner like Dad."

"Perhaps he asked them because there was some tax advantage if £450,000 was going to be placed into the trust fund," suggested Pete.

"But the trust fund wasn't even set up until five years later," replied Mark. "I don't think we are anywhere near solving this puzzle. However, I will agree with you on one point. The missing £450,000 is almost certainly the money that ended up in the trust fund. But how it got there is still a mystery."

They continued looking around the village, with some of them going in the church and others noting that the village still had its own school. It had been built in 1861, which must have meant that many of their forefathers had been pupils there.

Soon the twenty minutes were up, and it was time to board the minibus once more.

"We are off to Darley Dale to see where your grandfather moved to," said Simon. "It was also where he worked and where he met your grandmother."

Darley Dale was quite a large village, located halfway between Parwich and Chesterfield. Stan pulled up outside a garage with a sign outside with 'Off Road Racing' on it.

"We're not getting out here," said Simon. "But I wanted to show you where your grandfather used to work."

"Make a note of that," muttered Mark to Louise. "The next challenge might follow the same pattern as the last one."

"I will, but I don't think that's very likely," she replied. "After all, the second challenge was completely different from the first one."

"This used to be where Silver Service buses were based," Simon continued. "Your grandfather worked here between 1934 and 1938, first as a mechanic, then as a bus driver after passing his public service vehicle test in 1937. For the four years he worked in Darley Dale, your grandfather had digs above a shop in Chesterfield Road, which we will go past later. But next, we are going to visit the Whitworth Centre."

Setting off from the garage, they travelled to their next stop, a short distance away to what was now known as the Whitworth Centre but had been called the Whitworth Institute in the 1930s.

"We are going to get off here and have a look around," said Simon, "and there will be more tea and coffee for anyone who wants it."

The Whitworth Centre was a fine Victorian building in the gothic style.

"Sir Joseph Whitworth was a leading industrialist in the nineteenth century who lived in Standcliffe Hall, about a mile from the centre," said Simon. "He had wanted to use his great wealth to provide something of benefit to the local community, but he died in 1887 before his legacy could come to fruition. However, his wife ensured that his wishes were carried out and the Whitworth Institute was completed in 1890. Back then, the Institute had an indoor swimming pool, an assembly hall, and various reading and committee rooms. Eventually, a library, a billiards room, a museum of natural history, a hotel and a landscaped park were all added."

"It's amazing to find somewhere like this in a small Derbyshire village," said Mark. "Most bigger towns wouldn't even have had a facility like this when they were built."

"It was a tremendous resource to have on your doorstep in a rural area," said Simon. "Your grandfather made full use of it, especially the billiards hall. It was also here where he met your grandmother who was working as a clerk in the administration department."

They went inside and were met by June, the manager, who was going to show them around.

"Welcome to the Whitworth Centre," she said. "I understand that Simon has already told you a little about our history. However, I don't believe that he told you that our founder, Sir Joseph Whitworth made his fortune from machine tools and armaments. This centre was established after he died, and we still operate under the terms of his original endowment of 1890. When it was built, it included the hotel next door, but this was sold off a few years ago. Nowadays, we are the venue for numerous clubs, and we still have the billiards room where your grandfather played during the 1930s. We are particularly proud of our billiards room as it's one of the oldest in the country and is said to have two of the finest billiards tables in the world. If you'd like to follow me, I'll show you around."

The tour around the centre didn't take very long, and June left them in the Terrace Café afterwards where tea and coffee were being served. Zara, Jack and Hannah decided that they had already had enough coffee that morning and went for a walk around the grounds instead.

"You've been quiet today," Zara said to Jack. "Are you trying to avoid me?"

In reality, it was quite difficult to avoid Zara, as she was wearing a cropped top and a very short skirt.

"No," said Jack. "It's just that my dad doesn't like me being with you."

"And you're a little daddy's boy, are you?" said Zara.

"I'm not, but …" continued Jack.

"There's no but about it," interrupted Zara. "Either you're still a little boy doing whatever your daddy tells you to do or you're a grown man making your own decisions. You need to decide which one you want to be and, anyway, your dad is a real arsehole. He just opens his mouth and crap comes out."

Jack tried to think of a witty retort but by the time he'd decided what to say, Zara was already heading back indoors with Hannah in tow. He was quite taken aback by her departure. But then he thought that he'd at least know in future not to rely on his sister's support if his family ever came under attack again.

Once the rest of the group had finished their coffee, they all boarded the minibus again and headed for Chesterfield. First, they took a small detour to see St Helens, the church in Darley Dale where their grandparents were married. Before leaving the village, Simon also pointed out the digs their grandfather had lived in whilst he was working for Silver Service buses. Back in his day, the downstairs had been a corner shop. But the shop had closed down many years ago and the building had been converted into one large house.

They continued on towards Chesterfield where their next stop was St Augustines Road.

"When your grandfather got a job working for Chesterfield Corporation, this was the house your grandparents moved into," said Simon pointing at one of the houses on the right-hand side of the bus. "Your grandparents' house was number 76 St Augustines Road. It was also the house where your father was brought up and it will be of particular interest to you, Pete."

"Why's that?" he asked.

"Because you own it now," replied Simon.

Until that point, none of them had known where their new houses were located, other than the fact that they were all on the St Augustines estate. Now they were all keen to learn more about their new properties.

"Can we have a look at our houses as well?" asked Ben.

"I think we have enough time," Simon replied. "Actually, Ben, yours is next door at number 74 and the other two are around the corner on St Augustines Mount."

As they were pulling away, Pete commented that his house looked to be in fairly good nick except for a missing tile on the roof.

"Don't worry," added Simon, "all the properties will be thoroughly inspected, and any necessary repairs will be carried out before they are handed over to you. All the houses are currently let out on short-term tenancy agreements, which you will be able to end if any of you wish to move in."

"There's absolutely no chance of that happening," Pete replied.

"I will give you all the deed packs for your properties and copies of the tenancy agreements when we return to the hotel this evening," added Simon.

Stan turned left into St Augustines Mount where Simon showed them the other two houses. Next, they proceeded to Boythorpe Cemetery to see where their great-grandparents were buried. It was well maintained and on a far larger scale than had been the case with the churchyard in Parwich.

"It's far more impersonal," commented Mark.

The gravestone itself had a simple inscription which said:

Here lies
Herbert Ebenezer Bradbury
Died September 3rd, 1953
Aged 67

And his beloved wife
Julia Rose Bradbury
Died August 31st, 1953
Aged 64
Together Forever

This time it was Pete who got his mobile phone out and took a photo of their great-grandfather's grave.

"Isn't it romantic?" said Louise. "They died only four days apart. Your grandfather must have died from a broken heart."

"Either that or he caught what she had," added Pete rather disparagingly.

"But there's something more important than that," said Mark. "Look carefully and you will see that our great-grandfather died 56 years ago today. Not only that, but someone has put fresh flowers on his grave."

Chapter 17

Tuesday, September 3rd, 2019

"Anybody could have put the flowers there," said Pete. "It doesn't have to be a relative, it could be somebody who works in the cemetery. Perhaps they put flowers on the graves of people who don't have any relatives visiting them on the anniversary of their deaths."

"It's a cemetery not an old folks' home," said Jack as he looked at Zara to make sure she had noticed he was criticising his father.

Unfortunately for him, she was chatting to Hannah. So all he managed to get was a dirty look from his dad.

"No, Jack's right," said Mark. "The only people who would put flowers on a grave are either relatives or friends."

"It could be a lover," said Wendy. "I remember somebody put flowers of Lawrence of Arabia's grave for fifty years after he died. Nobody ever knew who she was."

"Lawrence of Arabia was single and only in his forties when he was killed," added Pete. "What you have here is the grave of a man who was buried along with his wife. Both of them were in their sixties when they died and that was 56 years ago."

He tutted before adding, "And you accuse me of being thick."

"Now then, you two," said Louise. "Let's not fall out about it. I'm sure there must be some logical explanation for the flowers."

"Yes, they've probably been put there this morning by James just to confuse us," said Pete.

A few minutes later, they all made their way back to the minibus.

"We are now going to drive past the registry office where your father and mother got married," said Simon. "By that, I mean Pete and Mark's mother, of course. After that, we are going to drive past the bus station on Vicar Lane where your grandfather used to work and then we are going for lunch."

In truth, there wasn't much to see at the old registry office, mainly because it was no longer used for that purpose. Instead, it was a recovery centre for people with addictions. Vicar Lane was pedestrianised, and new shops had been built on the site of the old bus station. Consequently, it didn't take too long before the group arrived at the Boythorpe Inn for lunch.

"The reason we are stopping here is because this is the pub your mother used to work in," said Simon looking at Rosie and Ben. "It was the pub where she met your father."

"Well, that explains something," said Pete. "I always thought Mum used to refer to her as the Boythorpe bike because she lived in the suburb of Boythorpe, not because she worked in a pub called the Boythorpe Inn."

"Can you please stop referring to her in that tone?" said Ben. "After all, she was our mother. Dad loved her and she died a horrible death 35 years ago."

"Allegedly," replied Pete.

The Boythorpe Inn was a Greene King pub these days and was located opposite the town's leisure centre. Its focus was more on price and quantity rather than quality. Given its location close to a large housing estate, this was not a bad strategy to have. It was the type of place which specialised in helping you to put back the pounds you had lost in the gym across the road. If you were a big fan of burgers and chips, fish and chips, or indeed anything served with chips, this was the pub for you. But if you had a passion for hand-dived scallops cooked in seaweed butter served on mustard mash with a Madeira wine jus, you might as well forget it. That said, it was smartly furnished, and Noel and Josh were both happy, as the pub had an extensive burger menu.

'The burgers are to die for, and the portions are massive,' one excited reviewer wrote on TripAdvisor. Obviously, they thought any place that could do burgers better than MacDonald's had reached the pinnacle of gastronomic achievement. Especially if they served large portions.

"At last," said Pete as he ordered a pint of Gloucestershire Gold, one of his company's best-selling brands, "a pub that serves a decent pint of cider."

The Boythorpe Inn was one of those pubs where you ordered at the bar and the food arrived fifteen minutes later. There was no Michelin starred chef leading a team of sous chefs in this pub's kitchen. Instead, there was a man who'd received his training at Chesterfield Technical College assisted by two kitchen porters, three microwaves and four deep fat fryers.

Still, the food was okay, considering most of it had gone straight from the freezer to the fryer.

"Remember the conversation we had at Haddon Hall?" said Rosie to Mark as he tucked into his southern fried chicken baguette.

Mark couldn't answer as his mouth was full.

"Remember how I said I thought James's whole involvement in this struck me as being a bit odd," she continued. "Well, the fact that his son has taken over today hasn't altered my opinion one iota. Both of them seem far too closely involved for my liking."

"If you remember, I asked Simon when we were in Parwich how he'd been able to find out so much about our family," Mark replied after having swallowed his food. "And he told me it was all down to research."

"Research, my arse," said Rosie.

Mark was tempted to ask her if you could get a government grant for that but decided against it. He let her continue instead.

"There has to be more to it than that and I intend to find out what it is," she added.

Simon was at the other end of the table from Rosie and Mark. He couldn't hear what they were saying as they were keeping their voices down. But he suspected that Rosie was talking about him. It was the way she kept looking at him whilst chatting to Mark that gave her away. So he decided to intervene and change the conversation.

"Have you all decided what you are going to do with your houses?" he asked them.

"I'm going to continue to rent mine out," said Mark. "I don't know what the rental income is but, given that it's a three bedroomed house, it must be about £1,000 a month."

"You're not in Reigate now," said Pete, "you can halve that figure up here."

"Pete is quite right," added Simon. "Rents are not as high in Chesterfield as they are in the south. All your properties are currently rented out on six-month lets at £575 per month. However, that still represents a good source of extra income for you all."

By asking around the table, it soon became clear that everybody was planning to keep renting out their Chesterfield properties. Only Pete still insisted that he was going to challenge the covenant.

Pete and Mark already owned their houses, although both of them had large mortgages. In contrast, neither Ben nor Rosie had owned a property before. However, they were both tied to southern England. For Rosie, it was because of the pub. For Ben, it was down to the fact that he had an audition for a part in *EastEnders* the following week.

"I'm confident of getting the role," he said. "It will be the breakthrough I've been looking for."

He puffed his cheeks out and ruffled his hair.

"You old slag," he added in a Cockney accent, demonstrating his complete mastery of the programme's dialogue.

After the meal was finished, it was time to move on once more.

"You'll be pleased to know that we've nearly finished the journey into the history of your family," announced Simon. "The only places we've still got to visit are the garage where your dad used to work, the pub where both he and your grandfather used to drink and the house where your father used to live."

They got back into the minibus and Stan headed out towards Walton, where their father had been a mechanic. There wasn't much to see at Walton Motors, as it was still a petrol station and garage, much as it had been when their father had worked there. The only thing that had changed was the addition of a minimart.

Then it was back the same way as they had come until they reached St Augustines Road once more.

"On your left was where the Walton Hotel used to be," said Simon. "It was your father and grandfather's local pub. Unfortunately, it was demolished in 2015, and now only the pub sign remains."

The group looked out of the minibus's window and could see the sign. It still said, 'Welcome to the Walton at Chesterfield'. The sign was poking out from beyond white security fencing, a somewhat forlorn reminder of past hospitality.

Shortly afterwards, they turned left into St Augustines Mount before finally arriving at the house in St Augustines Rise where their father used to live. It was an odd experience for Pete and Mark. This was the house where they had both spent the first few years of their lives. It should have brought back memories, but it didn't.

"I'm not surprised," said Louise to Mark. "After all, you were only two and Pete was barely four when you left. My earliest memory is just before my fifth birthday. Not many people have memories stretching back further than that."

"I'm amazed there isn't a blue plaque on the wall," commented Pete, trying to be ironic.

"What surprises me is that it isn't one of the houses the trust fund has given to one of us," countered Ben.

"That's because it's still owned by the council," said Mark. "You can tell by the roof. Most of the houses around here have been reroofed, but some still have their original roofs. The council must have carried out a schedule of improvements recently that included replacing the old tiles. The only ones that weren't replaced must be those that are in private ownership."

"Including mine," said Pete, "which explains why it's got a tile missing."

The visit to see their father's old house was the last thing on their itinerary. After that it was time to head back to Striding Hall.

"There's one final thing that I want to show you," said Simon as they pulled into the drive. "It's located in the grounds of Striding Hall."

They said goodbye to Stan and followed Simon through the grounds. They went across the minor road that ran past the hall and through a gate, which led down to the edge of the lake. Here they came across a teak bench seat. Mark had come across such benches before. They were usually put in place by families or friends of a rambler who had died, often denoting a favourite spot on a much-loved walk. This particular bench had two metal plaques, which revealed the names of the people who were being remembered.

"When your grandfather died, he wasn't buried in Boythorpe Cemetery like your great-grandfather," said Simon. "He was cremated in Chesterfield Crematorium instead. This chair was purchased in memory of him. It was originally located in the grounds of the crematorium. I believe it was moved here after your father died."

Everybody gathered around the bench in order to read the inscriptions on the two plaques. The first read:

In memory of
Robert Stephen Bradbury
Died 16.11.1983
Aged 68
A much loved husband and father

And the second read:

Also of his son
Andrew Graham Bradbury
Died 11.5.1984
Aged 34
Taken too soon

"Well, that settles it," said Pete who took a photo of the inscription. "Dad must have died in 1984 and been cremated just like our grandfather."

"It doesn't settle anything," Mark replied. "If Dad could fool the coroner and the press, he could certainly fool the person who commissioned this plaque."

"This throws up a whole series of new questions," said Rosie. "For a start, who paid for this seat to be made and why isn't our grandmother included in the inscription? Also, did the same person add the plaque in memory of Dad and why was the seat moved and brought here?"

"I've got another one," added Ben. "If our grandparents got married in 1938, why did they wait for another twelve years before having a child?"

"I bet you know the answers to all these questions," said Rosie, who was looking at Simon. "It's unfair of you to keep us in the dark any longer. You and your father both know far too much about our family for it just to be professional research. This has gone on for far too long. I demand you tell us here and now what really happened."

It was a forceful statement and the others backed her up by standing behind her, staring at Simon.

"I can't speak for my father," he replied. "But all this happened before I was born, and before my father joined the business. It happened back in my grandfather's day. I can assure you that I am not holding anything back from you, other than certain things that I have to under the terms of the trust fund."

"Like father, like bloody son," Rosie cut in and added in a mocking voice. "I don't know. It all happened before my time."

"I wasn't even supposed to come with you today," Simon continued. "I only stepped in for my father at the last minute.

Everything I've told you came from the notes he gave me and I wouldn't be at all surprised if my father originally got the notes from my grandfather. Here, take a look if you don't believe me."

He took some printed sheets from his jacket pocket and gave them to Rosie, adding, "I read them through three times before we went out today. I only brought them as a prompt in case I forgot anything."

"A likely story," added Rosie sarcastically.

"If you have any further questions, you can ask my father," said Simon. "He should be back at Striding Hall by now. But unfortunately, I have to leave. I will see you all at dinner this evening."

Pete saw that it was 2.55 and announced that he would have to leave as well. It seemed the only reason why James had come back to Striding Hall was because he had promised Pete that he could have a drive in the Overfinch.

"Let's think about this logically," said Mark to Rosie once Pete had gone. "We don't know when our grandmother died. But chances are it was after 1984. In which case, she could have paid for the bench, and both set of inscriptions. She could also have had it moved to its current site. It would explain why she wasn't on the inscription. There wouldn't be any family left to add her when she died, no family who knew about her, anyway."

"One possibility is that she isn't on it because she isn't dead yet," Ben cut in. "People do live a lot longer these days."

"Hang on a minute," said Louise and turned to Mark. "I thought you said your mother told you that both of your father's parents died shortly after your father abandoned you?"

"She did," said Mark. "But since we now know my grandfather didn't die until 1983, four years after my dad ran away, I am taking everything she told me about my father and his side of the family with a pinch of salt."

Even so, Mark had never considered the possibility before that his grandmother might still be alive.

"She might not be dead, but she'd have to be around 100 years old," said Mark. "We don't know when she was born. However, we do know she met my grandfather sometime between 1934 and 1938. Let's say she was 21 when she got married. That would make her 102 now. So the chances of her still being alive are pretty slim."

Realising they weren't going to be able to establish if their grandmother was still alive or not without further research, Mark instead turned to the question why their grandparents hadn't had a child until 1950.

"It's not uncommon," he explained. "Even back in the 1930s and '40s many couples waited until they were financially secure. Say our grandmother was born in 1921, she would still have been in her late 20s when Dad was born. Even if she was born in 1919, she would only have been 31. Perhaps they just wanted to have two wages coming in for as long as possible. Don't forget most women gave up work back in those days once they'd had a child. Then again, maybe she had difficulty in conceiving, which would explain why Dad was an only child. There was also the little matter of World War Two getting in the way."

"Some or all of those explanations could be correct, but I'm still not convinced," added Rosie. "The period immediately after the war was when all the baby boomers were born. The human desire to procreate and replace the lives lost with new life is a natural reaction to all the death and destruction caused by war. Yet, our grandparents still waited another four years. I wonder why that was?"

"Unless they weren't waiting," replied Mark. "As I said, perhaps they had difficulty conceiving."

They agreed that this was yet another unsolved mystery. But in the greater scheme of things, it was not that important. They decided to return to their rooms. However, just as they were going up the steps towards Striding Hall, Mark turned to the others.

"I've had an idea that might clear up some of these questions," he said. "I'm going to drive to Chesterfield Crematorium to look at their book of condolence."

"Why on earth would you want to do that?" asked Rosie.

"All crematoriums keep records of who they've cremated," Mark replied. "We know the date our grandfather died. So he should be easy to find. We also know the date when our father allegedly died. We don't know whether or not he was buried or cremated in Spain. I don't even know if they do cremate people in Spain, being as though it's a Catholic country."

"They do," said Rosie. "I know for a fact that our mother was cremated in Marbella and our grandparents brought her ashes back to this country."

"Right, so you can be cremated there," Mark continued. "But what if Dad wasn't. What if his body was brought back to this country and cremated in Chesterfield instead? If that was the case, then the crematorium records should prove it. As for our grandmother, that is going to be far more difficult. We don't know her date of birth or her Christian name, or even if she's dead yet. Mind you, if the crematorium has computerised its records, I would be able to look up all the Bradburys who've been cremated there in the last 35 years. That will enable me to see if any of them were born around 1920."

"It's got to be worth a try," said Ben.

The others agreed with him.

Mark took off to the crematorium, while Noel, Josh and Louise headed to the hotel pool for another swim. Zara and Jack had decided to take advantage of Pete's absence to go for a walk around the lake. That left Rosie, Frank, Hannah, Ben and Wendy, who opted to go and relax in their rooms.

Zara lit up a cigarette as soon as she was out of sight of the rest of the group, and she passed it to Jack. Jack had never smoked before. But since he wanted to look grown-up in Zara's eyes, he decided to take a drag. It was a mistake and it only served to make Zara laugh at him as he went purple and started coughing.

When he finally stopped, they lay down together on the grass bank a few feet away from the lake.

"It's lovely here," said Zara. "It's such a peaceful place."

Jack was in seventh heaven. He was lying next to a beautiful girl on a warm day at the end of summer. He wondered whether she would let him kiss her.

Then without warning, Zara sat up and said, "It's a warm day. There's nobody about and the lake looks inviting. Why don't we go skinny-dipping?"

"But its broad daylight," Jack protested. "Somebody might see us."

There was no stopping Zara, who had already started stripping off and was soon running down towards the lake.

Halfway there, she turned around and shouted, "Are you coming in or what?"

By this stage, she was down to her bra and pants. Soon she had gotten rid of them as well and had waded into the water.

Jack wasn't going to pass up the chance of going swimming with a naked girl, especially one he fancied. He hurriedly took off his clothes and was soon splashing into the lake just as Zara had done a few seconds earlier. It was freezing cold, but Jack didn't mind. He was in the water with the girl of his dreams. She was a few feet away from him and he started swimming towards her.

"I'll race you to the boathouse on the other side of the lake," said Zara as Jack got near her.

She set off with Jack in hot pursuit. He had absolutely no idea that Zara was a former county swimming champion and, instead of catching up with her, the gap got wider as they crossed the lake.

Soon Zara had reached the old stone boathouse where she waited for Jack to arrive. But just as he got there, she set off back for the other side again.

"I'll race you back," she said.

Jack swore under his breath and set off after her once more. But she was far too fast for him and he was still in the middle of the lake when she reached the shore.

It was then that Jack spotted another figure on the shoreline close to where Zara was getting out of the lake. He instantly recognised Hannah, and he noticed she was carrying one of the dressing gowns from the hotel.

Zara got out of the lake and, for a brief moment, Jack could see her perfectly formed backside before it was covered up by the dressing gown. It suddenly dawned on him that he'd been tricked, fooled by two girls of whom one was his own kid sister.

He was helpless as he saw the two of them gather up all the discarded clothes, including his own, before legging it back to the hotel. Just before she disappeared, Zara turned to where Jack was getting out of the water and blew him a kiss.

They'd planned it in advance, of course. Jack knew that. But his mind was now racing in order to work out how he could travel the half-mile or so back to the hotel, whilst at the same time preserving his dignity.

It was not going to be easy, but he was relieved when he spotted a piece of board floating near the water's edge. He pulled it out of the water, covered his manhood, and set off at breakneck speed back to Striding Hall.

He very nearly made it. But unfortunately for him, James and his father were returning from their drive in the Overfinch at that precise moment.

"I'd recognise that arse anywhere," said Pete as they pulled into the hotel driveway just behind a fleeing Jack.

If being spotted running naked up the drive wasn't bad enough, his humiliation was complete when Zara and Hannah, who were sitting on the hotel steps, started laughing at him.

"What have you got under that board, Jack?" shouted Zara. "Is it a little tiddler?"

"It certainly isn't a conga eel," added Hannah as both of them started laughing again.

And the taunting wasn't over yet.

"Put your rod away, Jack. Can't you read?" Zara continued.

Jack looked down to see what they were laughing at and to his horror saw that it was in fact a warning sign he'd picked up in order to protect his modesty. The sign said, 'No fishing'.

At this point, his father wound the window down and shouted, "Jack, what the hell do you think you're doing?"

Jack stopped immediately, realising he'd been rumbled and made his way over to the now stationary Overfinch. James was trying hard not to laugh and took the waxed jacket he kept on the back seat of his car and passed it to Jack.

"Well, it was a nice day and I decided to go for a dip in the lake," he said whilst putting the coat on, "and Hannah went and stole my clothes."

"I'll speak to her later," said Pete. "But why didn't you use the hotel swimming pool and why didn't you put your trunks on?"

"It was a spur of the moment thing," Jack replied. "The lake looked really inviting and I just thought, why not?"

"Well, we can be thankful for small mercies," added Pete. "At least, it was Hannah who pulled this prank and not that Zara girl."

Pete drove off into the hotel car park leaving a shivering Jack to make his way back to his room. Jack looked and felt like a flasher as he walked through the hotel lobby wearing only a coat. He could have sworn he saw the receptionist giggling as he went to collect his key from her. It was a hot day in early September, and he could only guess what she thought he'd been doing in a waxed jacket and no shoes.

As soon as he got back to his room, Jack showered and put the TV on.

"Bloody girls," he thought to himself, "who needs them?"

Shortly after six o'clock that evening, everyone was sitting in the bar drinking and chatting. Everyone, that was, except Mark who still hadn't returned from the crematorium. Pete hadn't been too hard on Hannah. He'd pulled a similar prank on Mark when they were young. For her part, Hannah hadn't ratted on Jack, never mentioning to her father the part Zara had played in the afternoon's fun and games.

However, that didn't make any difference as far as Jack was concerned. He had no intention of forgiving her. Instead, he sat as far away as possible from both his sister and Zara, staring at the two of them and showing his disgust. His mood was not helped when he overheard Zara telling Hannah a joke.

"What's the similarity between a dick and a fish that's just been caught by an angler?" she said.

"I don't know," Hannah replied.

"If it's small, you exaggerate its size. If it's large, you mount it."

Both girls fell about laughing once more whilst looking across the room at Jack.

"You know what Jack's dick reminds me of?" added Zara. "A fun-sized Mars Bar. I mean, what's the point of one of those? They never satisfy you. There's nothing fun about them. Personally, I much prefer the king-sized version."

This cued even more laughter from the two girls.

Pete was not amused and told Zara off for telling such rude jokes to his daughter, who was only fifteen.

"Don't worry, Dad," said Hannah. "I've heard far worse at school."

Her comment had precisely the opposite effect on Pete, who was now worried about what his daughter got up to with her friends. However, he soon forgot about that when he heard the sound of a car pulling up on the gravel outside. A few seconds later, Mark appeared in the room looking excited and bursting to tell everyone what he had discovered. But before he could open his mouth, Pete started speaking.

"I'm glad you're back, Mark, only I've been waiting for you to return before telling everyone what I discovered this afternoon, and I'm not referring to my son's lilywhite backside."

Jack just wanted to curl up and die at that point but thought better of it as he was as interested as the rest of the family in what his father had to say.

"You know I went out with James this afternoon in his Overfinch," said Pete, "and I have to say that it's a cracking motor. Anyway, whilst I was driving, James let something slip. I don't know whether or not he meant to, but he told me that Dad really liked performance cars. That shouldn't surprise anyone, as we know he owned a Porsche. But he said he was also a fan of Land Rovers and used to own one when he was a teenager. If James was only fifteen when Dad went off to Spain, that must mean he knew him when he was a child."

"Did you quiz him about it?" asked Rosie.

"Yes," replied Pete, "and he said he must have read it in his father's notes about the trust fund. But he looked rattled and I didn't believe him. I think he really did know Dad when he was a youngster."

"Let's quiz him about it tonight," said Rosie.

"That's just it," replied Pete. "That's another reason why I thought he was rattled. He isn't coming tonight. He said he had a lot of paperwork to do following his meeting today and told me he would meet us all at 9 am tomorrow morning in the bar."

"That's very interesting," said Mark. "Of course, he may be telling the truth. But from what you've just said, I think he may well have met our father when he was young and is really rattled. Either way, it doesn't answer the question whether or not Dad died in 1984. However, I may have made a discovery this afternoon that will answer that question."

The whole room went quiet and everybody turned towards Mark who continued.

"The first person's record I discovered was our grandfather's. This shouldn't come as any surprise since Simon had already told us he was cremated there."

"Personally, I don't believe a word that Simon says," added Rosie. "Or his father, for that matter."

"That's as maybe," Mark continued. "But there's something else he told us that I now know is correct. There are numerous bench seats in the remembrance garden at the crematorium and all of them look exactly the same as the one he showed us by the lake. Therefore, I have no doubt it was originally located there, just like he told us."

"So he's told us something that's true about a bloody bench seat," said Rosie. "Howdy bloody doody."

"Perhaps we ought to let Mark tell us what he's discovered," added Wendy, who was getting frustrated by Rosie's constant interruptions.

Rosie folded her arms and slowly breathed out.

"I had a spot of luck at the crematorium as the records have been computerised," Mark continued. "Not only that, but they also contain details of the deceased's next of kin. This was helpful as there have been numerous Bradburys cremated at Chesterfield Crematorium. I never realised that it was such a popular name in the town. Grandfather's next of kin is down as his wife, so she was still alive when he died. It gave her name as Helen Elizabeth Bradbury. Then I looked for Helen Elizabeth Bradbury to see if she had been cremated there as well, and ..."

Mark looked about to make sure that everybody was paying attention. But he needn't have worried about that. Everybody was listening intently. He continued.

"There is no record of her ever being cremated there, which must mean either she was buried or cremated elsewhere, or she is still alive. The latter, however, is highly unlikely since in all probability she would be over a hundred years old. Either way, it is a mystery."

Then he came to the bit of news everybody had been waiting for.

"Finally, I looked to see if there was any record of our father being cremated at Chesterfield Crematorium. In order for this to have happened, his body would have had to be repatriated to Chesterfield from Spain."

The tension in the room was palpable as Mark continued.

"I have to tell you that I did find his name in the records. He was cremated there in June 1984. Consequently, there can be no doubt about it. Our father really did die in a car crash in Spain in 1984."

Chapter 18

Tuesday, September 3rd, 2019

Once again, their father's death dominated the conversation during the evening, that and whether James had known their father when he was young. In James's absence, Simon had to field everybody's questions. But it became pretty clear early on that either he didn't know the answers or was not prepared to reveal them.

"I've arranged for Noel and Josh to have a golf lesson in the morning," Simon told Mark and Louise just before they retired for the night. "Then in the afternoon, Katie and I are taking them for a bike ride on the Tissington Trail."

"You don't think they are too young for golf?" asked Louise.

"The course here is only nine holes and they're all par three," replied Simon. "In reality, it's just a pitch and putt course."

"I can confirm that," said Wendy. "It's the ideal course for beginners."

With that settled, Simon left and, a few minutes later, the rest of them went up to their rooms.

The conversation about their father continued the following morning at breakfast. However, there was an additional topic. They were all speculating about what the day's challenge would entail.

Simon and Katie had met up with the group for breakfast and James joined them just before 9 o'clock.

"Are you two ready to play golf?" Katie asked Noel and Josh.

The two boys were extremely keen to get started. Simon and Katie took them to the hotel's small pro shop to get some clubs and balls.

"Let's go through to the bar where I will brief you about today's challenge," said James once Simon, Katie and the boys had left.

"We all want to have a serious conversation with you later on today," said Rosie to James as they were walking down the corridor. "And this time you aren't going to wriggle out of it."

James was unperturbed, however, and once they'd arrived in the bar, he began the briefing.

"Today, you will face your third and final task," he announced. "Yesterday, Simon told you a lot about your family history. He also showed you many places that were important in the lives of your forbears. Once again, you were told to take note of what you saw and heard, as it would help you today. The challenge you face today is a very simple one. I'm sure you all remember the entertainer, Ken Dodd. Well, your great-grandfather had something in common with him."

"Why?" asked Pete. "Did he fiddle his taxes?"

"I think you'll discover that Ken Dodd was found not guilty of defrauding the inland revenue," replied James. "No, it's because they both died in the same house where they were born. Your challenge is to find that house. That's your great-grandfather's house by the way, not Ken Dodd's. Once you have identified it, you need to discover what it says over the door. This will lead you to your final prize, which this time will be a mystery prize. In fact, the whole purpose of this challenge is to identify what the prize is. All you have to do is to return here and tell me what it is."

Whilst they were taking in what he had just said, he added, "Now, does anyone have any questions?"

"Yes," said Mark. "Yesterday, Simon told us our great-grandfather was born in Parwich and died in Chesterfield. So I don't understand the challenge?"

"Did he?" was the only reply they were going to get out of James.

"You have until 6 pm once more in which to solve the puzzle," he continued. "And that's the time I will meet you all back here in order for you to give me your answer. Good luck, everyone."

"Actually, he didn't say your great-grandfather was born in Parwich and died in Chesterfield," said Louise.

The moment James left the room, Louise assumed her role as team leader for the challenge.

"He just said those were the places where his parents lived when he was born and where his son and he both lived at the time of his death. The place where he was actually born and died must be somewhere else. But let's compile a list of what we know about him."

She went up to the flip chart, which was still in the bar and served as a reminder of their failure in the first challenge. She turned over the page, so she had a blank sheet to write on.

"We know that his name was Herbert Ebenezer Bradbury," she said writing his name on the board.

"He was the last Herbert Ebenezer Bradbury to run the Sycamore Inn in Parwich," added Ben. "His second son, Arthur took over from him when he retired, and he went to live with our grandfather after Arthur died of pneumonia."

"Correct," said Louise and wrote it on the board. "We know he was 67 years old when he died in 1953 and therefore must have been born in 1886."

"It was September 3rd when he died," said Pete looking at the photo he'd taken of their great-grandfather's headstone. "That means that he must have been born between September 4th, 1885, and September 3rd, 1886."

"I stand corrected," Louise replied. "We also know that, when he was born, his parents lived and worked in the Sycamore Inn in Parwich. In addition, we know that he was living with his son at number 76 St Augustines Road in Chesterfield when he died. So as you can see, we don't actually know where he was born or died. We assumed he was born at the Sycamore Inn and died at the house in St Augustines Road. But that can't be the case. His birth and death must have happened elsewhere. Now, is there anything else we know about him? Even things that may seem unimportant may contain a clue."

Pete was the first to reply. He was still looking at the picture he'd taken in Boythorpe Cemetery.

"We know his wife was called Julia. We also know she was three years younger than him and she died four days before him."

"That fact might be massively relevant," said Louise who was starting to relish her role as team leader. "What if they had had an accident that eventually killed both of them, a car crash for example?"

"But in that case, wouldn't they have died in a hospital?" asked Mark.

"Yes, but just suppose it was a small cottage hospital and it was the same one he was born in. It might have subsequently been converted into apartments. Don't forget that a hospital is highly likely to have an inscription over the door."

"Perhaps it said, 'abandon all hope, ye who enter here'," added Pete.

"Try being serious for a minute, will you, Pete?" said Louise.

"Well, there's a lot of ifs, buts and maybes in what you've just said," Pete continued. "And Parwich must be twenty miles away from Chesterfield. So why would he end up in the same hospital?"

"Because he'd lived in Parwich all his life," Louise replied. "All his friends would still be living in the village. It is quite feasible that he and his wife were going to visit one of them when they had an accident."

It was a long shot, but everybody agreed it made sense. Ben volunteered to look up anything he could find on the internet about cottage hospitals near Parwich.

"I could also look for anything about Herbert Ebenezer Bradbury on the internet," said Jack. "There may be something, you never know."

"Good thinking, Jack," replied Louise. "Is there anything else we know about your great-grandfather?"

"We know his father was also called Herbert Ebenezer Bradbury and, like his son, he was the landlord of the Sycamore Inn in Parwich," said Mark. "We also know his mother was called Mona Doris Bradbury and she died when she was 57."

"That might be relevant," said Louise. "My grandmother gave birth to my mother at her parents' house. She didn't have a good pregnancy. They decided she would be better off where her parents could look after her, rather than at home where her husband was at work all day. Your great-grandfather's mother died at a relatively young age. Perhaps she had always been a sickly woman?"

"I think 57 was considered to be a ripe old age back in 1924," added Pete. "However, even if our great-grandfather was born at his grandparents' house, why would he have died there as well?"

"Perhaps it was still owned by another member of his family," replied Louise.

Before anybody else had the opportunity to comment, they were interrupted by Jack who shouted, "Good grief, I don't believe it. I've found Herbert Ebenezer Bradbury. He's alive and still living in Parwich."

"How can that be?" asked Pete. "The last living Herbert Ebenezer Bradbury was our great-grandfather and he died in 1953. We've all been to his grave in Boythorpe Cemetery."

"That's as maybe," Jack replied. "But if that's true, then nobody bothered to cancel his entry in the phone directory. I've just discovered his telephone number."

"Perhaps he was buried along with his phone," joked Pete.

"It would be a massive coincidence if whoever he is had nothing to do with all of this," said Louise. "Mark, can you give him a call and find out what his story is?"

Mark took the number from Jack and went into the next room to make the phone call. Meanwhile, Ben had finished his search for cottage hospitals.

"I was quite excited there for a moment when I discovered that Parwich Hospital was built in 1812," he said. "But I discovered it's in Ashbourne not in Parwich. That in itself wasn't a problem since Ashbourne is just down the road from Parwich and could well have been where he was born. More of a problem, however, is the fact it is still open today. It hasn't been converted into apartments. Then I discovered there is a closed hospital in Bakewell. But I don't know if it's been converted into housing. Also, Bakewell is further away from Parwich than Ashbourne, which makes it less likely that he was born there."

"But we don't know that," said Louise. "It could be that Bakewell had a better hospital or it was the only one locally that had a maternity wing."

"We're talking about rural England in the 19th century, not the 21st century," said Pete. "Most pregnant women gave birth out in the fields, then got up and carried on bringing in the harvest. They didn't give birth in specialist neonatal units."

"Even so, it's still worth having a look," said an exasperated Louise. "Can anybody think of anything else about him? Is there anything we might have missed?"

"Well, we know his two elder sons died before him," said Wendy. "His eldest son, who was also called Herbert Ebenezer Bradbury, died in World War Two. His middle son, who took over the pub, died childless in 1952. That was why your great-grandfather had to move in with his youngest son in Chesterfield that same year."

Louise knew there was something highly relevant in Wendy's last statement. The problem was that she just couldn't pinpoint precisely what it was. Well, she couldn't until Mark came back into the room and dropped his bombshell.

"I've just been having an interesting conversation with our cousin," he announced. "Although, strictly speaking, he's our father's cousin, which would make him our second cousin. Or is it our first cousin once removed? I've never been able to work out how that works. Anyway, Bert as he prefers to be called, was born in 1938, and he's the only child of the Herbert Ebenezer Bradbury who died at the hands of the Japanese in 1943."

"Don't tell me?" said Pete. "I bet he's got a son who's also called Herbert Ebenezer Bradbury?"

"Actually, he has three daughters, all of whom have married and moved away from the village," Mark replied. "And that really does make him the last Bradbury living in Parwich."

"And was he able to tell you anything useful?" asked Louise.

"He told me that when his father died, his mother moved back in with her parents who ran the village post office. Eventually, he inherited it, but with nobody willing to take it on when he retired, he'd been forced to close it. He still lives in the flat above the old shop. But, more importantly, he knew quite a lot about our great-grandfather, who, of course, was his grandfather. He remembers him pretty well as he was fourteen when his grandfather left the village and fifteen when he died. He's quite sure that he was born in the pub, but he's absolutely sure where he died. That's because he and his mother were both at his bedside in the Royal Hospital in Chesterfield when he passed away."

Chapter 19

Wednesday, September 4th, 2019

"None of this makes any sense whatsoever," said Louise. "How could he have been born and passed away in the same house when we know he was born in a pub and died twenty miles away in a hospital?"

"If I could just say something," said Zara. "I think we're all overlooking something very obvious. We're assuming that the great-grandfather in question is Herbert Ebenezer Bradley, but don't forget that everybody has four great-grandfathers."

For a moment, you could hear a pin drop as the whole room went completely quiet. Zara added, "I wonder why none of us has thought of this before?"

There were several potential reasons for this oversight. Perhaps it was because all the information they had been given the previous day about Herbert Ebenezer Bradbury was nothing more than a classic piece of misdirection. Alternatively, it may just have been a case of them not being able to see the wood for the trees. Whatever it was, it slowly began to dawn on them that they had just wasted an hour and a half going around in circles. Herbert Ebenezer Bradbury was not the great-grandfather they were looking for.

"Even though everybody has four great-grandfathers," Zara continued, "if you rule out Herbert Bradbury, that only leaves one possible person. That's because Mum and Ben have a different mother to Pete and Mark. Consequently, it has to be your father's maternal grandfather."

It was perfectly logical. After all, everybody has one set of parents, two sets of grandparents and four sets of great-grandparents. However, now that they'd crossed off half the family, it left them with just two great-grandfathers, one of whom had already been ruled out. As a result, there could be no doubt that Zara had correctly identified the person they were looking for. It was definitely their father's maternal grandfather.

"Right, what do we know about him?" asked Louise.

"Absolutely sweet Fanny Adams," said Pete. "We don't know what his name was, where he was born, where he lived, what he did for a living, or where he died."

"We do know one thing about him," said Louise. "We know that his daughter married our grandfather."

"Yes, but we know virtually nothing about her either," Pete replied. "We don't know what her maiden name was, where she lived before she married our grandfather, or where she was buried or cremated. We're not even sure that she's dead."

"We do know a little bit about her," said Louise turning the page to reveal another blank sheet on the flip chart. "So let's have it. Let's list what we already know. If we can discover where she was born and brought up, I will bet you any money you like, it's the same place where her father was born and died."

It wasn't a long list. It simply said:

Helen Elizabeth Bradbury
Married Robert Stephen Bradbury in 1938
Worked at the Whitworth Institute ? - 1938
Lived at 76 St Augustines Rd Chesterfield, 1938 - ?

"How does that help us?" asked Louise.

"Well, if we can look up the census records, we will be able to tell in which decade she moved out of St Augustines Road," said Wendy.

"That's true," said Louise, "but I fail to see how that would move us forward."

"Hang on," said Pete. "I've just remembered that Simon gave me the deed pack for 76 St Augustines Road last night. Maybe there is something in it that would tell us about her."

"I doubt it," said Louise. "Don't forget your parents were council tenants not owners of the house. But I suppose we'd better leave no stone unturned."

Pete got up and went back to his room to look through the deeds.

"If we could get hold of our grandparents' wedding certificate, it should contain the address she was living at when she got married," said Mark.

"That's the best idea I've heard all day," said Louise adding, "Ben, can you get on to it?"

"No problem," came the reply.

"What about the Whitworth Centre?" said Frank.

"What about it?" replied Louise.

"Well, we know that your grandmother left in 1938," he continued. "So it's a very long shot. However, it is still owned and run by the same organisation as it was back then. Perhaps there are employment records going back that far."

"I agree that it's a very long shot," said Louise. 'Especially since we don't even know what her name was before she got married. But I'm ready to try anything. Why don't you and Rosie go and speak to June and see what you can find out?"

Shortly afterwards, Pete returned after sifting through the deed pack. He looked excited.

"They weren't just tenants," said Pete. "They bought the house under the Conservative government's right-to-buy scheme. They only paid £1,725 for it back in 1981, which is remarkable being as though that represents less than a month's salary these days. Mind you, this poses another mystery. I mean, what happened to the proceeds from the sale of the house after she died? After all, we are her closest relatives, and the money didn't go to any of us."

"Doesn't the deed pack tell you who the subsequent owners are?" asked Mark.

"No, it just states that our grandparents bought the house from the council in 1981 and the current owner is the Bradbury Family Trust Fund," replied Pete. "It doesn't say when our grandmother stopped living there, when the Trust Fund bought it, or indeed if there were any owners between our grandparents and the Trust Fund."

"The fact that the house has changed ownership doesn't mean your grandmother is dead," said Louise. "The house could have been sold in order to pay for her care. It may even have been sold relatively recently."

"Why don't Pete and I go to St Augustines Road?" said Wendy. "Your grandmother may still have friends living nearby who might know where she was born."

Louise agreed that it was another good idea. So Pete and Wendy set off to see what they could discover. Meanwhile, Ben announced that he had finished his investigation into their grandparents' wedding certificate.

"It's not good news, I'm afraid," he informed the rest of the group. "I can order a copy but it will take four days to get here."

"I knew it couldn't be that easy," said Louise. "We've got seven hours not four days. Never mind, Ben, it was worth a try."

"Is there anything we've missed?" Louise pleaded with them all to rack their brains. "What else do we know about her?"

"We know she had a son, our father," said Mark. "Other than that, I can't think of anything else, apart from the things we've listed already."

"There is something else," said Ben. "It's something we don't know about her. We don't know if she's alive or dead. If she's alive, given her age, she's almost certainly in a care home. Even if she isn't alive, there's a fair chance she ended up in one. Perhaps it's worth phoning all the care homes in the area and telling them we are trying to find a long lost relative."

"It's worth a try. Although, if she'd died, wouldn't she have been cremated like her husband?" Louise remarked.

"She may have requested a burial," Ben replied. "But as we've already agreed, we don't know if she's dead. She may be alive and just waiting to tell us where she was born."

"It's worth a try," said Louise. "I want Zara, Jack and Hannah to locate all the nursing homes within ten miles of Chesterfield. Once you've done that, you can phone them and find out if they'd ever had a Mrs Helen Elizabeth Bradbury as a resident."

Whilst all this was going on, Pete and Wendy had arrived in St Augustines Road. They had decided to ask the current tenant of number 76 whether he or she knew anything about their grandmother.

Pete knocked on the door but there was no reply, and they decided to try around the back. There they discovered a large woman standing in the garden with her back turned to them. She was scruffily dressed in a black tracksuit, pink trainers and a red baseball cap inscribed with the initials KFC. She'd presumably received it in recognition of her lifetime's consumption of bargain buckets. Her giant arse was the result of too many nights spent eating takeaway food whilst watching soaps on the TV.

"Rocky," she shouted and, just for good measure, she shouted it again even louder.

For a moment Pete and Wendy wondered whether she was shouting at the dog who was doing his business on the lawn, or her son who'd just kicked his football into next door's garden.

The answer soon became obvious when she bent over and gave the dog a slap.

"Good God," said Pete under his breath to Wendy. "The last arse I saw that was as big as that was on a police horse."

Then clearing his throat, he shouted out, "Hello."

The woman looked up and said, "If you're Jehovah's Witnesses, you can bugger off now."

"We're your new landlords and we've come to inspect our property," said Pete. "I hope you are going to clear up that dog shit."

As soon as he said it, the young boy who'd been playing football ran over to Pete and punched him right in the balls.

"Bruno," shouted the woman. "Stop that, you naughty boy."

Pete was doubled up in pain but still managed to say through gritted teeth, "I suppose you named him after Frank Bruno, the boxer?"

"No, he's named after Bruno Tonioli," said the woman. "You know, the judge on *Strictly*? I'm a big fan of his. He's so animated and enthusiastic just like my little Bruno here."

"Really," said Pete who was just beginning to recover from the excruciating pain in his groin. "I hope he takes after him in other ways. In which case, there will be no need to worry that he'll ever have brats of his own."

"Don't you call my little Bruno a brat," said the woman. "He's just highly strung."

"I didn't call him a brat," replied Pete. "I said there'd be no need to worry that he'll ever have brats of his own. Besides which, it was only a joke. Look, I think we've got off on the wrong foot. Let's start again. I'm Pete Bradbury and this is my wife, Wendy."

"You'd better come inside," said the woman. "My name's Tanya, Tanya Hyde."

As soon as she'd told Pete what her name was, he couldn't stop himself from giggling.

"Perhaps she's a dominatrix in her spare time," he whispered to Wendy. "I wouldn't fancy seeing her in a leather suit with a cat-o'-nine-tails in her hand."

"Go ahead and laugh. Most people do," said Tanya, who had overheard Pete's comment. "I didn't always have the surname Hyde. It's me married name and I'm thinking of changing it back again to me maiden name now that I'm divorced. At least, people won't laugh at me no more."

"I wouldn't be so sure of that," muttered Pete.

"Would you like a cup of coffee?" Tanya asked them.

"Thank you but we've just had one," replied Wendy.

That wasn't true. The real reason was because she was by no means certain about Tanya's hygiene standards. It was a feeling that was reinforced when she saw the rings inside her mugs.

"Anyway, if you're now me landlords, when are you going to get me fucking roof fixed?" Tanya asked them whilst pouring a mug for herself.

"I understand it will be fixed very shortly," Pete replied.

Through careful questioning, Pete and Wendy discovered that Tanya and Bruno had only lived in the house for three months and didn't know any of the neighbours.

"They're all snobs," she told them.

Pete thought it was unlikely that residents of an estate where most of the houses were still owned by the council would all be snobs. In reality, they were probably just ordinary hard-working people who didn't like having Tanya for a neighbour. Pete considered saying something to her to that effect, but then decided to hold his tongue.

"My grandmother used to live in this house," he said instead. "My wife and I are trying to find out when she moved out. Her name was Helen Bradbury. Can you help us at all?"

"I've never heard of her, duck," replied Tanya. "It must have been some time ago, as I still get post for lots of the previous tenants, but I've never had anything for a Mrs Bradbury."

Finally, Pete decided that they weren't going to get anything useful out of Tanya. So they made their excuses and left.

"We couldn't have inherited a worse tenant," said Pete after they'd left. "I think we are going to have some real issues with her."

"You're being a little harsh," replied Wendy. "For a start, she's obviously got a few health problems. She must be a little bit deaf, otherwise why does she need to shout all the time? And then there's the problem with her weight. She must be big boned."

"I think you are confusing a medical condition with just being common," said Pete. "Besides which, it's not having big bones that's made her arse so enormous."

"So what do you want to do next?" asked Wendy.

"I think we should ask the neighbours if any of them knew my grandmother," replied Pete. "The chances are that some of them must have lived here for a long time and might know her."

At the same time as they were doing this, Rosie and Frank were in Darley Dale. If Pete and Wendy hadn't learnt anything from their visit to see Tanya, then Rosie and Frank weren't faring much better at the Whitworth Centre.

"We keep minutes of all the committee meetings going back to 1890," June told them. "But we aren't as diligent when it comes to employment records."

Disappointingly, she couldn't help them in their quest to find an employee who had worked there back in the 1930s. However, she was able to tell them one thing that was useful.

"Back in those days, almost all of our employees would have lived within walking distance of the institute," she said. "Most of them walked to work. None of them came by car and even those who came by bicycle, still tended to live close by. As a result, it would have been highly unusual if your grandmother had lived more than two miles away."

Rosie thanked her and immediately phoned this information through to Louise, suggesting they do a search of the area. Her idea was to look at houses in and around Darley Dale, searching for any with inscriptions over the door.

The problem with that, however, was that there were at least a thousand houses within a two-mile radius of the Whitworth Centre. Even if you ignored all those built within the last 100 years, which you could do if Rosie's great-grandfather had been born there, there were still several hundred of them.

It was not going to be an easy search. They had no way of knowing whether their grandmother had lived in a terraced house, or in a large country property behind gates and a high fence. If it was the latter, it would be far more difficult to locate.

Whilst Rosie and Louise were chatting on the phone, Jack, Hannah and Zara had finished contacting all the nursing homes within ten miles of Chesterfield. Unfortunately, that particular exercise had turned out to be another dead end. None of them had any record of someone called Helen Elizabeth Bradbury.

Since they now had nothing to do, Mark suggested that he take them to join Rosie and Frank in their search of houses in Darley Dale. Louise, who had finished talking to Rosie by that stage, asked him to come straight back once he'd dropped them off. If anything else cropped up, she wouldn't have either the manpower or the transport to tackle it.

Meanwhile, Pete and Wendy were rapidly concluding that their grandmother must have left St Augustines Road a long time ago. None of the neighbours remembered her, even the ones who'd lived there for more than twenty years.

After having spoken to all the close neighbours, they decided to go back to Striding Hall. However, before they did that, Pete suggested they go around to their father's old house and see if they could discover anything there instead.

"I am not optimistic," said Wendy. "Your father was two generations removed from the person we are trying to find. Not only that, but your father left over forty years ago. The chances of anyone knowing where his mother was born are slim at best."

"Even so, we might as well try," said Pete, "especially as it's just around the corner."

The house in St Augustines Rise was only a short walk away, so they didn't bother taking the car. Pete approached the front door with quite a lot of trepidation. Apart from the previous day when he had seen it from the minibus, the last time he'd been in this house was when he was four years old. He composed himself and knocked loudly on the door. A lady in her early thirties answered. She was petite, softly spoken and quite pretty, the exact opposite to Tanya.

"I'm sorry to trouble you," said Pete. "My name's Pete Bradbury and this is Wendy, my wife. I hope you can help us, only I used to live in this house when I was a little boy. I'm trying to find out about my father who abandoned my brother and I when I was four."

"That's very interesting," said the woman whose name was Julie. "Why don't you come in and tell me more?"

She led the way into the kitchen, where she offered them coffee. This time Pete and Wendy did accept. Pete really wanted to be able to remember the inside of the house, but despite Julie giving him a guided tour, he couldn't remember a single thing.

"That's only to be expected," Julie told him. "The council substantially modernised all the properties on the estate back in the 1980s and again in 2015. The house today looks nothing like it would have done when you lived here."

"I haven't been inside this house since the 1970s," said Pete. "My mum took my brother and I to live in Gloucestershire in 1979 after our father ran off with a barmaid from the Boythorpe Inn. He'd just won a massive sum of money on the pools, and he left us with nothing."

"Wow, that's quite a story," said Julie.

"We are trying to discover what happened to my grandmother, who lived around the corner in St Augustines Road," Pete continued. "And we thought that if anybody knew our father back in the 1970s, then they might be able to point us in the right direction. You aren't able to help us, are you?"

Pete hadn't meant to be so open. He was normally the type of person who liked to keep his defences up. Perhaps it was because he felt so comfortable in his old home or perhaps it was because Julie was a good listener. But, either way, he ended up telling her everything. Julie took it all in before apologising to him.

"Sorry," she said. "I'm afraid I only moved to the neighbourhood with my daughter after I split up from my husband two years ago. I'm unable to tell you anything about any of the people who lived around here in the 1970s."

It was just as Pete and Wendy were about to leave that Julie turned to them and added, "I'm sorry I couldn't be of more help. But why don't you try Mr Richardson next door? He's lived in his house for over 45 years. He must have known your father."

Thanking her, they walked around to the next-door neighbour's house and knocked on his door. It was opened by a man in his seventies with grey hair wearing a sleeveless pullover.

"Mr Richardson?" said Pete. "My name is Pete Bradbury and I used to live next door when I was little. I'm trying to find some details about my family. Tell me, did you know my dad?"

Mr Richardson didn't reply straight away. Instead, he looked Pete up and down.

"Good God, it's little Pete," he said eventually. "The last time I saw you, you were wearing short trousers and had snot running down your face. Of course I knew your father. He used to be my best mate."

Chapter 20

Wednesday, September 4th, 2019

Mr Richardson invited them in and told them to call him Dave.

"I remember the day your dad won the pools as if it were yesterday," he told them.

He went to the cupboard and pulled out an old copy of *The Sun* and showed it to Pete.

"I kept this," he said. "Obviously, I didn't know he planned to abandon you all and bugger off with Miss Bristol."

"Miss Bristol?" said Pete. "I thought she came from Swindon."

"She did but we called her that because of her huge bust," said Dave. "You must know that Bristol City is rhyming slang for titty."

"Yes, I did know that," replied Pete.

"Mind you, after she ran off with your dad, we used to refer to her as the Swindon slapper," he continued.

"Really," said Pete, who made a mental note to tell Ben and Rosie.

Pete looked down at the article. The headline said, 'A million quid should come in Andy'. Immediately below that was a picture of his mum and dad in a pose that had obviously been staged by the newspaper. *The Sun* was notorious for its puns, and it must have taken some junior reporter all of five seconds to come up with that particular headline, which played on their dad's name.

He and Mark were also in the photo, looking perplexed as they gave a thumbs-up sign. The family all had huge smiles on their faces and were dressed in smart new clothes, which Pete guessed must have been bought especially for the occasion. His mum and dad both had a glass of champagne in one hand and, in the other, a large cheque for £1,002,172.48.

They looked like such a happy family. But it was the calm before the storm. Pete couldn't help thinking that they definitely wouldn't have been smiling if they had known back then what the future held for them all.

"It wasn't just the papers," added Dave. "You were on *Look North* as well. It stuck in my mind because they said you were from Yorkshire. Lucky pools winners from Chesterfield in South Yorkshire, they announced. I phoned up the BBC to complain. But all they said was 'Chesterfield is in South Yorkshire, isn't it?' That says everything you need to know about the BBC's attitude to North Derbyshire. It's been forty years since that happened and things haven't changed one bit. It's Yorkshire this, and God's own country that. Saying that if Yorkshire was a country, they would have won more gold medals at the Olympics than Italy. Then they go and include the women's hockey team in their totals, when only one of them comes from Yorkshire. They forget they serve this area as well. That Garry Hailsham, he's the worst. He never once uses the term 'our region', he always talks about Yorkshire and nowhere else. If you ask me, he should have retired years ago and gone to live with those two other professional Yorkshiremen, Dickie Bird and Geoff Boycott."

By this time, Pete had started to switch off and tried to change the subject away from Dave's rant.

"It's not just me who's returned to Chesterfield," announced Pete. "My younger brother Mark and his family are also with us. We are all staying at Striding Hall."

"Baby Mark, well I never," Dave replied. "How is he?"

"He's doing fine," replied Pete. "But he's not a baby anymore. He's a Chemistry teacher at a school in Reigate."

"Well, I never."

"I'd be grateful if you could continue telling me about my father and his pools win?" asked Pete.

"Nobody was more surprised than me that your dad ran off," Dave continued. "Not only that, but he pulled out of going to the Mansfield match on the Monday after his win. He came around and told me he wasn't feeling very well and couldn't make it. Not that he missed much since we lost 1-0. We had a crap end to the season that year. He was lying about being ill, of course, as we found out the following Thursday, when his win was splashed all over the papers. I only ever saw him once more after that, and that was when he came into the Walton Hotel the following Saturday. He bought everybody who was in the bar that night a drink and we all toasted his good fortune. Then he walked out, and we never saw him again. The next thing I heard was that he'd run away to Spain with the Swindon slapper. A few days after that, your mum took you and Mark back to live with her parents in Gloucestershire."

Pete was listening so intently he almost forgot the reason why they were there. Eventually, he asked Dave if he had known his grandmother.

"I most certainly did," replied Dave. "I'd known your father since he was a little boy. I've lived on this estate all my life and grew up only a few doors down from where your grandparents lived. I remember your granddad giving me a clip around the ear once for scrumping apples from his garden."

Pete thought back to his grandparents' former house that he had just visited. There were no apple trees in the garden anymore. They'd been replaced by dog turds.

"I don't suppose you know where my grandmother was born, do you, Dave?" he asked him once he'd composed himself.

He wasn't expecting that he would, which made him even more surprised by Dave's response.

"Yes, of course I do," he replied. "I told you I'd known her all my life. So it seemed only right that I should go to her funeral. She'd asked to be buried alongside her father and grandfather in the churchyard at Stanton in Peak. That was where she came from, Stanton in Peak."

It was the breakthrough they had been waiting for. Pete and Wendy were both congratulated for their initiative when they returned to Striding Hall.

"As a matter of interest, how far is Stanton in Peak from the Whitworth Centre?" asked Louise.

Ben looked it up on one of the Ordnance Survey maps left over from the previous challenge and reported back that it was three miles away.

"That knocks June's theory on the head," said Louise. "Your grandmother must have been a fit woman as it would have taken her over an hour each day to walk to work and to get home again in the evening."

"Mind you, that's relatively quick when you compare it with some people's commute into London nowadays," added Mark.

Louise phoned Frank.

"You can stop looking in Darley Dale and take the kids to Stanton in Peak instead," she told him. "Pete and Wendy have discovered that Rosie's grandmother was born there and she's buried in the village graveyard."

"Will do," replied Frank.

From the map, it was clear that Stanton in Peak was a far smaller village than Darley Dale. As a result, Louise presumed that it shouldn't take very long to find a house with an inscription over the door, especially with five of them looking.

"You can go and help them as well," she said to Pete.

"Is it okay if I go with him?" asked Mark, who felt they were getting close to the truth now. "I want to be there when any further revelations about our family come to light."

Louise reluctantly agreed. She couldn't really object, as she would still have Ben and Wendy with her.

Twenty minutes later, the two brothers arrived in the village and immediately spotted Rosie and Frank who were standing by their car. It was parked opposite the village pub, which went by the unusual name of the Flying Childers.

"Have you discovered anything yet?" Mark asked Rosie.

"Well, we've only been here for fifteen minutes," she replied, "and the kids haven't completed their search of all the houses. However, I'm already convinced that this is the correct place. That's because most of the houses in the village have an inscription above the door."

"That's not good news," said Pete. "We don't know which is the correct house. We all presumed there would be only one with an inscription, not lots of them."

"We don't need to know which one is the correct house," replied Rosie. "The inscriptions are the same. They all say WPT. Look, even the pub over there has WPT above the door."

They walked across to the Flying Childers and there, carved into the stone lintel above the door, were the initials WPT.

"We'd better go in and ask them what it means," said Mark who'd noticed the pub closed in the afternoon at two o'clock and, by his watch, the time was now 1.55. "Whilst you're doing that, I'll phone Louise and give her the news."

The Flying Childers was an old-fashioned type of pub where cobs and soup were the only food on sale. Its main purpose was to provide a social hub for the village. It was a place where people could enjoy a good pint and conversation.

Not too many years ago, there would have been many pubs like the Flying Childers in the Peak District. Nowadays, however, many had closed down or been converted into gastro pubs, with reviews on TripAdvisor complaining about the size of the portions, or the fact that they didn't cater for vegans. The original reason for their existence was long forgotten amongst the goose liver pâté, crispy kale and shiitake mushrooms.

Not so the Flying Childers where, despite the landlady's dismay at having three people walk in just as she was about to close up, they soon started to feel at home.

"You've got a lovely pub here," Rosie said to her. "My husband and I run a pub in Somerset but it's nothing like this. It's a biker's pub and we put on a lot of live bands."

As soon as she'd said that, the landlady, whose name was Tracy, welcomed them like long lost friends.

"So what does the name of the pub refer to?" asked Rosie as Tracy was getting their drinks. "It's quite unusual, isn't it?"

It was a question that Tracy had been asked many times before. So she knew the answer off pat.

"The Flying Childers was a racehorse foaled in 1714 and owned by the Duke of Devonshire," she told them. "He's often referred to as the first really great thoroughbred, since he was undefeated in all his races."

Mark had finished his phone call to Louise by this stage and had joined the other three in the bar. Rosie introduced him to Tracy.

"Do you mind me asking what the initials WPT above the door of the pub stand for?" he asked her.

This was another question that Tracy was used to answering.

"It stands for William Pole Thornhill," she told them. "His descendants still live in the village at Stanton Hall. William Thornhill was responsible for building a large part of the village including many cottages, the church and the reading rooms. This is the reason why so many houses carry his initials. He was also the High Sheriff of Derbyshire and the Liberal MP for North Derbyshire between 1853 and 1865."

"You say the family still live at Stanton Hall? Do you know them?" asked Mark.

Tracy laughed. "This is a small village," she said. "We know everybody who lives here, even those villagers who never come to the pub. However, we know the Thornhills particularly well, as we lease the pub from them."

It turned out that, over the years, the Thornhill family had sold off many of the properties their ancestor had built. But they had always held on to the village pub.

"Is there any way we could get to meet them?" asked Pete.

"Not at present," said Tracy. "The family are currently away on holiday."

It was only then that Mark explained the reason for them all being there.

"We are trying to find out about our grandmother's family, who we believe came from this village," he told her. "We're particularly interested to discover where she lived. Her married name was Helen Bradbury and we've been told that she's buried in the graveyard here. You don't know anything about her, do you?"

"Unfortunately not," Tracy replied. "My husband and I have only lived in the village for two years. We moved to Stanton in Peak from Matlock when we took over the lease of the pub. The name Helen Bradbury means absolutely nothing to me. Mind you, if you know what her maiden name is, it might help. There may be some of her relatives still living in the village."

As she was saying that, a party of fifteen walkers came into the pub. They either hadn't noticed or had chosen to ignore the sign that said the pub should have closed ten minutes earlier.

"I think we'll be closing late today," said Tracy. "I'm not going to turn their money away now they are here."

Whilst Tracy was serving the walkers, Mark went outside to phone Louise again. He wanted to ask her if she could find out anything about William Pole Thornhill of Stanton Hall. At this stage, he hadn't a clue whether the initials WPT referred to something completely different in the modern world or whether the answer lay in what it meant originally.

"Ben carried out an internet search on the initials WPT after your first phone call," she said. "And the only thing he could find was that they stood for the World Poker Tour. He looked at all the venues where the tour is being held and they are everywhere from Jacksonville to Johannesburg. But none of them are in Derbyshire and, as far as he could tell, there was no connection to the county."

"Well, keep looking," said Mark before saying goodbye.

As he put the phone back in his pocket, he spotted Jack, Zara, and Hannah walking towards the pub. They seemed to be in good humour, which Mark took to mean that the three of them had patched up their differences from the previous day. However, they didn't have any good news to give him as the only inscriptions they had managed to find were the initials WPT. Mark had been hoping one of the houses would have different letters above the door, an inscription that would lead them in a totally different direction. But it was not to be.

They went to join the others in the bar where Tracy had just finished serving the walking party.

"Why don't you go to the cemetery and find her grave?" she suggested. "It's only just up the road. It's near the church on the opposite side of the road. Quite a lot of families from the village are buried together and her gravestone might give a clue to her maiden name."

"I think we're past that point," said Mark. "If the only inscription we can find is WPT, then that must be the clue. If that's the case, it doesn't matter what her maiden name was, or indeed where she lived."

Despite his reservations, Mark agreed to go and take a look. If nothing else, it would provide a missing piece of the family jigsaw. He and Pete set off for the cemetery whilst the others remained in the bar. They'd decided to do some brainstorming to see if they could work out what the initials WPT could mean.

Once at the graveyard, it didn't take long for Pete and Mark to discover their grandmother's headstone. It was fairly plain and just said:

Here Lies
Helen Elizabeth Bradbury
Died November 17th, 1989
Aged 72
A Daughter of this Parish

"Well, she was 72 when she died," said Pete. "But other than that, it doesn't tell us very much."

But Mark had already moved on from looking at their grandmother's grave. He was staring at the inscriptions on some of the nearby graves instead.

"Good grief," he said pointing. "I don't believe it. Her gravestone might not tell us much but look at the gravestones next to hers."

Pete could hardly believe what he was looking at. For the surnames on the gravestones close to their grandmother's revealed they were all members of the Knight family. But it was the two adjacent gravestones that particularly caught his eye. They were the grave of James Simon Knight who'd died in 1971 aged 83 and that of Simon James Knight who'd died in 2013 aged 92.

Chapter 21

Wednesday, September 4th, 2019

Mark and Pete returned to the Flying Childers to tell the others what they had discovered. The Knight family were related to them through their grandmother on their father's side.

"Her maiden name was almost certainly Knight, as she is buried in the Knight family plot," said Mark. "Not only that, but the Knights appear to reverse the name of their first-born son with each generation. The first son of James Simon is always Simon James and vice versa."

"If what you're saying is true, then James Knight's father, the person who drew up the trust fund, was actually our father's uncle," said Rosie in utter amazement.

"It has to be," replied Mark. "We always wondered why our father used a solicitor from Matlock and why James knew so much about our family. It's because he's part of our family. He's Dad's cousin, which makes him our first cousin once removed. Or at least I think it does, I'm still not a hundred percent certain how that works."

"He hasn't got the Bradbury nose though," added Pete.

"That's because he's not a Bradbury," Mark replied. "He's related to us via the female line. We inherited our distinctive noses via the male side of the family, which is why Rosie and Ben here look so much like us, but James and Simon don't."

"I can't get my head around all this," said Rosie. "A few days ago, I only had one brother and a daughter. That was the sum total of all my known relatives. Now I've got two half-brothers, five nephews and nieces and numerous second cousins and first cousins once removed."

"We can always draw up the family tree later," said Pete. "In the meantime, we now know the name of the great-grandfather whose house we need to find. His name is James Simon Knight and he is the grandfather of the current James Knight."

"What's the betting it's the same house that our James Knight lives in?" Mark added. "After all, any family that keeps the same Christian names for each generation, just reversing them every time, are probably going to live in the same house for several generations as well."

"Well, there's one way to find out," said Pete. "Let's ask Tracy if she knows him. His father and grandfather are both buried in the churchyard. So if your theory is correct, he must live in this village."

The last of the walking party had just left and Tracy was putting a tea towel over the hand pumps as Pete and Mark approached her again.

"Don't worry," he said. "We're going to leave soon as well. But before we go, I wanted to thank you for making us go and visit the graveyard. We found our grandmother's grave and also discovered that her maiden name was Knight. So that then begs the question, is there anybody called Knight living in the village? And if there is, can you tell us where they live?"

"There's no one by that name living here," Tracy replied, which caught them both by surprise.

"But there must be," said Pete. "We were told that our grandmother came from this village. It's obvious that she did as she's buried in the churchyard with written on her gravestone 'a daughter of this parish'. Her grave is right next to her father's. He's called James Knight, which is the same name as the man who's in charge of our trust fund."

"Hang on, I know that name," said Tracy. "James often comes into the pub, sometimes with Simon, his son. But you're wrong about him living in the village. He doesn't, he lives in Stanton Lees, one and a half miles away."

On quizzing Tracy, they discovered that Stanton Lees was a small hamlet on the road between Stanton in Peak and Darley Dale. It comprised just a few houses and a chapel. Anyone who was a member of the Church of England, however, would have to worship at Holy Trinity in Stanton in Peak. That was why Helen's gravestone was correct when it said 'a daughter of this parish'. Stanton Lees was part of the parish of Stanton in Peak.

"That explains why Dave Richardson thought she was from Stanton in Peak," said Pete. "He wouldn't have known that this parish included Stanton Lees. He must have presumed that she came from Stanton in Peak when he saw her being buried in the graveyard here next to her father."

"It also proves that June was correct about members of the institute's staff walking to work," added Mark. "Stanton Lees is less than two miles away from the Whitworth Centre."

Tracy gave them directions to James Knight's house and, after Mark had thanked her, they set off to find it. It was only then that a relieved Tracy locked the front door of the pub, some one and a half hours later than usual.

Jack, Zara and Hannah all opted to go with Rosie and Frank, as their car was much larger and more comfortable than Pete's. It was only a short journey, but Mark had enough time to phone Louise to update her about their discovery regarding the Knights.

"I'm pretty confident that the inscription we are looking for is at James Knight's house," he told her. "So you can stop looking on the internet for anything about William Pole Thornhill or the letters WPT."

"Does he live in Stanton in Peak, then?" asked Louise.

"No, he lives in the neighbouring village of Stanton Lees," Mark replied, "which is where Pete and I are right now."

Pete had driven past the village sign as Mark was talking to her.

"If what you are saying about James Knight is correct, there's going to be an interesting conversation around the dinner table this evening," said Louise.

Stanton Lees was such a small place that it didn't take them very long to find James Knight's house. Mark was still on the phone when he spotted the inscription above the door. It wasn't carved into the lintel like those in Stanton in Peak. Instead, it was engraved on a metal plaque and said SK1854. Mark read it out to Louise and agreed to stay on the phone whilst Ben looked it up on the internet.

"I'll put the phone on speaker, so you can hear what he's got to say," she said.

It didn't take Ben long to discover that the first item in the Google search showed that SK1854 was a scheduled SAS flight between Alicante and Stockholm.

"And there's some good news," he said.

"What?" asked Mark.

"The flight's on time," Ben replied.

"Very funny, Ben," said Louise sarcastically.

"Look," said Mark. "You give some thought as to what it might mean and phone me back if you come up with anything. I need to point the inscription out to the others and see if they can work out what it means."

He ended the call and went to speak to Rosie and Frank who had parked behind them. He showed them the plaque, but they were as much in the dark about its meaning as Pete and Mark.

"Why don't we take a moment to think about what SK1854 might mean and how it could be a clue to the mystery prize?" said Mark. "Maybe we could all go for a coffee at the Whitworth Centre, sit down and have a brainstorm together?"

Rosie and Frank thought that was a good idea and a few minutes later all seven of them were huddled around a small table in the Terrace Café.

Meanwhile, Louise, Wendy and Ben decided to do the same thing and were having a brainstorming session of their own in the bar at Striding Hall.

"Obviously, SK are the initials of Simon Knight, an ancestor of our James and Simon Knight," said Mark. "1854 must be the year the house was built. The clue might have changed from WTP to SK1854 but the problem remains the same. We have to work out if SK1854 means anything in the modern world, or if the answer is based on what it meant originally."

"Jack, can you ask one of the staff members what the wi-fi code is?" said Pete.

With the code tapped into the iPad, Jack immediately started looking for anything he could unearth about SK1854 or Simon Knight. But the only thing he could find was the same SAS flight that Ben had already discovered. There were quite a few Simon Knights listed, including a plastic surgeon, as well as their very own Simon Knight LLB, partner in the firm of Knight and Son, solicitors.

"Perhaps the clue is a reference to our Simon Knight," said Rosie. "We need to speak to him."

"That will be difficult," replied Mark. "He and Katie have taken Noel and Josh cycling on the Tissington Trail this afternoon. They could be absolutely anywhere and we don't have his mobile number."

"Perhaps we could phone his office and get it," said Rosie. "You could spin them a yarn about needing to speak to Noel and Josh."

"Hang on," replied Mark. "Noel's got a mobile. I could phone him and ask to speak to Simon."

Mark pulled out his own mobile and rang Noel. A few seconds later, he was swearing at his phone, which did no good whatsoever, but at least it made him feel better.

"Bloody hell," he said. "If I've told that kid once I've told him a thousand times not to switch his phone off."

"Never mind," said Pete. "We'll just have to revert to Rosie's plan."

"There's no need for that," said Frank. "I think I've solved it."

The rest of them had been so intensely involved in the discussion, they hadn't realised that Frank had gotten up from the table. He had wandered over to a framed Ordnance Survey map that was hanging on the wall and was staring at it intently.

"I think SK1854 is a map reference," he said.

"Why do you say that?" asked Mark.

"Because it's the map reference for Parwich," Frank replied.

Chapter 22

Wednesday, September 4th, 2019

"How can that be?" asked Pete. "How can the inscription on our great-grandfather's house lead us to the village where our other great-grandfather lived? The two families wouldn't even have met until our grandfather and grandmother got married and that was in 1938. That plaque must have been made 84 years before that."

"It doesn't make any sense at all," replied Mark. "However, I reckon that Frank is right. Whatever we are looking for, is somewhere in that village."

After a brief discussion, they all set off on the fifteen-minute journey to Parwich. None of them had any idea what they were looking for, but Rosie had come up with the best idea how they might find out.

"Whenever you want to know what's going on in a village, the best place to ask is in the village pub," she said. "Even if the landlord doesn't know, chances are that one of the locals will."

They agreed to go straight to the Sycamore Inn and ask Alan, the landlord, if he knew James Knight. If he said yes, they planned to tell him their story and ask if he had any idea what they were looking for. Even if he said no, they were still going to do the same, as at this stage they didn't have a plan B.

Mark phoned Louise from the car to tell her what Frank had suggested.

"It makes sense if it's something in Parwich," she said. "But then again, I haven't a clue how this whole mystery fits together. Why don't you stay on the line whilst I ask Ben to look up SK1854 Derbyshire on Google Images?"

A few minutes later she read the results out to him. In total, there were twelve things listed:

The old Post Office in Parwich
The parish boundary between Tissington and Parwich
Parwich village taken at distance
A minor road near Middlemoor farm
A slurry store
A ruined barn above Parwich
Dam Lane entering Parwich
A corner of Parwich
The Royal British Legion clubhouse and bar
A footpath in Parwich
The Sycamore Inn
St Peter's church graveyard

"I don't know if that helps us," said Mark. "Our prize can't be the church. It can't be the pub for that matter, being as though it's owned by Robinsons Brewery. It must be something else. Hopefully, it isn't the slurry store."

"It could be absolutely anything in the village," said Louise. "It doesn't necessarily have to be on Google Images. I presume that whatever the prize is, it has to be quite valuable."

"I reckon it's another property," said Mark.

"Hey, you don't think that Parwich is an estate village like Beeley?" asked Louise. "Perhaps our prize is the entire village."

"I doubt it," said Mark. "If that were the prize, then the trust fund would be worth far more than five million pounds."

As soon as Pete and Mark arrived in Parwich, Louise wished them luck and ended the call. Pete headed straight for the Sycamore Inn. Frank wasn't far behind and a few seconds later the Jag pulled up alongside Pete's BMW in the pub's car park. Theirs were the only cars in the car park, and it didn't take a genius to work out that the pub was closed.

"Bugger, bugger, bugger," said Pete. "What time does it reopen?"

The sign on the door told them that the pub opened again at 6 pm, which was no good as that was when they had to be back at Striding Hall. Mark looked at his watch, which said 4.40.

"Right, if we allow half an hour for the journey back to Striding Hall, that leaves us fifty minutes to find whatever it is we are looking for," he announced.

"It doesn't help that we don't know what it is though," said Rosie.

"Well, we can't help that," Mark replied. "Can anybody come up with any idea what we could do?"

"Yes, let's go around the back and see if they're in," said Rosie. "They will almost certainly live above the pub."

She set off to see if she could find the entrance to their private quarters. A minute or so later she was back.

"They don't appear to be at home," she announced after having knocked on all the pub's doors.

They were just beginning to give up hope when another Jag pulled into the car park. They recognised Jenny and presumed that the driver was Alan, her husband. Rosie immediately went over to grab them as they got out of the car.

"Sorry for calling whilst the pub is closed," she said. "But we urgently need to speak to you."

"That's absolutely fine," said Jenny. "Alan and I just popped into Ashbourne to do the banking and some shopping. What can I help you with?"

While they were talking, the others had walked over to join them.

"The reason we are here is because we are looking for something," Mark told them, "and we believe it's here in Parwich."

"Tell us what it is, and we'll see if we can help you," said Alan.

"That's just it. We don't know what it is that we are looking for."

"Only it must be quite valuable," added Rosie.

"Can you tell us if you know a man called James Knight?" asked Mark.

"I certainly do," replied Alan. "I had a meeting with him only yesterday."

"But I thought you were in a rent review?" said Rosie.

"So I was. James Knight is the person I was having the rent review with. He's our landlord's solicitor. Whilst I was with him, he also briefed me that the freehold of the pub was about to change hands."

"But hang on," said Mark, "I thought this was a Robinsons pub."

"Well, it was," said Alan. "But four years ago, they put the freehold up for sale. Jenny and I would have loved to have bought the freehold but they were asking silly money for it. Anyway, it was bought as an investment by a trust fund, which James Knight manages. It's worked out really well for us as we are paying the same rent as we did when Robinsons owned the pub. But since we are now free of the tie, we are paying far less for our beer, even though we stayed with Robinsons because the locals like it."

Mark had stopped listening to what Alan was saying once he'd mentioned the pub had been purchased by a trust fund. But then he composed himself and asked Alan a question.

"You said that James told you in the meeting yesterday that the pub had changed ownership. Do you mind if I ask you who the new owners are?"

"I don't mind at all," replied Alan. "It's all of you guys. You're the new owners."

Chapter 23

Wednesday, September 4th, 2019

"James told me he expected you to come back today," Alan informed them. "This would mean that it was time to transfer ownership of the pub from the trust fund to the family. And here you all are, just like he said you would be."

"But you were out when we got here," said Pete. "Shouldn't you have stayed here until we arrived?"

"We had to go into Ashbourne at some point today," said Alan, "and James didn't tell us what time you'd get here. The only thing he told us was that if we did go out, we must be back by 5 o'clock, as that would give you enough time to find out about the pub and return to your hotel. We had to be back by five anyway as we've got to have our evening meal before opening up again at six. And whilst we are on that subject, I have to apologise to you as we've got to do precisely that."

After saying their goodbyes, Alan and Jenny disappeared inside.

"I think I'd better phone the others to give them the good news," said Mark as he dialled Louise's number. She answered immediately. It was obvious that she'd been waiting for the phone to ring.

"You'd better put me on speakerphone so that the others can hear the good news," said Mark.

Louise did as Mark instructed.

"You've solved the puzzle, then?" she said.

"We have," he replied, "and we are now the proud owners of a quarter of the Sycamore Inn in Parwich."

"But I thought it was a Robinsons pub," said Louise.

"It was until four years ago, when it was bought by our trust fund."

"So how did you solve it then?"

"It was very easy in the end. We knew that the prize was somewhere in Parwich and Rosie suggested that we ask Alan and Jenny at the pub if they could help us discover what it was. In the end, they were able to do far more than that. They confirmed that the pub is owned by the trust fund and that James had already told them that it's about to be transferred to us."

"Well, we could do far worse," said Louise. "It's a fine pub in a wonderful village."

"It is," replied Mark. "So put the champagne on ice and we should be back with you shortly."

Pete was a little less keen on the idea of owning a pub. He'd come to Striding Hall hoping to go away with a load of cash. Instead, he'd ended up with a former council house, a quarter share in a pub and a shedload of new relatives.

"Well, I think it's cool that we own a pub," announced Jack once the phone call was over. "We'll be able to get groceries and free drinks whenever we want them. Don't forget it's a shop as well as a pub."

"I don't think you understand," replied Pete. "We own the building not the business. That's still owned by Alan and Jenny. We are their landlords, just like we're the landlords of the fat bird with the big gob and huge arse, the one your mother and I met earlier."

"The only difference is that she is a tenant whereas Alan and Jenny are lease holders," said Rosie. "That means they have security of tenure and a fully maintaining and repairing lease."

There was a blank expression on the faces of some of the others. She explained what she meant.

"In other words, we can't throw them out unless they breach the terms of their agreement and they have the right to sell the lease at any time. It also means that they are responsible for any repairs that need to be done to the building. So if there is a tile missing from the roof, that's their responsibility not ours."

Everybody seemed satisfied with Rosie's explanation, and they continued to speculate about their latest prize.

"I wonder what rent they are paying for the pub?" said Pete who'd realised that he would receive a quarter of the rental income each month.

"We can always ask James," replied Mark.

"We also need to ask him how long the lease is for," added Pete. "We won't be able to sell the pub with vacant possession until it's expired."

"Not with security of tenure, we won't," said Rosie. "When the lease expires, we'll have to offer them another one."

"In which case, we'll have to sell it as an investment, with Alan and Jenny as sitting tenants," Pete continued. "Mind you, knowing James, he will almost certainly have put the same covenant on the pub as is on our houses. In which case, I doubt if we'll be able to sell it for the next twenty years."

"This discussion is all very well and good," said Mark. "But being as it's now a quarter past five I think we need to get back to Striding Hall and continue it there."

"That's a good point, well made," said Pete, who had no desire to lose his share of the prize by being late.

Thirty minutes later, Striding Hall appeared in the distance, looking truly spectacular in the early evening sun, its reflection shimmering in the lake. Pete and Frank pulled into the car park and everyone got out. However, instead of going through reception this time, they all went straight to the terrace in front of the bar, where Louise, Ben and Wendy had already opened the champagne.

"Here's to our family," said Pete after he had poured a glass for himself. "May our tenants never cause us problems, especially those of them with fat arses."

Everybody raised their glasses and joined in the toast.

"I hope there's some of that for us?" came a man's voice approaching them through the French doors.

It was James and he was accompanied by Simon, Katie, Noel and Josh.

"After all, we're part of the family as well, as I'm sure you know by now," he continued.

"We do, and it goes a long way towards explaining what's been going on around here," added Pete as he filled three more glasses.

Louise hugged Noel and Josh and asked if they had had a good time.

"I think you've got a couple of budding Rory McIlroys here," said Katie. "Are you sure they haven't played golf before?"

"And the bike ride was fantastic," added Josh. "I got to wear a crash helmet and I didn't fall off once."

"I already know you've succeeded in solving the day's challenge," James explained. "Alan phoned me a few minutes ago to inform me. So well done everyone and charge your glasses. It's about time I made a toast."

James, Simon and Katie each grabbed a glass and Pete poured some more champagne. Once he'd done that, he summoned one of the waiters.

"Two more bottles of Laurent Perrier Pink, please," he said.

"To all my relatives," said James holding up his glass. "May we always stay in touch with each other and, by that I mean not just with a card at Christmas."

Once more, the champagne was downed and there were shouts of "hear! hear!" Afterwards, the conversation was as free flowing as the champagne. Everybody had loads of unanswered questions and realised this might be their last opportunity to get some answers.

"So James," said Rosie, "did you often see our father when he was a boy?"

"Fairly often," he replied. "I remember him as a good-looking young man who used to drop in to see my mother and father and me when he was driving around the Peak District in his Land Rover."

"Can you tell us if the Sycamore Inn has the same covenant as our houses on the St Augustines estate?" asked Mark.

"Yes, it does, I'm afraid. So you won't be able to sell it for twenty years. But I wouldn't let that concern you. Alan and Jenny are paying £24,000 in rent per annum, which means that each of you will receive £1,500 per quarter."

"What I don't understand," said Pete, "is why the inscription on the plaque above the door of James's house is the map reference for the Sycamore Inn in Parwich? I mean, I presume that SK are the initials of one of your ancestors."

"One of our ancestors," James corrected him.

"And that the house was built in 1854," Pete continued. "But surely it's too much of a coincidence that the initials of the person who built it and the year in which it was built should turn out to be the map reference of the pub where our grandfather was born."

"Let me explain," said James. "Firstly, as you now know, it has been tradition on my side of the family that the first-born sons all have the same names, only reversed. The son of James Simon is Simon James and vice versa. Consequently, it should come as no surprise to discover that my middle name is Simon and Simon's middle name is James."

"You don't say," added Pete sarcastically.

"It has also been the tradition that the first-born son inherits the house," James continued. "In days gone by, when families were a lot larger than they are now, this was a way of ensuring that a house stayed in the family rather than being sold off with the money split between all the beneficiaries. It must have caused a lot of problems for the other children, who inherited nothing at all. But that was the way it was. It was exactly the same problem that the Dukes of Devonshire had, albeit on a much larger scale. Fortunately, it is a problem that I won't have since Simon is an only child."

"Thanks, Dad," said Simon as he held up his glass in salute.

"You should be aware by now that your grandmother, my aunt, was one such sibling," James continued. "That was why she ended up inheriting nothing, even though she was four years older than my father. With regards to the house, I had that plaque made in 1997 after I'd devised the challenges. I put it above the door this morning and it's only stuck there with Blu-Tack."

"Typical," added Pete.

"The house was actually built in 1847 by my four times great-grandfather whose first name was James not Simon. I intend giving the plaque to Alan and Jenny now that the challenges are over."

"But why go to all the trouble of having a false inscription made?" asked Mark.

"The original brief of the trust fund was just that you had to understand your family history," James replied. "It laid out that you needed to discover what your ancestors' values were, where they lived and worked, and what happened to them. It was my idea, after I'd taken over as trustee, to encapsulate all this into the three challenges. For the last challenge, I had to find some way to steer you towards the Sycamore Inn in Parwich. Its map reference is SK1854 and with our surname being Knight and half my ancestors being called Simon, the idea just came to me."

"So it was all a lie when you said you knew nothing about the terms of the trust fund," commented Pete.

"Oh, but that's not what I said. What I actually said was that I was limited by the terms of the trust fund what I could reveal to you. It was never my role to question the terms of the fund, only to implement them. There is a subtle difference."

There was no point in arguing with James. After all, he was a trained solicitor and could tie them all up in legal knots if he wanted to. Besides, there were still some unanswered questions to sort out.

"It's all very well and good for you to say you wanted us to know about our family," said Rosie, "and I'd be the first to admit I know a hell of a lot more about them now than I did before. But there is still an awful lot that we don't know. For example, why was the trust fund set up after our father died? Other things that do not make sense include the lottery tickets, the Maxell cassette, why all the pools money wasn't deposited in our father's account, why his body was flown back to

Chesterfield to be cremated and what happened to the money raised from the sale of our grandparents' house after they died. These are just some of the things we don't have answers to yet."

"I'm not the best person to answer these questions," said James. "But if you'd all like to turn around for a minute, I can introduce you to the man who will clear these things up for you once and for all."

With that, the entire group turned as one and saw a man in his seventies standing in the open French doors. The most obvious thing about him that they all noticed immediately was that he had the distinctive Bradbury nose. Everybody stared at him in silence until Ben hesitantly broke the silence.

"Dad," he said. "Is it you?"

Chapter 24

Wednesday, September 4th, 2019

"I'm not your father, Ben," the man replied. "He died in a car crash in Spain in 1984. I know this because I identified his body and I also arranged for him to be flown back to Chesterfield to be cremated here."

"So who are you?" asked Mark.

"Isn't it obvious?" the man replied. "I'm your uncle Tony, the person who established your trust fund. You thought the letters AS in the name AS Bradbury stood for Andrew Stephen, your father. But they didn't. They stood for Anthony Stuart. In other words, me."

"But we don't have an uncle," said Pete. "Dad was an only child."

"According to your mother, I suppose," replied Tony. "She told you that so that you wouldn't start looking for me. She was not good to your father. Don't misunderstand me, he was no saint either. But she was as much to blame for what happened as he was. She made me promise that I would never get in touch with you whilst she was still alive, and that is why I had waited until now."

"But that didn't apply to us," said Rosie. "Why didn't we know about you either?"

"That's slightly different," replied Tony. "I didn't really know you or your grandparents. In fact, the only time I'd met your grandparents was whilst I was out in Spain after the crash. It was not a pleasant encounter as they blamed my brother for the death of their daughter. Why would they mention me to you? After all, they wouldn't have had any reason to do so. In fact, I wouldn't be surprised if they eventually forgot about my existence."

"What I want to know, is where you got the money to put into our trust fund," snapped Pete.

"Can't you guess? It was some of the money we got from winning the football pools."

"But it was Dad who won the pools, not you," Pete replied.

Tony just smiled.

"Let me explain," he continued. "I think it's about time that I told you the whole story and, hopefully, that will answer all your questions."

Everyone went quiet. They were hanging onto Tony's every word as he began to tell them what had really happened.

"I was the oldest, a baby boomer born just after the end of the war. Andy was four years younger than me but despite the age difference, we were inseparable. He used to follow me everywhere and I took care of him making sure nobody ever bullied him at school."

"So our grandmother didn't wait until she was 33 before having her first child," said Mark. "She'd have been 29 when you were born."

"That's correct," Tony replied. "I was born in 1946 and your father was born in 1950. Back when we were young, it was all open fields at the top of St Augustines Road, and we used to play there all the time. We'd go fishing with nets and jam jars in the stream. We'd visit the annual fair that was held there each summer and we'd ride on the dodgems and the helter-skelter.

Beyond the fields was the golf course where Andy and I would volunteer to caddy for the golfers. In the autumn, we'd pick conkers from the horse chestnut trees and have conker fights. In December, we'd pick holly and go sledging when it snowed. They were happy carefree days full of fun and new discoveries. We'd often walk as far as Striding Hall where we'd throw stones into the lake and pick wild blackberries and damsons. It was a private house back then and we used to say that, one day, once we'd made our fortune, we'd buy it. We both really loved this house, which is why I placed the memorial seat here, looking out over the lake."

"That's another mystery solved then," exclaimed Louise.

Tony merely smiled. "For Christmas 1964, Dad bought us a fifteen-year-old Land Rover. It cost him £25 and was in a right state. It didn't have an MOT, wouldn't start and it hadn't been driven for two years. I was eighteen at the time and had already passed my test. Your dad was fourteen and, although he was too young to drive, he was a fantastic mechanic. He took after our dad in that respect. Personally, I never liked tinkering around with cars. I much preferred working with wood and, by the age of eighteen, I was apprenticed to a French polisher."

Tony was going all misty-eyed as he recalled events from 55 years ago.

"Andy and I loved that Land Rover," he continued. "Your dad stripped the engine, replaced the broken parts with ones we bought for next to nothing from a salvage yard and got it through its MOT. Then it was over to me, as I was the one who could drive it. We used to put ten bobs' worth of two star in it and head off into the Peak District."

"Fifty pence worth of petrol wouldn't get you very far today," said Mark.

But Tony was on a roll and kept talking.

"Of course, even though your dad wasn't allowed to drive on the road, there was nothing to stop him from doing so off-road. And that is exactly what he used to do. We also regularly visited some of the Derbyshire pubs. The Devonshire Arms in Sheldon was one of our favourites as it was one of the few where they would serve Andy, despite him being underage."

"Which explains why the Devonshire Arms in Sheldon featured in the second challenge," muttered Pete.

"Back in those days, we'd drive all over Derbyshire looking for pubs and girls. It was the girls who eventually came between us. As the eldest, I was the first to get a girlfriend when I fell in love with Lynne, a girl who lived just down the road from where we were. We married when we were both 23. Andy was nineteen by then and he was the best man at our wedding. I'd bought a Ford Anglia the previous year. So I let Tony keep the Land Rover. After all, it would have been scrapped years before if it hadn't been for him. Later, we found out that Lynne couldn't have children, which was devastating news for both of us. She died of breast cancer in 1985."

As he said it, a tear appeared in the corner of one of Tony's eyes. He wiped it away with his hanky.

"She was only 39, my first and last girlfriend and the love of my life. Andy, however, had numerous girlfriends and he met your mother whilst on holiday in Newquay when he was 25. He got her pregnant and felt obliged to marry her. As a result, he was trapped."

"So they didn't fall instantly in love then?" said Pete. "Dad put her up the duff, instead."

"If you want to put it that way, then yes," replied Tony. "Your dad never really settled into married life. Although what had happened to him did bring the two of us closer together once more. He and your mum were given a council house just around the corner from the one we lived in, on the same estate where we had been born. We used to meet up every Saturday and go to the match and for a drink in the Walton Hotel. Our good friend Dave Richardson always came with us."

"Ah, Dad's next-door neighbour," commented Pete, "who must have known all about you. So why didn't he say anything when I called on him?"

"That was my fault, I'm afraid. I warned Dave that you would probably be coming around to see him and would be asking questions about Andy. I asked him not to mention me to you. Sorry about that little deception. Anyway, your dad was never happy. He thought there must be more to life than working in a garage and living on a council estate. Your mother didn't help the situation. She knew Lynne was desperate to have children and was only too pleased when she offered to look after the two of you. It meant she could have a Saturday job in Boots. However, she got jealous of the bond Lynne was building with you two. She even threatened to replace her with a child minder. It was only her refusal to pay someone that prevented her from doing it. She was jealous of the amount of money the two of us had. I was making a good living as a French polisher. Also, with both of us in full-time employment and having no kids, we were fairly well off. That said, we would willingly have swapped all that to have had a child of our own. But your mum wouldn't accept that and told Lynne she didn't believe she couldn't have children. She said we had chosen not to have any, as we were a selfish couple who just wanted to spend our money on ourselves. It was very hurtful and couldn't have been further from the truth."

"That doesn't sound like the mum I knew," said Mark. "She didn't have a malicious bone in her body."

"Your mother must have changed after 1979," said Tony. "I wouldn't know. I never saw her again after she moved back to Gloucestershire. The Sharon I knew back in the 1970s was a manipulative woman, with very little money and living in a council house. She went from that to being a middle-class doctor's wife in the Cotswolds. So obviously something changed."

"I still don't believe it though."

"Mark, I'm not trying to change your opinion of your mother. It's just that the woman I knew was totally different to the one you remember. Anyway, I never let the things your mother said about Lynne ruin the relationship between Andy and me. In fact, Andy was more upset about it than I was, saying that he wished he'd never let her trap him into marrying her. Anyway, it was around this time that he started seeing Joanne. It was pretty obvious what he was doing. I used to joke about it although I never pulled him up over the affair. After all, if their marriage had been more loving, the relationship with Joanne might never have started."

"Or Dad might just have been a shagoholic," said Pete.

"Trust me, he wasn't," replied Tony. "Anyway, on May 19th, 1979, our whole world was turned upside down. That was the day your dad and I won the pools."

"You won it jointly then?" asked Mark.

"That's correct," Tony continued. "The two of us had been doing it together for years. It started when we didn't have much cash and, in the end, it just became a habit. One week I'd complete the coupon. The other week would be your dad's turn. That particular week, I had completed it and, on the way to the match that Saturday, I gave your dad a list of the games I'd chosen. We won a truly vast amount of money, over a million pounds, £1,002,172.48 to be precise. We were the first people ever to win more than a million pounds on the pools."

"I didn't know that," said Mark.

"There's no reason why you should," replied Tony. "Not only were we the first, but it was also on the last Saturday of the football season that we won the jackpot. Those two facts were of massive significance to the pools company, as they were due to switch over to the Australian league the following Saturday. This was something that was necessary every summer for the company to survive financially. But most English people knew absolutely nothing about Australian football teams and the majority of punters stopped filling in their coupons during the summer months, resulting in a big fall in revenue for the pools company. Consequently, there couldn't be better news for them than a family becoming the first ever pools millionaires. The publicity it generated was bound to boost their sales substantially throughout the lean summer months. There was one minor problem though. I'd put a cross in the box that said 'no publicity'."

"So how come everyone knows about Dad, but no one knows about you?" asked Pete.

"Let me explain," he replied. "Over the next few days, your dad and I came under increasing pressure to forgo our right to anonymity. The pools company even offered us an extra £50,000 each if we allowed them to publicise who we were. I refused point blank. After all, I valued my privacy. I didn't want all the begging letters and my friends turning their backs on me just because I now had a bit of money. No, as far as I was concerned, they could stick their £50,000 up their corporate arses. I was not going to change my mind. Your dad, however, was minded to take the cash. Looking back on it now, it was probably because he'd already decided to go to Spain and just thought why not? I mean, he was planning on leaving his friends behind anyway. He wouldn't be getting any begging letters where he was going, especially since nobody would know where he was living."

"Sorry," said Pete. "I still don't see how the pools company could release Dad's name, but not yours."

"The fact that he had accepted and I hadn't posed a real problem for the pools company. That is why all the headlines referred to the winners being the Bradbury family rather than Andy Bradbury. Now, anybody reading the headlines would assume that they were referring to Andy and Sharon rather than Andy and me. That was one of the reasons why your mum hated me. The other was because I'd told her I'd known about his affair with Joanne when she'd asked me. When she wanted to know why I hadn't told her about it earlier, I told her straight. I wasn't the type of person who would rat on his brother. And even if I was, she would have been the last person I'd tell, seeing as though she'd been so rotten to Lynne. I later regretted the harsh words I'd spoken to her. So I went around to Sharon's house and offered her £20,000 from my share of the pools win, but she threw it back in my face."

"Now, that does sound like Mum," added Mark.

"Shortly afterwards, your mother packed up and left Chesterfield," Tony continued. "But not before she'd made me promise not to get in touch with either her or her children ever again. She told me that if I did, she'd tell the press I'd shared the pools prize with Andy and my anonymity would be blown wide open. Andy and I differed more than I'd ever thought.

We'd shared so much, been through so much together and yet, in many ways, we were complete opposites. Andy wasn't happy with his lot. He wanted more excitement and glamour in his life. That was why he ran away to Spain with Joanne. However, I valued my family and my friends. Perhaps it was the fact that Lynne and I couldn't have children that made me appreciate those things more than Andy. But I'd like to think it was just because it's the way I am. I like where I live. It was where I was brought up. It is where I belong. I like my job. I like going to the football on a Saturday and going for a pint in my local. I could never give up those things."

"Each to his own," muttered Pete.

"For me, winning the pools was never going to mean I'd buy a Porsche. In fact, I bought a Lada Niva instead. They used to call it the Russian Range Rover, although you could buy four of them for the same price as a Range Rover. It was a great car and since it was really cheap, nobody suspected how much money I had. Even these days, my car is a Suzuki Swift for exactly the same reason. Winning the pools for me meant I'd have financial security for the rest of my life. What it didn't mean, was that I was going to trade in my pint of bitter for a glass of champagne or my fish and chips for lobster thermidor. However, I did buy my council house in 1981. Mrs Thatcher had brought in the right-to-buy scheme by then. I also bought Mum and Dad's house for them at the same time. Eventually, I inherited it when they died. That was when I transferred it to the trust fund."

"That explains how their house in St Augustines Road ended up in the trust fund," said Mark.

"Our parents knew the truth about the win of course, as did my cousin Simon, James's father. I told no one else, not even

Dave. He still doesn't know that I shared the prize with Andy. Mum, Dad and Simon knew that I didn't want my pools win publicised, and I knew I could trust them to keep quiet about it. Although my secret was safe, absolutely everybody knew what Andy had done. Our parents were ashamed of him and the fact that he'd abandoned their two grandchildren. They were really upset that they no longer had access to you two, when previously they'd seen you most days of the week."

"It sounds like there was a side to Mum that I never knew," said Mark with a tinge of sadness in his voice. "She told us that they both died shortly after Dad."

"Well, as you now know, your grandfather lived until 1983 and your grandmother didn't die until 1989. By which time, you'd have been twelve and Pete would have been fourteen."

"So why didn't they ever come to see us?"

"Because your mother wouldn't let them. But it was worse than that. In 1979, your mother sent back all the Christmas presents your grandparents had bought for you. I'd never before seen my dad this angry. He was a placid man. But when your mother did that, he flew into a rage. I found him later sobbing like a baby in my mother's arms. Dad never really recovered from the humiliation of what your father had done. He was a broken man and that was probably what killed him four years later. Andy didn't even come to the funeral, although I'd like to think it was just in case he was arrested for stealing from your mother."

Tony took a deep breath before continuing his explanation.

"Whilst all this was going on, I'd taken an interest in different ways to invest the money I'd won. Even though I have to say it myself, I was rather successful. I never became a full-time investor, however. I loved my French polishing business too much. Investing was never more than a hobby for me, albeit a highly lucrative one."

"Well, you don't appear to have done too badly out of your hobby," added Wendy.

"What you've got to remember is that the early 1980s were boom time in the City thanks to Mrs Thatcher's policies. It was also a good time to invest in property. House prices seemed to be rising on a daily basis and, as a result, it was extremely easy to make money back then. I'd never taken an interest in share portfolios or property prices before, mainly because I didn't have enough money to worry about things like that. But now I was hooked, and the value of my assets kept on rising rapidly. I often thought back on our childhood and the wonderful times we had here in the garden of Striding Hall. So in January 1984, I bought the hall for £66,000 and moved your grandfather's memorial seat here from the crematorium. I wanted it to be in one of my favourite spots, overlooking the lake. It was somewhere I could sit during the summer months and remember all the good times from my childhood. Later that same year, Andy died and I had a second plaque made for the seat. Its location was now even more poignant as it looked out over the lake where we played when we were boys."

"That explains the location of the seat and the two plaques, then," said Mark.

"Yes, that was down to me," added Tony. "You can hardly believe that I only paid £66,000 for this place, can you? It must be worth at least thirty times that amount now. But in the early 1980s, nobody wanted to buy grand country houses. They were expensive to maintain, you see. Up and down the country many of these houses were being demolished. For me, however, it was the fulfilment of a dream that your dad and I had when we were children. But I had no desire to live here. I was happy in my house on St Augustines Drive. After all, what would I do with all these bedrooms? Besides which, it was too far away from a decent pub."

"It's a pity more people don't think like you," muttered Frank.

"I had a different vision for Striding Hall," Tony continued. "I wanted to turn it into a country house hotel and that was precisely what I did. The building was in a right state, and it ended up costing me three times more to convert it than it cost to buy. But it was still a good investment. The hotel made money from the day it opened. It's in an ideal position, you see. It's very close to Chesterfield and yet, it feels as if it's in the middle of the Peak District."

"You certainly did a good job," said Mark. "This place is a credit to you."

"Thank you very much," replied Tony. "Of course, whilst I was investing my money, your father was squandering his fortune on flashy cars and fancy clothes. I knew it wouldn't last forever, but I was shocked when I heard he'd died. I'd never been to see him in Spain when he was alive. But I flew out immediately upon hearing of his death. I had to identify his body for a start, which was one of the saddest things I'd ever had to do. Joanne's parents were there as well to identify the body of their daughter, arrange her funeral, and to look after Rosie and Ben. If things had been different, Lynne and I would have offered to take the two of you. But given the circumstances of your mother's death, I knew perfectly well that your grandparents would never even entertain the idea. In addition, Lynne had already been diagnosed with breast cancer by then and was undergoing chemotherapy, which was why she wasn't with me. I decided that the best course of action would be to employ a Spanish lawyer in order to protect the family money. It was so there would be a little left over for all of you. However, as you now know, the few thousand pounds that were left all went to your mother."

"She never told us about that," added Mark.

"That doesn't surprise me," Tony replied. "Of course, it was me who brought your father's body back to Chesterfield to have him cremated. I also set up the trust fund for you. Initially, I started it with £50,000. But when it became clear that most of your father's estate would be swallowed up by damages and your mum would inherit the rest, I topped it up and have been doing so ever since."

"Which is something we are all very grateful for," said Rosie.

She looked around and saw that even Pete was nodding in agreement.

"The following year, Lynne died, and I have another seat in my back garden dedicated to her. It's similar to the one by the lake and is another place where I can sit on sunny days and remember the happy times. Only with that seat, it's the happy times that Lynne and I had together."

Tony was getting emotional again and his voice was starting to waver. He broke off from the story for a couple of seconds to compose himself before he continued.

"When Simon died in 2013, it left James and his son as the only relatives I had regular contact with. I knew about my cousin Bert in Parwich, but we had never been close. I haven't seen him since we were boys and he's probably forgotten I exist. In many ways, his story is similar to yours, a father who died young and whose son lost touch with his father's family. That was why I wanted you to discover your family history. I discussed it with James, and he came up with the idea of the challenges shortly after he'd taken over control of the trust fund in 1997. I liked his idea because the challenges made you find out things for yourselves, rather than just being told about them. As a result, you are far more likely to remember them. However, I was concerned what you might think if you failed the first challenge, which is why I recorded the message that was played to you."

"And if you didn't record the message until 1997, it explains how you were able to record it on a Maxell Metal Vertex cassette," said Frank.

"It also explains why the message was recorded without video," added Pete. "We'd have seen straight away that it wasn't Dad who was speaking if you had."

"Precisely," replied Tony. "As well as suggesting the challenges, James also suggested the prizes and I take my hat off to him. He got them spot on. The first one, the one you didn't win, was supposed to make you think about what you would do if you won a large amount of money. By the time James was drawing up these challenges, the National Lottery had largely taken over from the football pools. With half a million pounds worth of lottery tickets, it would have been inevitable that some of them would have been winning tickets. One of them could well have been a major prize, perhaps even the jackpot. The prize for this challenge was designed to make you think about what you would do if you won a large amount of money. Would you spend the money rashly, would you give some to charity, something like Cats Protection, for example? Would you buy a posh house or a flashy car? Would you give up work? Or would you just invest the money and carry on as normal?"

"We'll never know now," said Pete, "unless we ask the cats."

"Very funny, Pete," said Tony. "The second prize, the houses on the St Augustines estate, was designed to tie you to the place where your father and I were both born. Pete and Mark were born here as well, and it was also the place where your grandparents lived. You could decide to live here yourselves. After all, there are far worse places you could choose to settle."

"I doubt it," muttered Pete.

"Alternatively, you could rent the houses out. In which case, you will still need to visit occasionally in order to keep an eye on your assets."

"I think you can pay people to do that sort of thing nowadays," said Pete.

Tony ignored Pete's interruption.

"The third prize, the pub in Parwich, was meant to keep you together as a family. After all, you each own a quarter of the freehold, which you can't sell for the next twenty years. You'll need to visit it regularly to make sure the terms of the lease are being adhered to. You'll need to get together every five years with Alan and Jenny to carry out rent reviews. If they ever want to sell their lease, the four of you will need to approve the people they are selling it to. If they want to build an extension, you will have to approve their plans."

"We get the picture," said Pete.

He was starting to get dirty looks from the others by this stage. They were really interested and just wanted to hear Tony's story.

"There was another reason for choosing the pub in Parwich. It was the pub that was run by four generations of our family. It broke my grandparents' hearts when the family had to surrender the tenancy. After that, both of them started to go downhill rapidly. It was no surprise when my grandmother died less than a year after moving to Chesterfield. With her death, Granddad had nothing left to live for and he died four days later. I was only eight when my grandparents died, and I remember all the stories my dad used to tell me about them. Like, for example, how Granddad would sometimes play the piano in the bar. How he'd always be smartly dressed wearing a waistcoat and a bow tie, even after he'd retired. How my grandmother would always have a cauldron of soup on the boil and plenty of homemade cobs for sale. I still put flowers on their graves once a year close to the anniversary of their deaths. I like to think they'd both be looking down, smiling because the family now owns the pub they once ran."

"And that clears up the mystery of who put flowers on the grave in Boythorpe Cemetery," said Jack.

"I'd made a promise to Sharon, and I meant to keep it. I was worried about what would happen if I died before her. So I made James and Simon promise that they would carry out my bequest if that were to happen. As you know, it never came to that as she died earlier this year leaving me free to get James to contact you and arrange all of this."

Tony fell quiet. Then he looked up and smiled while taking in the faces of all his relatives.

"That's about all I've got to tell you. I hope you understand why it had to be this way. Now, do any of you have any questions?"

"Yes," said Pete. "If we'd failed all three challenges, would you really have let us inherit nothing at all?"

"That's a good question, Pete, and I hope you believe me when I say that I wouldn't have done that. You must realise by now that my main motivation for doing these challenges was to get you to understand your family history and to meet and stay in touch with the rest of the family. Therefore, it was always my intention to give you the houses and the pub, even if you had failed all three challenges."

"That's easy to say now, being as though we achieved those two tasks," added Pete.

"Yes, but if you don't believe me, ask James. I instructed him to transfer the deeds of the properties over to you three weeks ago."

"That's correct," added James. "And I've already informed the Land Registry."

"So what about the lottery tickets?" asked Rosie.

"That's slightly different, I'm afraid. I love cats, as did Lynne. They've always been a part of my life and I already give an amount to Cats Protection each month. I've got two at the moment called Rhubarb and Custard, and they both came from Cats Protection. The money from the first challenge is really going to them. I'd still have given them a donation even if you'd achieved the task."

"Lucky old cats," added Pete.

That was the last of the questions, and the room went quiet as they all took in what Tony had just told them. Pete and Mark had arrived at Striding Hall as part of a family of eight. They were leaving with a family of nineteen, possibly even more if Bert's three daughters had husbands and children. That was something they promised to discover as soon as possible.

That evening they all sat down for a final meal together. This time, Tony joined them and so the family was more or less complete. Not only that, but the Bradburys now knew about all the things that mattered to their family.

They laughed and joked about everything they had been through and all the things they had discovered over the past six days. Everybody had a really enjoyable evening, with plenty of good food, good wine and good company.

The next morning as they were all preparing to leave, they pledged to stay in touch with each other.

"Not that we have much choice in the matter as our uncle stated yesterday," said Pete. "By the way, I wondered if any of us have reconsidered moving here? I can't see myself doing it. I'll continue to rent the house out. How about you guys?"

"Nothing has changed for Frank and me," said Rosie. "We still plan to continue renting out our house, being as though we've got the pub in Weston to run."

"Me too," said Ben. "I can't see myself moving to Chesterfield, even if I fail to get the part in *EastEnders*, which I won't."

"It's highly unlikely that Louise and I will move here," added Mark. "There are just too many things to tie us to Reigate."

It was nearly time to leave. They all said goodbye to one another, exchanged hugs and kisses before they went on their separate ways. Mark and Louise were taking Ben home, of course.

It was only when Mark had been driving for half an hour, that a thought suddenly crossed his mind, which he shared with Louise and Ben.

"You know," he said. "The first prize was worth half a million pounds. The four houses were probably worth £125,000 each, making another half million. If we say the freehold of the pub was also worth half a million, that makes the total one and a half million pounds. So what happened to the other three and a half million?"

Chapter 25

During the years that followed

Ben was the first to move to Chesterfield. Phil storming out and abandoning him at Striding Hall had been a sign that their relationship was at an end. Since Phil owned the flat in Brighton, this left Ben with nowhere to live. After he failed to get the part in *EastEnders*, it seemed like the logical thing to do.

He really had nothing to lose. With no proper job, no accommodation in Brighton and a house he owned outright in Chesterfield, it was a no-brainer. He gave notice to his tenant and, by the beginning of the following year, he'd moved into his house in St Augustines Road.

He didn't know what he was going to do for work. There wasn't much call for failed actors or antique shop managers in Chesterfield. He knew that he needed to get his life together and was just deciding what to do about it when James phoned him and offered him a job. They'd got more business than he and Simon could handle and needed somebody they could trust to join the firm. Who better than another member of the family?

Ben started as a clerk. But James encouraged him to enrol in a part-time law degree at the Open University, where he qualified as a solicitor five years later. A year after that, he became a partner in the business. The office in Matlock wasn't too far from his house in Chesterfield and he bought himself a

Tesla for the commute. It was a far flashier car than he really wanted. In fact, he was considering getting a Renault Clio but James dragged him to a proceeds of crime auction and insisted he buy something more in keeping with the image of the partnership.

Things were a lot slower on the romantic front for Ben in Chesterfield than it had been in Brighton. But eventually, he met Richard, a plumber who'd come to service his central heating boiler and ended up servicing him as well.

"It came as a complete surprise," said Ben at the time. "I never realised Richard came as part of my maintenance contract with British Gas, otherwise I'd have taken out a policy with them years ago."

They started going out and it wasn't long before Ben's garage was full of copper pipes, which told everyone that they were now a couple and were living together. They eventually got married, much to Rosie's surprise, who had long believed that her brother was a commitment phobe.

Pete was next, which was as big a surprise to him as it was to everybody else. The years following his return from Striding Hall were not good for him. First, he lost his seat on Stroud District Council to the Liberal Democrats. Or the wishy-washy *Guardian*-reading soap dodgers as Pete usually referred to them. Then he lost his job after a reorganisation at West Country Cider. He couldn't believe it. He always thought he was destined for the top. He'd given the company twenty-five years of constant sales growth. But that cut no ice with the new managing director, who told him the company wanted to move in a different direction.

"I know the direction you mean," he said as he stormed out of his boss's office, "fucking backwards."

Despite his outburst, they offered him a job as a key account manager but that was a demotion. It would have meant he'd have to give up his BMW for a Ford Focus and that was more than he could take. So he opted for redundancy instead.

He thought he'd get another job straightaway. But he was 47 by then and kept on losing out to younger candidates. Eventually, he realised that he was being rejected before he'd even had an interview. It was a depressing time for him as he moped about at home.

It was also a depressing time for Wendy, having Pete at home all the time, constantly getting under her feet. The strain got too much for her and that was the main reason behind them splitting up. This occurred just after Hannah had gone to university and Wendy had to face up to the fact that she and Pete were now classed as 'empty nesters'. She couldn't bear being cooped up in the house all day with only Pete for company. So she upped sticks and walked out, never to return. Eventually, they got divorced and she and Pete had to sell the house in Stroud. The divorce settlement wasn't helped by the fact that Pete owned a property in Chesterfield that he couldn't sell. In the end, Pete kept his house on St Augustines Road and his pension, whereas Wendy got the equity in the Stroud house once the mortgage had been paid off. She subsequently married a local farmer who used to supply the milk for her cheese and set up quite a reasonably sized cheese factory in one of his outbuildings.

With no job, no house and no family in Stroud anymore, Pete decided to move to Chesterfield. He had to give notice to his tenant first, who was so pissed off that she stopped paying her rent. Pete initially felt a little guilty about making her and Bruno homeless. But that stopped when he discovered that Bruno had been taken into care the previous year.

Tanya was rehoused in a one-bedroomed flat three months later, which allowed Pete to move in once the house had been fumigated and redecorated. Six months after that, Pete opened a delicatessen in the Market Hall. To show there are no hard feelings, he sells some of Wendy's single and double Gloucester cheese in his shop. He's very happy, working five days a week, nine till five, and enjoys being his own boss. He even likes living on St Augustines Road and really loves the fact that Ben is his next-door neighbour.

Remarkable as it may seem, Pete and Ben struck up quite a friendship. After all, other than Tony, Ben was the only person Pete knew in Chesterfield when he moved there. He even gets on well with Richard, despite always calling him Dick. Mind you, Pete is always careful to refer to him as Ben's partner rather than his bum chum.

You would never have believed Pete and Ben would become so close if you had seen them when they first met at Striding Hall. But people change and few changed more than Pete Bradbury, as exemplified when he agreed to be best man at Ben's wedding.

That said, a bit of the old Pete did reappear when he asked Ben whether he wanted him to be best man or to give him away. He claimed he wasn't certain who did what at a same-sex wedding and said he hoped for their sakes that it wasn't the same for the two of them on their wedding night.

Pete's best man's speech contained a few rude jokes. He had this to say about Richard.

"You know that Ben has always been looking for a Dick and now he's finally found one. Not only that, but I hear that he's got a massive plunger and Ben tells me it's absolutely amazing what he can do with a length of pipe."

It was a good speech, though, and was widely enjoyed by all the guests at the reception in Striding Hall. That was despite all the references to plumber's mates and servicing old boilers.

Eventually, Pete found love again in a relationship with Julie, the lady who lived in the house where he'd been born. She took some persuading to give up her house and move in with him. After all, she didn't want to give up her benefits. But he persuaded her, and now Pete has both her and her teenage daughter living under his roof. Sometimes they give him hell, but he is very happy with his new family on the whole.

Jack passed his A levels with good grades and got a place at Bristol University to study history. He graduated with a two-one and subsequently got a job as a graduate trainee with Thatcher's Cider in the sales department. This amazed and delighted his father in equal measure. Amazed, because Jack had never shown the slightest interest in either cider or a role in sales. Delighted, because Thatcher's were a major competitor of his old firm, and he was finally able to get his revenge on the very people who'd made him redundant. He passed on details of his old customers to his son, telling him what discounts they were on. He even phoned some of them up to make appointments for Jack.

Jack eventually married his boss's secretary and they moved into a lovely cottage in Chew Magna. They still live there and have twin daughters called Rosé and Katy. There was some question when they were born whether they were named after Jack's relatives or after Thatcher's cider brands. However, the fact that neither name ends in an ie, tells you that it was the latter rather than the former.

Hannah did even better in her A levels than Jack, getting three A stars and one A. She was accepted to study medicine at

Leicester University and, five years later, she found herself working as a ship's doctor on a cruise liner in the Mediterranean.

"All you'll be doing is handing out sea sickness pills and prescriptions for Viagra," said Pete when she phoned him up to tell him the news. "And I hope you realise that the only people who go on cruises are newly-weds and nearly deads."

Hannah just bit her lip. She knew better than anyone that it wasn't a good idea to disagree with her father.

Rosie and Frank continued to run Scallys in Weston, but they hankered after a quieter life. So they contacted Alan at the Sycamore Inn and asked if he and Jenny would give them first refusal if they ever wanted to sell the lease. It was another four years before they finally phoned them. By then, Alan and Jenny had grown tired of the long hours and endless complaints about the roast beef on TripAdvisor. It was always either too rare or too well done. Sometimes, the reviews were even on the same day about the same joint of beef. They had decided to sell up and buy a bed and breakfast instead, which was far less time-consuming. As a result, Rosie and Frank bought the lease from them and moved to Derbyshire.

It was an odd situation, them owning the lease and also a quarter of the freehold. It made for interesting conversations when it came to rent review time. Still, they were happy in their country pub and cousin Bert was happy that one of his relatives had moved into the village. He wouldn't be the last Bradbury in Parwich after all. In fact, it seemed as if he had almost been hanging on until Rosie had moved there, as seven months later he had a heart attack and died. While he might not have been the last member of the Bradbury family to live in Parwich, he was the last of the Herbert Ebenezer Bradburys. That was unless you counted Rosie's little Shih Tzu, which she'd named in honour of all her forefathers who had run the pub. Also, when Rosie added her name to the list of licensees on the wall, she made sure it said Rosie Stephenson (née Bradbury).

Rosie was extremely proud of her family history in both the village and the pub. Unlike her cousin, she made sure that the family graves in the churchyard were well maintained and even put flowers on them from time to time.

Zara had moved out long before her parents moved to Parwich. She got into De Montfort University in Leicester and graduated with first class honours in underwear design. She was in her third year when Hannah started her medical degree and the two of them shared a flat for a while.

After university, she got a job with a well-known fashion house in London and eventually started up BraZars, her own business making designer bras. She is doing really well and now employs 75 people in both the UK and Turkey. She's had numerous lovers of both sexes over the years, but so far has never settled down with any of them.

Mark and Louise were the only beneficiaries of the trust fund who didn't move to Derbyshire. It would have made perfect sense if they had. After all, Mark could easily have gotten another teaching job and the house on St Augustines Mount had three bedrooms. So the boys wouldn't have had to share a room anymore. In the end, it was the fact that they had too many ties to Reigate that stopped them. For a start, it was where all their friends lived, and the boys were happily settled in school. Mind you, they did seriously consider a move, especially in the early days. That was until Mark was promoted to head of science, which finally settled the matter once and for all.

With Mark's additional salary and the extra income they were getting from their rental properties, they were able to increase their mortgage and have a loft conversion done. It was the best possible outcome for them, as they really liked their house and this way the boys got a bedroom each without them having to move home.

Noel eventually trained as a vet at Nottingham University and is now working at a practice in Helmsley in North Yorkshire. He's married to Vanessa, a veterinary nurse at the same practice. They don't have any children yet, just Ralph the labradoodle, a parrot called Fritz, four geese, six hens, Horace the cat, and Porky Scratching, the Kunekune pig.

Josh didn't go to university but got an apprenticeship as an engineer in the RAF instead. He's currently stationed at RAF Brize Norton in Oxfordshire where he's considered to be one of the most eligible bachelors on the station.

As for Tony, he grew old surrounded by his family, as now he had Pete and Ben living just around the corner. Not only that, but Mark and Louise would always visit him whenever they came to Chesterfield. He had his friend Dave living close by and the two of them would continue going to all of Chesterfield's home matches. They also went to some of the away games, providing they weren't too far away. The one game they never missed was the one at Mansfield Town. After each match, they would always moan about the lack of passion and commitment shown by their team. It was all part of the woes of supporting a side in one of the lower leagues. But despite it all, they kept on going and would never dream of switching their allegiance elsewhere.

They went to the pub every Saturday night, only now it was to the Boythorpe Inn, as the Walton Hotel had been demolished. A care home was finally built on the site in 2022.

"It's going to be a home for the bewildered," said Dave when the plans were announced.

"I'd be careful what you call it," replied Tony. "You and I could end up there one of these days."

Not that either of them ever did.

James retired a couple of years after Ben was made a partner. He got himself a lady friend called Emily and they spend a lot of their time going on cruises. Hannah has proven very useful in that respect as she usually gets them her staff discount when they book to go on the ship where she works.

When they are not on a cruise, they like to go for walks in the Peak District followed by a pub lunch, usually at the Sycamore Inn where Rosie only charges them half price. James eventually got rid of the Overfinch and bought another car at a proceeds of crime auction. This time it was a Maserati Levante.

As promised, he presented the metal plaque with SK1854 on it to Alan and Jenny who screwed it to one of the outside walls of the Sycamore Inn. It was still there when Rosie and Frank took over, and it sure sparked many conversations. Many of their customers wanted to know what it meant. People were often heard saying things like, "But I thought the pub was far older than that and who was SK?" Very few people knew what it actually meant, although you occasionally got the odd rambler looking at his Ordnance Survey map and scratching his head.

Simon and Katie eventually had two children of their own, a boy and a girl. They called the boy James Simon and the girl Alice Katie, which are Katie's Christian names reversed.

As she said at the time, "What's sauce for the goose is sauce for the gander."

They live in a lovely cottage in Darley Dale in the knowledge that they'll move to Stanton Lees one day.

Life continues for the Bradbury family. They have their ups and downs but they always stay in contact with each other. They know who they are, what their family history was and where they came from.

They are the Bradburys from Derbyshire.

Epilogue

Thursday, May 19th, 2039

"There's post for you," said Vanessa as Noel walked through the door. "It's the usual rubbish, but I think there's also a letter from your uncle."

Letters were a rarity these days with most correspondence being carried out by email. However, Royal Mail kept going, delivering Christmas cards, junk mail and the odd piece of formal communication. Mind you, their main job these days is delivering parcels, as most people buy everything online.

Noel had had a bad day at work, having to put down three dogs and two cats. He was looking forward to a night in with a bottle of wine watching repeats of his favourite comedies on Dave.

It had been Vanessa's day off and she had driven into Thirsk to do the week's shopping. Noel kept saying it would be far less time-consuming if she ordered groceries online and let the supermarket deliver them instead. But she preferred to do her shopping the old-fashioned way.

Noel took his work clothes off and went to have a shower. He'd been caught earlier when a cat had relieved herself on the examination table. It was one of the occupational hazards of being a vet. He put on joggers, a baggy T-shirt and his slippers. Now he could relax.

Going into the living room, he picked up the post and quickly found the letter Vanessa had referred to. It was franked with the name of his uncle's solicitors practice in Matlock. So he opened it and started to read.

Knight and Bradbury
Solicitors and Commissioners for Oaths
12 Riber View
Matlock
Derbyshire DE4 7JH
Tel 01629 583127

May 17th, 2039

Mr N Bradbury
Rose Cottage
87 Bridge Street
Helmsley
North Yorkshire
YO62 5XD

Ref: Bradbury Family Trust

Dear Noel,

I hope you and Vanessa are both well. Apologies for the formal nature of this letter. But I am writing to you today in my formal capacity, that of trustee of the Bradbury family trust.

Even though you were just a boy when we all met twenty years ago, I am sure you remember the events from back then as well as I do. After all, the things we discovered about our family in those few days will live with us forever.

You will recall that the properties your parents and your aunts and uncles received at Striding Hall all had restrictive covenants lasting twenty years. Those covenants are about to expire, which means they will be free to sell them if they so wish. I personally do not want to sell, but what the rest of the family decide to do with their properties is entirely up to them.

One question remained unanswered twenty years ago. If the trust fund was valued at five million pounds, why were the prizes only worth one and a half million? The answer to that question is simple. The trust fund is a family fund. It was never meant for just one generation.

You will also recall that your great-uncle Tony died last year. He'd had a good innings and was 92 when he passed away.

I was his solicitor and I have to tell you that he left all his assets to the trust fund in his will. As you can imagine, Tony's assets were substantial and, when combined with the existing monies in the fund, it comes to a very large amount of money. In fact, thanks to prudent investment over the years, the fund now stands at over £61 million.

You, your brother and your three cousins are all named as beneficiaries of the trust fund. That is why I have written to all five of you inviting you to attend a series of three challenges at Striding Hall commencing on Friday, September 2nd at 5 pm.

I can tell you that these tasks will be totally different from the ones your parents had to face all those years ago. Simon and I have given much thought to what challenges we are going to set you. After all, we've had twenty years in which to decide on the right ones. These challenges will be thought-provoking and, hopefully, they will also be rewarding for you.

I look forward to seeing you on September 2nd. In the meantime, if you have any queries, please do not hesitate to contact me. I'm sure you will understand that, under the terms of the fund, I am restricted as to what I can tell you.

Yours sincerely

Ben Bradbury LLB (Partner)

Noel put the letter down.
"Good grief," he thought to himself. "Here we go again."

The end

Author's Notes

One of the great things about writing a novel is that you can incorporate some obscure things from your past into the storyline. In this book, the inspiration for the father and son reversing their names came from two former customers of mine who owned a wine bar in South London. They were Turkish Cypriots and the father's name was Yusuf Mehmet. His son was called Mehmet Yusuf. It was a tradition in their family that the first-born son always had his father's names reversed.

Also, some people really do name their children after alcoholic drinks, just like Jack and his wife did towards the end of the story. The chef at our pub in North Yorkshire had two boys and a girl, who were called Caffrey, Bailey and Tia Maria.

In addition, I have one of the waitresses from our pub in North Yorkshire to thank for telling me about the BA course in underwear design at De Montford University.

Where some of the other things in this book are concerned, I played the Red-Blue challenge when I was on a cross-functional teambuilding course whilst working for Courage Brewery. After much deliberation, both teams worked out what the objective of the game was and both played red every time. The inspiration for the photograph challenge came from another course I attended.

Many of the houses in Stanton in Peak do have WPT carved above the door as they were built by William Pole Thornhill and the map reference for the Sycamore Inn in Parwich is really SK1854.

Bet Lynch was the loudmouthed landlady of the Rovers Return in the long running soap, *Coronation Street.*

The Riley graves in Eyam are so called even though it's the Hancock family who are buried there. This is because they are located next to Riley House on land that belonged to the Riley family. The graves are in an egg-shaped drystone enclosure called Riley's Field.

Little John, the ironically named and trusted lieutenant to legendary rebel Robin Hood, is reputedly buried in the churchyard of Saint Michael's church in Hathersage. His grave is one of the main tourist attractions in the area.

Please note that in Chesterfield, St Augustines has no apostrophe as the name is the plural for two saints called Augustine.

I have a personal connection with the football pools, which started in the UK in 1923. Two years later, Joseph Walker, my grandfather who was a French polisher, won the jackpot. The pools were still in their infancy back then. So the jackpot was not as large as it would become later on. Nevertheless, he was able to move out of the rented house he shared with my grandmother and my aunt. He bought a new detached house half a mile away, still close to his family and friends. They were also able to afford to have another child, my father.

When my wife and I owned the pub in North Yorkshire, one of our locals told me a story about his uncle who had also won the pools. Following his win, he went into his local pub in Doncaster and bought a drink for everybody who was in the bar that night. That was the last time any of his friends ever saw him. This got me thinking about the choices people make when they win a large amount of money. Either they make small changes to their lives, staying in the same area with their friends and family. Or they change completely, abandoning everything to do with their old life. This was the idea on which this story was based.

The largest pools win in 1979 was actually £882,000. The first jackpot of over £1 million wasn't won until 1986.

Please note that the football results and fixtures mentioned from the 1970s are all correct. I attended the Sheffield Wednesday match referred to in Chapter 1. However, the match against Mansfield Town in 2019 did not take place as Chesterfield had been relegated from the football league the previous year. As a consequence, the Spireites were in the National League in 2019, one tier below both Mansfield Town and Forest Green Rovers. Nobody ever supports a side in the lower leagues for the glory. Supporting a team like Chesterfield is 50% disappointment, 50% frustration and only 10% joy, to paraphrase Pete Bradbury.

About the Author

Ian Walker was born in Chesterfield in 1956. His father was the chief clerk of a brewery in town and his mother was a ballet teacher.

He went to Chesterfield School before gaining a place at Leicester University where he studied Chemistry and Maths.

After graduating, he got a job working in the laboratory at Truman's Brewery in Brick Lane, London. The following year, he transferred to Watney's Brewery in Mortlake, where he moved into the sales department eighteen months later.

Several sales roles followed until he became Regional Sales Director for Scottish and Newcastle in the West Country.

All this came to an end in 2006 when, aged just fifty, he suffered a stroke and had to give up work. After twelve months of physiotherapy, he felt sufficiently recovered to buy a pub in the North York Moors along with his wife Euníce.

In the eight years that they owned the pub, they achieved listings in both the *Good Beer Guide* and the *Good Pub Guide*. They were also included in *The Times* list of the top fifty places to eat in the British countryside.

In 2016, he decided to retire and move back to Chesterfield after forty years. He and his wife now live just around the corner from the house where he grew up.

He has two grown-up sons from a previous marriage.

Family Trust is his fifth published novel.